SI..... ......

They say the first forty-eight hours are critical on a homicide case, and that's true, but, frankly, a lot of murders can be solved in the first eight. Sometimes it's obvious—the boyfriend standing there with a guilty look and blood under his nails rambling about a "masked robber." Sometimes the neighbors can tell you they heard a knock-down, drag-out fight. And sometimes . . . there are tracks in the snow.

"Nah. I didn't make them prints and ain't no reason for my boys to be out there," Amos told Grady. He said "there" as *dah*, his German accent as broad as his face. "But lemme ask 'em just to be sure."

He started to stomp away. I called after him. "Bring the boys out here, please."

Amos Miller shot me a confused look, like he hadn't expected me to be giving orders. I arched an eyebrow at him—*Well?*—and he nodded once. I was used to dealing with men who didn't take a female cop very seriously. And I wanted to see the boys— wanted to see their faces as they looked at those tracks.

My first impression of Amos Miller? He looked worried. Then again, he was an Amish farmer with two boys in their teens. A beautiful young English girl—the Amish called everyone who was not Amish "English"—was dead and spread-eagled in his barn. I'd be worried too.

KINGDOM
COME

JANE JENSEN

BERKLEY PRIME CRIME, NEW YORK

BERKLEY
PRIME
CRIME

An imprint of Penguin Random House LLC
375 Hudson Street, New York, New York 10014

This book is an original publication of Penguin Random House LLC.

Library of Congress Cataloging-in-Publication Data

Jensen, Jane.
Kingdom come / Jane Jensen.—Berkley Prime Crime trade paperback edition.
pages cm.
ISBN 978-0-425-28289-2 (paperback)
1. Women detectives—Fiction.   2. Murder—Investigation—Fiction.
3. Amish—Pennsylvania—Fiction.   I. Title.
PS3560.E5919K56   2016
813'.54—dc23
2015027689

PUBLISHING HISTORY
Berkley Prime Crime trade paperback edition / January 2016

PRINTED IN THE UNITED STATES OF AMERICA

10 9 8 7 6 5 4 3 2 1

Cover photo: *Trees & Barn in a snow shower* © Minden Pictures/Masterfile.
Cover design by Sarah Oberrender.
Interior text design by Kristin del Rosario.

Penguin
Random
House

For Bill Holmes.
Thank you for the bottomless well of support you give your family,
even your add-on members like me.
Would that we could all live as long as you
and be as sharp, loving, and happy when we get there.

ACKNOWLEDGMENTS

When my husband and I moved back to rural Pennsylvania four years ago, I was a little like Elizabeth Harris in this novel— seeking peace and beauty in a hectic life. We have loved living in Lancaster County. In the summer months, eating almost exclusively from the bounty of our local Amish farms is one of my favorite things in life.

I grew up the daughter of a conservative fundamentalist minister and yet a free-spirited liberal at my core. That conflict still plays out in the things that I admire and the things that I fear, much of which are given voice in this novel.

The people in this book are entirely fictitious. I have taken some liberties with the reach of the Lancaster City Bureau of Police. And as far as I have been able to tell with my research, no crime like this has ever happened in an Amish community.

Knock on wood.

CHAPTER 1

The Dead Girl

"It's . . . sensitive," Grady had said on the phone, his voice tight.

Now I understood why. My car crawled down a rural road thick with new snow. It was still dark and way too damn early on a Wednesday morning. The address he'd given me was on Grimlace Lane. Turned out the place was an Amish farm in the middle of a whole lot of other Amish farms in the borough of Paradise, Pennsylvania.

Sensitive like a broken tooth. Murders didn't happen here, not here. The last dregs of sleep and yet another nightmare in which I'd been holding my husband's cold, dead hand in the rain evaporated under a surge of adrenaline. Oh yes, I was wide-awake now.

I spotted cars—Grady's and two black-and-whites—in the driveway of a farm and pulled in. The CSI team and the coroner had not yet arrived. I didn't live far from the murder site and I was glad for the head start and the quiet.

Even before I parked, my mind started generating theories and scenarios. *Dead girl*, Grady had said. If it'd been natural causes or an accident, like falling down the stairs, he wouldn't have called me in. It had to be murder or at least a suspicious death. A father disciplining his daughter a little too hard? Doddering Grandma dipping into the rat poison rather than the flour?

I got out and stood quietly in the frigid air to get a sense of place. The interior of the barn glowed in the dark of a winter morning. I took in the classic white shape of a two-story bank barn, the snowy fields behind, and the glow of lanterns coming from the huge, barely open barn door. . . . It looked like one of those quaint paintings you see hanging in the local tourist shops, something with a title like *Winter Dawn*. I'd only moved back to Pennsylvania eight months ago after spending ten years in Manhattan. I still felt a pang at the quiet beauty of it.

Until I opened the door and stepped inside.

It wasn't what I expected. It was like some bizarre and horrific game of mixed-up pictures. The warmth of the rough barn wood was lit by a half dozen oil lanterns. Add in the scattered straw, two Jersey cows, and twice as many horses, all watching the proceedings with bland interest from various stalls, and it felt like a cozy step back in time. That vibe did not compute with the dead girl on the floor. She was most definitely not Amish, which was the first surprise. She was young and beautiful, like something out of a '50s pulp magazine. She had long, honey-blonde hair and a face that still had the blush of life thanks to the heavy makeup she wore. She had on a candy-pink sweater that molded over taut breasts and a short gray wool skirt that was pushed up to her hips. She still wore pink underwear, though it looked roughly twisted. Her nails were the same shade as her sweater. Her bare feet, thighs, and hands were blue-white with death, and her neck too, at the line below her jaw where the makeup stopped.

The whole scene felt unreal, like some pretentious performance art, the kind in those Soho galleries Terry had dragged me to. But then, death always looked unreal.

"Coat? Shoes?" I asked, already taking inventory. Maybe knee-high boots, I thought, reconstructing it in my mind. And thick tights to go with that wool skirt. I'd *been* a teenage girl living in Lancaster County, Pennsylvania. I knew what it meant to care more about looks than the weather. But even at the height of my girlish vanity, I wouldn't have gone bare-legged in January.

"They're not here. We looked." Grady's voice was tense. I finally spared him a glance. His face was drawn in a way I'd never seen before, like he was digesting a meal of ground glass.

In that instant, I saw the media attention this could get, the politics of it. I remembered that Amish school shooting a few years back. I hadn't lived here then, but I'd seen the press. Who hadn't?

"You sure you want me on this?" I asked him quietly.

"You're the most experienced homicide detective I've got," Grady said. "I need you, Harris. And I need this wrapped up quickly."

"Yeah." I wasn't agreeing that it could be. My gut said this wasn't going to be an open-and-shut case, but I agreed it would be nice. "Who found her? Do we know who she is?"

"Jacob Miller, eleven years old. He's the son of the Amish farmer who lives here. Poor kid. Came out to milk the cows this morning and found her just like that. The family says they've got no idea who she is or how she got here."

"How many people live on the property?"

"Amos Miller, his wife, and their six children. The oldest, a boy, is fifteen. The youngest is three."

More vehicles pulled up outside. The forensics team, no doubt. I was gratified that Grady had called me in first. It was good to see the scene before it turned into a lab.

"Can you hold them outside for five minutes?" I asked Grady.

He nodded and went out.

I pulled on some latex gloves, then looked at the body, bending down to get as close to it as I could without touching it. The left side of her head, toward the back, was matted with blood and had the look of a compromised skull. The death blow? I tried to imagine what had happened. The killer—he or she—had probably come up behind the victim, struck her with something heavy. The autopsy would tell us more. I didn't think it had happened here. There were no signs of a disturbance or the blood you'd expect from a head wound. I carefully pulled up her leg a bit and looked at the underside of her thigh. Very minor lividity. She hadn't been in this position long. And I noticed something else—her clothes were wet. I rubbed a bit of her wool skirt and sweater between my fingers to be sure—and came away with dampness on the latex. She wasn't soaked now, and her skin was dry, so she'd been here long enough to dry out, but she'd been very wet at some point. I could see now that her hair wasn't just styled in a casual damp-dry curl, it had been recently wet, probably postmortem along with her clothes.

I straightened, frowning. It was odd. We'd had two inches of snow the previous afternoon, but it was too cold for rain. If the body had been left outside in the snow, would it have gotten this wet? Maybe the ME could tell me.

Since I was sure she hadn't been killed in the barn, I checked the floor for drag marks. The floor was of wooden planks kept so clean that there was no straw or dirt in which drag marks would show, but there were traces of wet prints. Then again, the boy who'd found the body had been in the barn and so had Grady and the uniforms, and me too. I carefully examined the girl's bare feet. There was no broken skin, no sign her feet had been dragged through the snow or across rough boards.

The killer was strong, then. He'd carried her in here and laid her down. Which meant he'd arranged her like this—pulled up her skirt, splayed her thighs. He'd wanted it to look sexual. Why?

The doors opened. Grady and the forensics team stood in the doorway.

"Blacklight this whole area," I requested. "And this floor— see if you can get any prints or traffic patterns off it. Don't let anyone in until that's done. I'm going to check outside." I looked at Grady. "The coroner?"

"Should be here any minute."

"Good. Make sure she's tested for any signs of penetration, consensual or otherwise."

"Right."

Grady barked orders. The crime-scene technicians pulled on blue coveralls and booties just outside the door. This was only the sixth homicide needing real investigation I'd been on since moving back to Lancaster. I was still impressed that the department had decent tools and protocol, even though I knew that was just big-city arrogance talking.

I left them to it and went out to find my killer's tracks in the snow.

This winter had been harsh. In fact, it was shaping up to be the worst in decades. We'd had a white Christmas and then it never really left. The fresh two inches we'd gotten the day before had covered up an older foot or two of dirty snow and ice. Thanks to a low in the twenties, the fresh snow had a dry, powdery surface that showed no signs of melting. It still wasn't fun to walk on, due to the underlying grunge. It said a lot about the killer if he'd carried her body over any distance.

There was a neatly shoveled path from the house to the barn. The snow in the central open area in the driveway had been stomped down. But it didn't take me long to spot a deep set of prints heading off across an open field that was otherwise pristine. The line of prints came and went. They showed a sole like that of a work boot and they were large. They came from, and returned to, a distant copse of trees. I bent over to examine one of the prints close to the barn. It had definitely been made since the last snowfall.

A few minutes later, I got my first look at Amos Miller, the Amish farmer who owned the property. Grady called him out and showed him the tracks. Miller looked to be in his mid-forties with dark brown hair and a long, unkempt beard. His face was round and solemn. I said nothing for now, just observed.

They say the first forty-eight hours are critical on a homicide case, and that's true, but, frankly, a lot of murders can be solved in the first eight. Sometimes it's obvious—the boyfriend standing there with a guilty look and blood under his nails rambling about a "masked robber." Sometimes the neighbors can tell you they heard a knock-down, drag-out fight. And sometimes . . . there are tracks in the snow.

"Nah. I didn't make them prints and ain't no reason for my boys to be out there," Amos told Grady. He said "there" as *dah*, his German accent as broad as his face. "But lemme ask 'em just to be sure."

He started to stomp away. I called after him. "Bring the boys out here, please."

Amos Miller shot me a confused look, like he hadn't expected me to be giving orders. I arched an eyebrow at him—*Well?*—and he nodded once. I was used to dealing with men who didn't take a female cop very seriously. And I wanted to see the boys— wanted to see their faces as they looked at those tracks.

My first impression of Amos Miller? He looked worried. Then again, he was an Amish farmer with two boys in their teens. A beautiful young English girl—the Amish called every- one who was not Amish "English"—was dead and spread-eagled in his barn. I'd be worried too.

He came back with three boys. The youngest was small and still a child. That was probably Jacob, the eleven-year-old who'd found the body. His face was blank, like he was in shock. The next oldest looked to be around thirteen, just starting puberty. He was thin with a rather awkward nose and oversized hands he still hadn't grown into. His father introduced him as Ham.

The oldest, Wayne, had to be the fifteen-year-old that Grady mentioned, the oldest child. All three were decent-looking boys in that wholesome, bowl-cut way of Amish youth. The older two looked excited but not guilty. I suppose it was quite an event, having a dead body found on your farm. I wondered if the older boys had gone into the barn to get a good long look at the girl since their little brother's discovery. Knowing how large families worked, I couldn't imagine they hadn't.

Each of the boys glanced at the tracks in the snow and shook his head. "Nah," the oldest added for good measure. "Ain't from me."

"Any of you recognize that print?" I asked. "Does it look like boots you've seen before?"

They all craned forward to look. Amos stroked his beard. "Just look like boots, maybe. You can check all ours if you like. We've nothin' to hide."

I lifted my chin at Grady. We'd definitely want the crime team to inventory every pair of shoes and boots in the house.

"Would you all mind stepping over here for me, please?" I led them over to the other side of the ice-and-gravel drive, where there was some untouched snow. "Youngest to oldest, one at a time."

The youngest stepped forward into the snow with both feet, then back. The others mimicked his actions obediently, including Amos Miller.

"Thank you. That's all for now. We'll want to speak to you a bit later, so please stay home."

They went back inside and Grady and I compared the tracks.

All three of the boys had smaller feet than the tracks in the snow. Amos's prints were large enough but didn't have the same sole pattern. Besides, I was sure Grady wasn't missing the fact that the prints came and went *from* the trees, since the prints heading that direction overlaid the ones approaching the barn.

"I think Ronks Road is over there beyond those woods." Grady sounded hopeful as he pointed across the field. "Can it be that easy?"

"Don't!"

Grady cocked an eyebrow at me.

"You'll jinx it. Never say the word 'easy.' That's inviting Murphy, his six ex-wives, and their lawyers."

Grady smirked. "Well, if the killer dumped her here, he had to come from somewhere."

I hummed. I knew what Grady was thinking. I was thinking it too. A car full of rowdy youths, or maybe just a guy and his hot date, out joyriding in the country. A girl ends up dead and someone gets the bright idea to dump her on an Amish farm. They drive out here, park, cross a snowy cornfield, and leave her in a random barn.

It sounded like a stupid teenage prank, only it was murder and possibly an attempt to frame someone else. That was a lot of prison years of serious. A story like that—it would make the press happy and Grady fucking ecstatic, especially if we could nab the guy who wore those boots by tonight.

"Get a photographer and a recorder and let's go," I said, feeling only a moment's silent regret over my good black leather boots. I should have worn my wellies.

It wasn't that easy.

The tracks crossed the field and went into the trees. They continued about ten feet before they ended—at a creek. It hadn't been visible from the barn, but there was running water here, a good twelve feet across. The land dipped down to it, as if carved out over time. The snow grew muddy and trampled at the creek bank. The boot prints entered the water. They didn't reemerge on the opposite side.

"Cattle use this creek?" I asked Grady, looking at the mess of mud and snow and hoofprints along the bank.

Grady sighed. "Hell. It's not legal, but a lot of the farmers do it, especially the Amish. It's hard to explain to a man whose family has farmed the same land for generations why politicians in Baltimore don't want his animals to have access to the free and plentiful water on his own land."

I really didn't give a toss about the pollution of Chesapeake Bay at the moment. But our possible killer's footprints, so clean in the snow, had vanished into a churned-up creek bed that had been literally ridden herd over. I walked up and down the bank as carefully as I could, trying not to step anywhere there might be evidence. There was chicken wire strung up across the creek to the north, and a matching wire wall glinted to the south. Presumably, this kept the farm's animals from escaping the property.

The freaky thing was, there were no signs of tracks on the other side of the creek anywhere between those two makeshift fences. I rubbed my forehead, a sense of frustration starting in my stomach.

"Damn it!" Grady cursed, apparently reaching the same conclusion.

"How far is the road?" I asked.

As if to answer my question, an SUV lumbered past, visible through the trees on the far side. There was a road maybe thirty feet beyond the other side of the creek.

In a righteous world, the boot prints would have climbed out the opposite bank and led right to that road. In a righteous world, there'd be tire tracks off the side of the road over there, tire tracks we could attempt to trace.

No one had to tell me it wasn't a righteous world.

I looked at the creek again, then went back to look at the boot prints. The prints with the toes facing the creek definitely overlaid the prints with the toes facing away. Unless the killer had walked backward in both directions—one way carrying a dead body—he hadn't come from the farm.

Grady stood there shaking his head. I decided, *Screw it*, and shucked my boots and rolled up my pant legs. At least this suit was a trendy wash-and-wear and didn't require dry cleaning.

"You don't have to do that." Grady sounded uneasy.

I ignored him. If there was one thing I knew for sure about being a woman on the police force, it was that you didn't turn up your nose at getting physical or messy. You didn't wait for some guy to do it. If you wanted respect, you had to be willing to jump into the shit headfirst.

But, goddamn, this sucked. I waded into the ice water masquerading as a creek and followed the bank to the chicken-wire obstruction.

"Anything?" Grady called to me as I ran my hand along the chicken wire and stepped deeper into the creek.

When I reached the middle, the frigid water was streaming painfully around my upper thighs.

"Damn," I muttered as I felt along the fence.

A few inches below the surface of the water the wire ended. To be sure, I sent one leg forward on a foray. It swept through nothing but water. No wonder our Jane Doe had gotten wet. The killer had pushed her under these barriers and then likely followed by ducking under himself.

"Bastard walked through the creek," I said, my voice shaking with cold and not a little disgust. "He came in and out under one of these fences, but he had to leave the water somewhere. We need to search the banks upstream and down from here. We'll find his tracks."

I sounded confident. And I did believe what I was saying. We were talking about a man, after all, not a superhuman, not a ghost.

I was wrong.

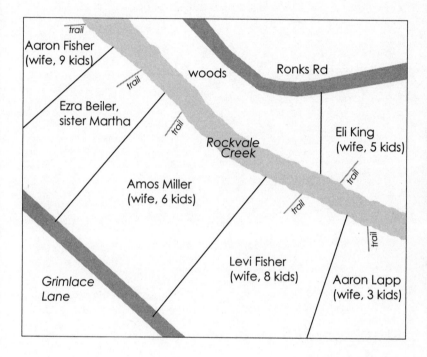

CHAPTER 2

Fistful of Seeds

I sat at my desk and stared at the situation board I'd set up right behind me. The mug in my hands was warm, but its heat ended where porcelain met skin. Nothing could penetrate the chill I lived with. It was psychological, or so my therapist had said, the one they made me see after what went down in New York. That didn't make it any damn less unpleasant.

Always so cold, deep down inside. Moving back here to a simpler life was supposed to change that.

The property survey map in front of me had been marked up with permanent pens and Post-it notes. It'd been only twenty-five hours since I'd pulled up to that barn yesterday in the pre-dawn hours to get my first look at Jane Doe. By now I knew this case wasn't going to be one of the quick ones.

The teams had crawled all over the countryside yesterday. Grady even called in reinforcements from Harrisburg. We'd carefully gone up and down that creek bed for several miles in either direction. The killer's tracks never emerged from it.

Which led me to one inescapable conclusion, and I'd marked it on the map.

As for our Jane Doe, we hadn't found her coat and shoes. The coroner was almost certain her death was caused by asphyxiation. The autopsy would reveal more. The time of death was a bit of a surprise—between ten the previous morning and four in the afternoon, depending on how long she'd been in the cold water. And we knew she'd been moved to the barn most likely between midnight and two A.M., giving her clothes and hair a chance to mostly dry before Jacob found her at five.

It was still dark outside, but there were rousing sounds of life in the sparkling new facility that was the Lancaster City Bureau of Police. I saw Grady in my peripheral vision. Like me, he'd gone home after midnight and was back before dawn. He wheeled over a roller chair and planted himself next to me, a mug of joe in his hands. He yawned hugely, making no attempt to cover it up. I smiled to myself. I appreciated the fact that Grady treated me like one of the guys. And I liked his wife, Sharon. The wife of the last partner I'd had in New York had hated me at first glance and was always going into jealous rants on the phone when we had to work late. But Sharon was a petite, redheaded spitfire whose passion was the LGBT youth center in Lancaster. She and Grady had three boys and they were solid. They'd had me over for dinner a few times. Sharon didn't find me a threat.

Detective Lieutenant Mike Grady wasn't my type anyway, even if I'd been into home wrecking—which I wasn't—even if I'd had any interest in sex at all since Terry died—which I didn't.

Grady ran the Violent Crimes Department for the Lancaster City Bureau of Police. He was in his late thirties and, like many Pennsylvania men, he was big—six foot two and at least two hundred fifty pounds. He'd probably played football or wrestled in high school. He had short, curly brown hair, beefy hands and shoulders, and a reddish complexion. A lot of years behind the desk and serious home cooking had given him a belly and bulky heft all over. Grady was a nice guy. Then again, most people who lived here were.

I was from here originally too, but my "nice" had been hammered down by ten years of being a police officer for the NYPD. I had to be tough because a) I was a woman and b) I had a tall but somewhat fragile build and a pretty face to overcome. Everyone thought I was crazy when I decided to join the police academy. I'd never been a natural jock. But I liked that—liked the fact that it was something that really challenged me, that I was going against type. I loved being sweaty and tough. I'd worked my ass off, trained hard then—and still did. No perp was going to take advantage of me, and no fellow police officer either. I wore my dark hair pulled back in a bun and little makeup to work. That didn't keep men from being, well, *male*, but most of them knew better than to treat me like a dumping ground for their hormones. At least they did after the first time they tried it.

"No matches in missing persons," Grady said by way of greeting. "Today I'm sending Hernandez and Smith out to talk to all the high school principals in the area, show them her picture. And we'll send out a missing persons bulletin to all the Mid-Atlantic precincts. If we don't get an ID on her today, I'll have to do a press alert."

I hummed. I knew a press alert was the last thing we needed.

I was surprised the story had been kept quiet so far. We'd been lucky that the area where the farm was located was well off the beaten track.

"I want to interview everyone at those farms today," I said, nodding at the map.

Grady sighed. He was silent for a good while as we both regarded the layout. "Talk to me, Harris," he said in a tone that acknowledged that he wouldn't like what I had to say. "What are you thinking?"

I stood up and drew my finger down six lines I'd drawn with a brown pencil. Each one ran from the creek—which we'd since learned was called Rockvale Creek—to the farms. The lines were on the Millers' property and five of their neighbors'.

"The killer used one of these animal trails to get in and out of the creek. Had to. We didn't find his prints leaving the creek because they were trod over at some point after he left her body at the Millers', covered up by hoofprints."

I looked at Grady. He was frowning, but he didn't say anything.

"We saw dairy cows out in a couple of these fields yesterday." I tapped two Post-it notes I'd put up with cow stick figures. My attempt at high art. "So for sure he could have used either of these trails. As for the others, all these farms have at least a horse or two for the buggies. We'll have to interview the farmers to know if their animals were out between midnight and when we were looking, I'd say as late as ten A.M. yesterday."

"He could have kept to the creek. Could've walked miles," Grady countered.

"Even in the water, it wouldn't have been easy to manage a

dead body, and it was damned freezing. Plus, we looked up and down both banks of the creek and didn't find fresh prints coming out of it for at least a mile. And there aren't any more animal tracks along it for a good ways either." I tapped the paper. "He used one of these trails, Grady. Which means he *knows* this place. He knew where those trails were and when the animals moved. He came from one of these farms."

It was the first time I'd said it out loud, but I'd started thinking it yesterday afternoon. I knew Grady didn't want to hear it. Then again, I didn't want a lot of the shit that had happened to me. Life sucked that way.

Grady rubbed at his jaw. He looked around as if worried about being overheard. But most of the detectives didn't get in until after seven. He still lowered his voice.

"Okay, I agree that he knows the area. That doesn't mean he's Amish. He could be someone who works with the Amish—a driver, someone who picks up dairy or produce. Hell, a mailman. Or a customer."

He grabbed my Post-it pad and began scribbling. He tore off the top page and slapped it over one of the properties marked *Fisher.* "Eggs and dairy," he said, repeating what he'd written on the note. He scribbled another one and put it on the map. "Chicken coops." Another. "Baked goods." Another. "Mules." He waved his hand. "All these farmers sell goods directly off their farms, which means they have customers driving in and out all the time. Any of those customers could have thought, *Gee whiz, where should I dump this body? How 'bout where I buy my eggs? No one would ever guess because I'm such a clever bastard.*"

"Just because you stop in someone's driveway to buy eggs

doesn't mean you can see the creek or the animal trails leading to it. The creek's in a gully."

"Maybe they wandered around a bit one fine spring day. Maybe their dog took off across a field and they chased it. Maybe they chatted with the farmer and he mentioned it. Could have been months ago, even years, and only now they had a reason to use that information. Hell, it could have been a fisherman or hunter who wandered up and down that creek in his youth. These farms have had cows and horses living there for a hundred years, which means those trails have been there forever."

He had a point. Maybe I was getting ahead of myself. "Right. We should get started on customer lists, and lists of anyone who visits these farms regularly. But . . . I'm gonna say this, Grady, at least once."

I waited until he looked at me.

"I'm not ruling out anything, not yet. These farmers and their families have to be considered suspects, at least until we can cross them off officially."

I made it sound logical, but it was more than that to me. It was a gut feeling, a feeling that said the killer knew this area like he knew his own skin.

Grady's frown deepened. "Look, Harris, I hired you because you've got the best homicide training from one of the biggest cities in the world. So I'm glad I have you available for something like this. But you're not from around here, so you don't know the Amish."

I huffed. "I was born and raised in Quarryville. You know that."

"Yeah, but you probably had about as much dealings with

them in high school as I did, which is to say the occasional ogle at a horse and buggy. I've been an officer of the law in Lancaster County for fifteen years and I know their culture. There's never been a murder among the Amish—ever. And I especially can't imagine one involving a beautiful young English girl in the middle of the night. Why would she even be out there with them? These people don't associate with girls like her. Somebody she knew killed her and dumped her out there, someone with a car. We need to find that person."

I bristled instinctively. Jane Doe was young and perhaps a little too made-up, but that didn't make her a "like her" in my mind. I was defensive of my vic, which was foolish and sentimental, but it was a sentimentality I'd been prone to ever since I became a cop. It helped me stay motivated when things got tough, so I didn't fight it. But I didn't have to voice it and make myself look like a sap either.

"I don't disagree. It's probably an ex-boyfriend or a stepdad, someone she knew well. I'm just saying we need to look at all possibilities with a clear eye, not go into it with a list of won'ts and couldn't-bes, because that's the surest way to screw yourself over." I folded my arms over my chest, prepared to be stubborn. They'd brought me in to do a job, and I was going to do it.

Grady visibly relaxed. "I'm not asking you to ignore them. Just—we have to be circumspect. Know what that word means, Harris?"

Now he was just yanking my chain. I laughed. "Circumspect? Kind of a personal question, isn't it? Are you asking me if I'm Jewish? I don't even have the equipment for that, in case you hadn't noticed."

Grady rolled his eyes. "That's just gross. I'll take that for a no. Which is why you and me are partners on this case."

"What?"

I thought for a moment that Grady was still pulling my leg. There were a whopping eight investigators in the Violent Crimes Unit, including Grady himself. I wasn't surprised to be partnered up for a case this serious, but I had no idea Grady still took cases himself in addition to overseeing the lot of us.

"This could get ugly," Grady said quietly. "I need your expertise, Harris, because it has to be solved fast. But I need to be in it myself. I know the area. I know the people and the . . . delicacies, for lack of a better word. I already discussed it with the chief. He thinks it's a good idea."

I couldn't help thinking they wanted a man involved, maybe because the Amish would take a man more seriously. But the goal was to solve the case. I wasn't going to argue with what would work.

"Are you going to want to lead the interviews?" I asked in a neutral voice.

"Nah. Like I said, you've got a lot more recent homicide experience than me. Besides, I want to see you in action." He smirked.

"Okay," I said slowly. "If you watch me very, very carefully, you might learn something."

Grady snorted. "Like how to wipe my ass and text at the same time the way you New Yorkers do? Lookin' forward to it. Hell, let's go get started on those interviews. The Amish are early risers."

It was mid-afternoon when Grady pulled into Ezra Beiler's farm. On my iPad were interviews with every member over the age of ten in the Miller family, the King family, the Lapps, and both sets of Fishers. Aaron Fisher's family and Levi Fisher's family both lived on Grimlace Lane, and it turned out Aaron and Levi were cousins. The audio interviews were on my iPad as well as photos. The Amish dislike having their photos taken, but I'd insisted to Grady and he'd backed me up. With so many Samuels and Miriams, I had to have the photos to keep them all straight. The organization geek in me was already planning out my situation board in my head.

Of all the people we'd interviewed, no one admitted to recognizing the dead girl from our photo of her face, and if any of them were lying, the natural wall of their reticence around strangers hid it well. In a sense, everyone had an alibi, and in another sense, they didn't. At the time the body was moved, between midnight and two A.M., everyone was in bed. Wives claimed husbands never stirred all night, and husbands said the same about their wives. Most of the children in these large families slept two or more to a room, and siblings swore no one had gotten up and left for more than a bathroom run last night.

There's no more annoying alibi than "He was sleeping beside me all night." Wives will tell you they are such light sleepers they wake at the drop of a pin, and husbands aren't about to contradict that and admit that their wives could sleep through a brass band in the bedroom, because that would break their own alibi. Siblings are unlikely to rat on their own flesh and blood out of fear of retaliation, if not loyalty.

We'd asked each family to make a list of anyone who visited

their farm on a regular basis and we had a long list of names to check already.

Our last stop was Ezra Beiler. I knew nothing about Beiler except that he owned the farm at 467 Grimlace Lane and that his twenty-five-acre farm was one of the ones with an animal trail to the creek. As we pulled in I saw a sign: *Beiler's Molly Mules.* A number of the long-faced creatures were grazing in the fenced pasture along the road. They were big, magnificent animals, light tan in color with tightly groomed manes and squarish heads. They didn't look anything like donkeys, which is what I would have guessed. They looked more like very homely Clydesdales. I was staring at them as Grady stopped the car and flipped open his notepad.

"Ezra Beiler. Widower. No children. Maybe this one will be quick."

He sounded relieved. I couldn't blame him. Birth control was not the Amish way, and we'd interviewed enough people already today to make my voice hoarse and my mind spacey with the weight of all those blank stares. I was looking forward to a hot meal and getting back to the station to put my thoughts in order.

As we got out, I took stock of the property. The farmhouse was a bit small, an old clapboard two-story, the top of which had strongly sloped eaves. I imagined there were only one or two rooms upstairs, the kind where you had to duck your head. But though rough, the house was freshly painted white and had a porch with welcoming tan rockers. In front of the house on the driveway's left was the winter shell of a kitchen garden. What looked like grapevines and possibly berry canes stretched bare branches along a trio of thick wires. It was neat and clean and probably quite a sight in the summer.

The barn was directly opposite the house on the gravel drive. Everything else appeared to be fenced-in pasture. In the distance I could see the line of trees that marked the creek.

Grady and I looked at the house and the barn for a moment. It was silent, so silent that I could hear the crunch of the mules' hooves as they walked through the snow and the creak of the trees in the wind. Damn, it was cold. I desperately needed some coffee.

Grady nodded his head at me. "Check the barn. I'll try the house. After this, we're going to get some damn lunch."

I had no argument. I headed for the barn.

The barn was at least a few hundred years old but well kept. There was a big door on a slider and a smaller, human-sized door with a small cement step in front of it. It had a black latch rather than a knob. I opened it.

I'm not sure why, but something compelled me to move quietly. I stepped inside the barn, which was considerably warmer than outside, and closed the door behind me. I turned around—and stared.

An Amish man had his back to me as he stood against a horse stall. One arm was on a post that he leaned against in a posture of despair. His head was laid on his raised arm, his face turned down. His other hand stroked the jaw of a mule that was inside the stall. Its champagne-colored head nuzzled the man's shoulder playfully. It managed to knock off his hat, revealing a head of long, shining blond hair streaked with the natural light and dark undertones of someone who spends hours in the sun.

I suddenly couldn't get enough air. The scene was so private and sad. And . . . something else I couldn't get a handle on. The word "raw" didn't fit, or "powerful," though it was both of those things. It was *honest* in a way that dug little stinging prickles into my numb heart, made the hurried rush of my life stop and be still. The man was frankly beautiful. He wore the common black pants of the Amish. Made of some kind of polyester-like fabric, they stretched and clung to his narrow hips and long legs. His shoulders were broad in a plain white shirt crossed with black suspenders. He had one leg cocked at the knee to rest against the half wall of the wooden stall. I hadn't even seen his face yet, and I felt like I'd been kicked in the head. I wasn't sure I *wanted* to see his face. In fact, I was pretty sure I should turn around and leave.

The spell was broken, and my hopes for escape dashed, when the mule noticed at me and made a blowing noise. The man whirled.

For a second, he seemed embarrassed that I'd caught him in a private moment. But quickly his face fell into a hard stoic expression—or lack thereof.

"What d'ya want?" he asked bluntly. He ran a hand through his hair, noticed his hat on the ground, and did a graceful swoop to pick it up. With it on he looked even more Amish. His complexion was very fair, almost that of a redhead. He had freckles despite the fading tan of summer, and his eyelashes were a light reddish-blond. It was hard to tell the color of his eyes, because after that first glance, he wouldn't look directly at me and I felt uneasy looking directly at him because, yes, he was even more attractive from the front.

"I'm, um, looking for Ezra Beiler. He around?" My voice sounded softer than my usual bite. I cleared my throat and glowered a bit to make up for it.

"I'm Ezra Beiler." He walked over to me, stopping a good few feet away, and put his hands on his hips in a way that felt defiant.

"Is . . . do you have a father, Ezra Beiler, who lives here?" I was confused. According to Grady, Ezra Beiler was a widower. This man looked to be in his twenties and he was clean-shaven. Amish men grew a beard once they married.

"I have a father, sure. His name's not Ezra and he don't live here. I own this farm. What is it you need?"

"Oh. Right. Sorry. I . . . I'm Detective Harris with the Lancaster police." Christ. I wasn't the type to get tongue-tied over a good-looking man, especially since Terry's death. But there was something about Ezra Beiler that was throwing me sideways. I resolutely stuck out a hand for a shake and then regretted it. Police detectives didn't shake hands with persons of interest. Keeping a distance helped create just that extra ounce of authority. But it was too late to pull it back now.

Beiler looked at my hand for a second, then took it. His was rough and warm. So warm. My own hand felt like an icicle in his.

Greenish-brown. His eyes were brown flecked with green, like a summer field.

The door behind me opened, causing me to pull back my hand too quick. *God, E, get a grip.*

Grady came in. "I see you found him."

"Yes, this is, uh, Ezra Beiler. Mr. Beiler, this is Detective Grady."

Ezra nodded but didn't offer a greeting or his hand.

I put the stiff back in my spine. "Does anyone else live here, Mr. Beiler?"

"Ja. My sister Martha."

"Anyone else?"

Ezra shook his head, his face unreadable. The warmth of the barn was starting to sink in and all of a sudden I felt exhausted.

"I see. Perhaps you heard about what happened down the road?"

"I heard. You know they say the only thing that travels fast with the Amish is news." Ezra studied my face and his eyes softened. "Would youse like to come in the house and have some coffee? We can talk better at the table."

I glanced at Grady. He looked as relieved as I felt.

"I'd love a cup of coffee, thank you," Grady said.

Inside, the house was plain but cozy. There was a round pine table in the kitchen, and we sat there while Ezra made coffee in a regular coffeepot. A lamp on the kitchen counter shone bright in the late afternoon gloom. I knew by now that many of the Amish homes in this area had power—either through gas-powered generators or windmills or solar panels. Power itself wasn't against their creed, apparently, just being hooked up to the grid. It was reliance on an outside agency they wanted to avoid.

"Is your sister Martha, here? We'd like to speak to her too," I asked, trying to avoid looking at Ezra's strong, work-toughened hands as he arranged coffee cups and spoons on the table.

"Ja. I'll call her out."

He vanished from the kitchen momentarily and returned

with a very large and plain-faced Amish woman. She had Ezra's blond hair and fair, freckled skin, but she was a big girl—at least five eight and well over two hundred pounds. The bold features on her round face, and the way her hair was pulled back tightly under a white cap, did nothing to soften her. She regarded us with wary interest.

"Martha, this is Detective Harris and Detective Grady, here to ask you and me some questions. Why doncha put some cake out?"

Martha complied without a word. A few minutes later the four of us were seated at the table with coffee and a plate of sliced pound cake. I was starving and I didn't refuse, nor did Grady, as Martha lifted slices onto four small dessert plates and passed them around. The cake was lemon flavored and good. The coffee was better. Dear God, I needed that.

"Thank you," I told Ezra with a reluctant smile. "This hits the spot. It's been a long day."

"Ya looked tired," Ezra mumbled, dropping his gaze to his plate.

It was the first time we'd been offered anything all day, even a seat. I suspected it was because we were police more than the fact that we weren't Amish. Everyone had been cooperative. They'd stood and responded to what was asked, but had been neither welcoming nor overly forthcoming. I'd gotten the impression they wanted us to leave as soon as possible, that they understood our purpose there but didn't believe it ultimately had anything to do with them. Sitting here in the Beiler house was the first time I'd felt any spark of human connection, though I was probably exaggerating the importance of coffee and cake out of sheer gratitude.

I pulled out my iPad. "I need to record this for our files. And I'd like to get a photo of each of you, for our internal records only."

Ezra and Martha looked at each other and nodded. I took the photos right there at the table and then turned on the audio recorder. "This is Detective Elizabeth Harris. Detective Mike Grady and I are interviewing Ezra Beiler of Grimlace Lane and his sister Martha Beiler. It's"—I looked at my watch—"three twenty on Thursday, January twenty-third, 2014."

I looked at Martha to find her staring at me. She quickly lowered her eyes.

"Martha, can you tell us where you were Tuesday between ten in the morning and four in the afternoon?"

"I did laundry in the mornin' and cleaned some. After lunch I was workin' on a baby quilt for my sister Jane till suppertime."

She poked a finger at a crumb and didn't raise her eyes from her plate. Her cheeks reddened a bit.

"So you were in the house that entire time?"

"Ja."

"Was there anyone here with you?"

"Ezra was outside."

I looked at him expectantly. "What were you doing during those hours?"

"Tuesday I took some rockers over to Hennie's on Route Thirty. I make rockin' chairs for 'em."

"What time was that?"

"Left 'bout eight, after the mornin' chores."

"What time did you get back?"

"Well, after I left Hennie's I stopped at a feed store—Miller's in Paradise. Got home 'bout noon. Had lunch with Martha 'n' did some work out to the barn."

Martha's color had deepened. When I looked at her again, I caught her staring at me. She looked down at her cake immediately.

"Did you know your brother was gone Tuesday morning?" I asked.

"I 'member now he went to Hennie's after breakfast. Didn't know he'd been gone so long already."

"I see."

If Ezra was telling the truth, it would be easy to corroborate at both stores.

"What about last night? Can you recount what you did?"

Ezra and Martha looked at each other. Martha got a bit of a frown between her brows, but she didn't speak.

"I had a bad birthin' last night," Ezra offered in that broad accent of his. "Had to call the vet. First time I needed help with a birth in a couple a years, but it was twins and the first one was turned and sort of hooked 'round the other. Mother was bleedin' bad."

"What time was the vet here?"

"I called around half past eleven. Guess it took him 'bout three-quarters of an hour to come. He was here till nearly mornin'. Had a molly and a john born. We lost the john but saved the molly and the mother."

"A molly and a john?" Grady asked.

"Mules. A molly mule's a girl and a john mule's a boy."

"Ah."

"How did you call the vet?" I asked. "Do you have a phone?"

Ezra pulled a cell phone out of his pocket. "It's allowed, for business use only."

He wasn't the first Amish farmer I'd seen with a cell phone, so I wasn't surprised. "Do you have the vet's name?"

"Ja. 'Twas Dr. Lane, Ag Vet Associates."

I glanced at Grady. A vet who'd been in the area overnight could be an important witness.

"During the night, maybe when you were out waiting for the vet to come, or taking a breather, did you see or hear any movement outside, at your neighbors or at the road? A car? A buggy? Even anything you might have thought was normal?"

Ezra gave it a moment's thought. "Didn't see anything before the vet come—came. And afterwards things were too worrisome in the barn for us to notice anything, I guess."

"And you, Martha? Were you assisting with the birth?"

She looked at her brother worriedly, as if asking what she should say.

"Martha was abed," Ezra answered. "She don't do well with blood. Anyhow, no point in both us losin' sleep. There was nothin' she could do."

"Ja. Slept gut." Martha had her hands in her lap and her eyes fixed on them.

"Always somethin' bein' born on a farm," Ezra added, as if to assure his sister it was no big deal she hadn't helped. He looked at her with something like fondness.

Grady nudged me. Crap. I'd lost the thread of the conversation, too busy staring at Ezra while he was looking at his sister. I straightened up and took a manila folder out of my portfolio. "I have to ask you to look at this photo and tell me if you recognize this girl. It's a bit grim. I apologize for that, but it's vital that we learn who she was."

The photo actually wasn't too gruesome. It was a close-up picture of the dead girl's face. Her eyes were open and staring but the blood on the skull wasn't visible.

Ezra looked at it for a long moment. He shook his head and pushed it across the table toward Martha. She glanced at it, shook her head hard, and looked away, uncomfortable.

"You've never seen this girl before? Are you certain?"

"Don't know her." Ezra closed the folder and pushed it back toward me, but he didn't look me in the eyes.

Not that I'd expected a different answer, but these two were the last on Grimlace Lane we had to question, and I felt a burn of disappointment in my throat that we still had no idea who Jane Doe was.

"Right. Last thing. You raise mules for sale?"

"I do."

"Do you have customers come here? Buyers for the mules or anything else?"

"People come by to see the mules sometimes, and sometimes they order them on the Internet and have a trailer pick 'em up."

"What about your carpentry?"

"Used to have furniture for sale on the farm but closed that up 'bout a year ago. Now I sell direct to the stores."

"What about the people who run the stores? Do they ever come here to pick the furniture up?"

Ezra nodded. "Sometimes. And sometimes I take things in if they fit in the buggy. That's what I did on Tuesday."

Grady spoke up. "We'd appreciate it if you could make us a

list of any English who come by here, anyone at all that you can remember, even if it's been a few years."

"Don't know names for most the people who stopped by, but I can give you some."

"Just do the best you can."

I handed over a notepad we'd been using for the purpose and Ezra and Martha set to work on a list.

Ten minutes later, Ezra walked us out and stood in the doorway as we stepped off the porch.

"Thanks for the coffee," I said. I paused, debating with myself. Then I dug a card out of my pocket. "If you can think of anything, anything related to the case or to last night, will you call me?"

Ezra took the card and looked at it a moment too long, as if checking the spelling of my name or memorizing the number. When he looked up he met my eyes, and for a moment I saw something in them other than politeness or distance. It made my stomach flop over. I looked away.

"If I think of anything, I will."

"Thanks," I said brusquely as I turned to go.

By the time I'd gotten into the passenger seat of Grady's car, the door was closed and Ezra was gone.

CHAPTER 3

Bread and Milk

For the next three days we organized, correlated, and tracked down leads working from seven in the morning till after ten at night. Every name the Amish on Grimlace Lane had given us was checked out with the help of Detectives Hernandez and Smith. Though it was faster to call people, I preferred to go to their homes. You could tell a lot about someone by seeing where they lived and looking them in the eye while you asked questions. Most of the time, that personal touch yielded nothing of interest, but sooner or later it would. I was counting on it.

One of our first stops was Ag Vet Associates. The place was pleasant and clean, and a receptionist confirmed that the vet in question, Dr. Lane, had indeed been called to Beiler's farm the night of the murder. Dr. Lane was on a farm visit, but he offered to stop by the station when he was done.

He came by, and Grady and I took him into a little room for the interview. Bill Lane was a man in his early thirties who still had the clean-cut vibe of a Boy Scout. He confirmed everything Ezra had said. He'd been at Ezra's farm from about quarter past midnight until a little after four A.M. Unfortunately, he didn't recall seeing anything on his drive in or out—no parked cars, headlights, walkers, or anything else of note. And they'd both been very consumed with the emergency in the barn while he was there. Dr. Lane knew most of the families in the area and, as far as he was concerned, they were all good people, especially Ezra Beiler.

I attended the autopsy. I hate them with a passion and they usually give me nightmares, but I felt I owed it to Jane Doe—to be willing to see what had really been done to her for myself, not to ignore the grim horror of it, not push it off to a paper report I could review over a cup of coffee or a statistic I could tabulate. She was so young, her body only newly ripened as a woman. It would never grow old now.

I met with Grady in his office afterward and told him about the findings.

"The blow was right here." I cupped my hand around the left back side of my skull. "There were no signs of struggle, nothing under her fingernails. So he hits her from behind—she doesn't see it coming. Then, when she's unconscious, he suffocates her like this." I put my hand over my nose and mouth. "That was the cause of death—asphyxiation. The capillaries of her eyes were all blown and she had foam in her airways."

Grady shook his head at the mental image. "So was it an argument? If she wasn't in his face, why'd he hit her?"

I picked up my cup of coffee from where I'd parked it on his desk and tapped the side thoughtfully. "Okay, bear with me; this is all hypothetical. What if she arranges to meet a guy, they go park on a rural road for a little make-out action, and he pushes too far or wants something kinky. She says no, and gets out of the car. Her back is to him, maybe she's calling her dad or a friend to pick her up. But the guy's all jacked up and doesn't want to hear no. He picks up a rock, comes up quietly behind her and—" I mocked a blow to my own head.

Grady made a face. "That's pretty far to go to get into someone's panties. And she didn't show signs of penetration or semen."

"I know. But let's say our perp didn't mean to hurt her that much. The ME's pretty sure the weapon was a rock—that's a weapon of opportunity, not premeditation. Maybe he just meant to stun her so he could have his way, or he just reacted in anger. But the blow does more damage than he intended. Now he panics. He can't take her to the hospital without getting himself in trouble. Maybe he feels he's got no choice but to finish the job, hush her up. So he covers up her mouth and nose."

Grady nods. "Yeah. I could see that. If he'd meant to kill her, he could have kept hitting with the rock, but he only hits her once, right?"

"Right. The fact that he switched methods in the middle indicates some kind of shift in mood or intent. And putting your hand over someone's nose or mouth who's unconscious—that's a coward's act, right? It's bloodless and it's easy. You don't need rage for that. Hell, it's the common choice of mercy killers. We saw a few of those when I was in New York."

"Okay. But why the long time between when he killed her and when he put the body in Miller's barn?"

I dropped into the chair in front of Grady's desk and took a sip from my cup. One thing I loved about the Lancaster police station—they had damn good coffee. "I think he was working it out. He didn't expect to kill her. Suddenly, midday, he's got a dead body. So he hides her and tries to figure out what to do. That night, when it's dark and he can get away with it, he gets rid of her."

"So he, what, put her in his trunk till then?"

I bit my lip. "Maybe. They haven't found any fibers on the body, but she was dragged through the water. Trace evidence could have gotten washed away. But the coroner thinks she spent several hours outside in the snow, postmortem. There was skin tissue damage that indicates contact with ice or snow."

"So he doesn't intend to kill her. It happens. He hides the body outside, goes home, and tries to figure out where to dump her. He remembers this area of Amish farms, with the creek and the trails the animals use to get to the water, and he decides to put her there."

I nodded. "He'd have to know the area well, but yes."

"Either he figures there's no way the family there would be blamed for it, or he's looking for a scapegoat."

"It's hard to believe he'd think anyone at Miller's would be a suspect. The father's unlikely and the oldest boy isn't mature enough, if you ask me." Wayne Miller was a farm boy, so he was strong, but he wasn't all that big and he still gave off the impression of a boy still too naive to have had dealings with a girl like our Jane Doe.

"What if the killer made a mistake? What if he thought he

was putting the body in someone else's barn, someone he thought he could frame?"

"Anything's possible," I admitted reluctantly. "But at some point you have to stop reaching for straws and investigate the most likely theories. Otherwise you'll just chase your own tail and get nowhere."

"Yeah," Grady agreed. "Unfortunately, the boot prints aren't likely to pan out. They're a common Everly farmer's boot that's been in production forever, and from the way the pattern is worn down, they're old."

"Any chance of checking online sales records?"

Grady gave me a you-gotta-be-kidding-me look. "Online! You buy boots like those at a feed store, and you pay cash. That's how farmers work. And yeah, I'm having Hernandez check out the local stores, but honestly, I doubt we'll get a lead."

Damn. I'd pinned some hope on those boot prints.

"So . . . profile. You sure the killer's a man?" Grady asked.

"The scenario we just laid out—it makes more sense if it was a man. But maybe she got in a fight with a girlfriend or a woman jealous because she was flirting with her boyfriend or something. The blow to the head—the ME says it was a strong blow but can't rule out a woman. The suffocation afterward, that definitely could have been a woman. But the way the body was transported . . ."

"Yeah."

"I laid awake thinking about that last night," I admitted. It hadn't been a pleasant evening. "I kept thinking about the killer pushing Jane Doe's body under those chicken-wire fences and then diving under himself—sinking down completely into that freezing cold water in the middle of winter with a dead body *right there*. And then, when he gets to Miller's, pulling her out of the water, lifting that body, carrying it across a field of snow in the night air while soaking wet. That took a lot of strength, but also balls of steel. It was a low of twenty degrees that night. How desperate did the killer have to be to do that? He was desperate to hide what he'd done. Like, crawling-over-broken-glass-to-escape-a-fire desperate."

Desperate . . . why? Desperate to hide his sin? I didn't say it out loud, but my gut had a pet theory. I wasn't convinced a modern person could have done that. We're too soft, too lazy. The killer was someone used to physical hardship, used to doing unpleasant things, a person driven by overwhelming guilt or fear of being found out.

"Yeah," Grady agreed. "We're looking for a man."

"Well, there was no sexual assault, so we can't entirely rule out a very strong woman with big feet, but again—"

"No point wearing yourself out chasing the unlikely. I agree."

"Here's another thing—the Millers don't have a dog. How'd the killer know that? I'd expect most big farms to have a dog. Both of the Fisher farms and the Lapps do. A dog would have woken up the family. That was a big risk to take unless he knew for sure. Maybe that's why it was *that farm*."

"Yeah, you're right. He must have known the Millers. Which brings us back to our list of service providers and customers to those farms."

Or the people who live there, I thought. I'd interviewed everyone who lived at those farms and they all seemed to be as impeccable and forthright as you would expect from the Amish, and there was nothing to connect them to Jane Doe. And yet . . .

Grady saw it on my face. "You're still thinking it's a resident, aren't you, Harris?"

"Not ruling it out."

"They all have alibis—"

"If you consider not waking up a spouse or parent while they're sleeping an alibi. Didn't you ever sneak out of the house when you were a teenager?"

"—and they're all in good standing in the community. Well, the only one who isn't has the most solid alibi of them all." Grady took a sip of his coffee.

A distant alarm bell rang in my head. "What? Who are you talking about?"

He grunted. "Ezra Beiler. I talked to Aaron Lapp. The Millers, the Fishers, the Kings—all of them are beyond reproach in Lapp's eyes. And he's a deacon of the church himself. Ezra's the only one who's not in good standing at the moment, and he had the vet there all night."

I stood up and shoved my empty coffee cup onto his desk, paced. I felt a weird mix of emotions. Annoyance was definitely in there.

"When did you talk to Aaron Lapp about this?" I asked Grady tersely.

"I stopped by there on Saturday after I talked to Klein's Dairy. It was nearby and I wanted to speak to someone high up in the Amish community, get their impression of those farmers."

"And you chose Aaron Lapp? He's one of them!"

Grady got a frown on his brow—part irritated, part guilty—

like he wasn't sure what I was objecting to but he felt maybe he'd done something wrong all the same. "Well, that was sort of the point, Harris. He'd know his neighbors better than anyone, wouldn't he? And he's a deacon. It wasn't like he was trying to put suspicion on anyone. He's positive it couldn't have been an Amish—which I agree with, by the way. He only mentioned the thing with Ezra when I pressed for people's standing in the church."

Everything Grady said made sense, and I would have asked Aaron Lapp those questions myself, had I thought of it. But I didn't like being left out of the loop, especially when the resultant conversation was *mano a mano*. "I'm just surprised you didn't mention it."

"Yeah, I shoulda. But really, I didn't learn anything new except about Ezra, and he's airtight. My focus has been on this other list."

I forced myself to relax. There was no point in broadcasting my sensitivity and being labeled touchy. Been there, done that, learned my lesson. I forced a smile. "Right. So what did Lapp say about Ezra Beiler?"

Grady blew out a heavy breath. "He told me—with reluctance, mind—that Beiler has been struggling since his wife's miscarriage and subsequent death. When I pushed him for more, he said Ezra hasn't been attending meetings like he ought. I thought there was more, but Lapp wouldn't tell me. I wondered—it's a bit odd that Beiler is clean-shaven. The Amish grow beards when they get married, but it's not common for them to shave it off if they're widowed, not that I've seen. Anyway, Lapp just said they were praying for him and it was 'in God's hands.' I got the impression they were giving him some time to straighten out due to his mourning. If he doesn't, he'll likely be in trouble."

"Trouble?"

"Well, nothing legal. Every Amish Ordnung has rules, and members of the church are expected to follow them. If they don't, they'll be given warnings, and if they still don't comply, eventually they'll be shunned."

I knew what shunning meant. I wondered how close Ezra Beiler was to that eventuality and exactly why. I was reminded of the attitude of despair in which I'd first seen him. I knew all about despair. We were bosom buddies. Maybe that's why that man had gotten under my skin.

"Just saying," Grady went on. "I'm glad Beiler has a strong alibi. He seems like a nice kid to me. I don't give a rat's ass if he misses church or shaves his damn beard. I'm just glad we don't have to consider him a suspect. As for the rest, I don't see it."

"I know," I said, in a conciliatory voice. *I know you don't.*

"You're the one who said there's no point grasping at straws."

"Yeah. And that's exactly what I meant. So let's go over the list of people who visit those farms."

Grady was correct about grasping at straws. I'd done some research online. Not that I was trying to prove him wrong, but there were other Amish communities outside Lancaster and I was curious if there'd ever been an Amish murder anywhere. I couldn't find any reference to a deliberate homicide being done by an Amish ever, which is amazing if you think about it. I did, however, find other vices. Drug trafficking, for one, among the Amish youth. Numerous cases of animal abuse and a few of domestic abuse.

I'd seen plenty of families in my time as a cop in New York

that had no real parenting, no structure, no moral code. By comparison, the tight-knit families of the Amish were a dream. I may not have believed in God the way they did, but as a cop I couldn't argue against their sense of morality and community. But the fact was, the Amish were not eunuchs and not saints. They were human like all the rest of us and were capable of grievous wrong. But if they were capable of abuse and drug trafficking, wasn't it just a small step to homicide?

I hoped I was wrong.

"Detective Harris," I said, showing the guy my badge. "And this is Detective Grady. May we come in?"

Larry Wannemaker was a driver for Klein's Dairy. He drove a truck that did a pickup round to thirty-one farms, siphoning up milk into the company's refrigerated tanker truck. His run included Grimlace Lane Monday through Friday and had for several years.

"What's this about?" Larry was playing it tough. He guarded the door to his little ranch-style house like he was Cerberus on the banks of the River Styx.

"It's about a police investigation," Grady said flatly, looming even taller. "You can let us in, or we'd be happy to take you down to the station to chat."

Larry scratched his side, where a stained red hunter's vest covered a gray thermal shirt. He looked nervous. "Fuck it. I don't have time for that shit. Give me a minute though."

He disappeared back inside, shutting the door. I heard movement as he apparently straightened up. There was the sound of an old window being forced. Grady looked worried for a second but I just rolled my eyes. The guy wasn't trying to escape; he was airing out the place. I could smell the pot from the doorway.

Finally, Larry let us in.

Larry Wannemaker was in his late twenties, though he looked older. His long brown hair was back in a ponytail and he had a goatee. He was lean going on skinny and could be considered good-looking if you disregarded his crooked yellow teeth and the lecherous gleam in his eyes as he looked me over. He got high regularly, I guessed, and not just on beer and pot either. Still, his place was fairly clean and his employer seemed happy enough. Larry might be a partier, but he was straight when he needed to be. You didn't run a milk route if you were irresponsible. This much I knew.

A stack of porn magazines featuring big-breasted women left no doubt as to his sexual orientation. Charming.

"You work for Klein's Dairy doing a pickup route in Paradise," I began coolly.

"Yeah." Larry sounded wary. He didn't offer to let us sit down. He stood nervously and folded his arms tight across his chest.

"So you know that area pretty well then, huh? Ronks Road, Lenore, Grimlace Lane."

"Yeah. What's this about?"

"Ever seen this girl before?" I pulled out the photo of our Jane Doe and handed it over.

Larry stared at the picture. I could swear I saw recognition on his face, but it passed quickly. He shoved the photo back to me. "No idea."

"Really."

Larry shrugged. "Why the hell should I know who that is?" He chewed on a thumbnail.

I stared at him. I wasn't getting a good vibe. I was pretty sure he was lying. And why was he so nervous? Was it just because he had drugs in the house?

"Do you hunt?" I asked, nodding at his vest.

"Huh?" He looked down in surprise, as if expecting to see a gun he'd forgotten he was carrying. "Oh, the vest. Yeah, I do. Sometimes."

Brilliant.

"When? What do you hunt?"

"Just deer. I go every year. A friend of mine hunts bear, but I've never gone. I mean to someday though." He chewed on the nail again. His eyes slid to my chest and stayed there. Apparently my B cups held his interest just fine even though they were mostly hidden by my open wool coat and suit jacket.

I leaned forward a bit, tilting my head down in an obvious bid to get him to look at my face. "Mr. Wannemaker? Ever hunt along the creek there by Grimlace Lane?"

Caught, he looked guilty. "No. We go up to the state game lands. Why? Was someone shot?" His gaze flickered anxiously between Grady and me. "Hey, I haven't been out hunting since last September. Like, *at all*."

I wondered if he was being coy, if he really hadn't heard about the dead girl found in the Millers' barn. Ezra said that news traveled fast, but it might not travel at all between the Amish and a man like Larry, even if he did pick up their milk. It was hard to imagine Amos Miller and Larry Wannemaker having much to say to each other.

I gave Grady a slight nod.

"Where were you this past Tuesday, between ten A.M. and four P.M.?" Grady asked.

Larry crossed his arms again and huffed. "Workin'. I drive my route six to two, Monday through Friday, and I usually don't pull out of the dairy till three."

"According to Klein's, you take a lunch break every day from eleven to noon," I said. "Do you park somewhere and eat a bag lunch?"

"Yeah. So?"

"Where'd you do that on Tuesday?"

Larry scratched his forehead with one overly long thumbnail. *Cocaine.* Either that or he was a fan of Dracula.

"I, um, I dunno. I usually pull the truck into a park, the one on London Vale Road. But maybe—no, I think it was Monday, I had to run some errands."

I looked at him without blinking. That was almost coherent. "So you were at the Paradise Community Park on Tuesday?"

"I think so. Yeah."

"Anyone see you there?"

"Well, I guess. I mean, people are around the park usually. Probably not in January though."

This guy was full of certitude.

"Ever meet up with a girl on your break? Get a little action?" I raised an eyebrow slyly.

"What? No! Not in the company truck, man!" He laughed as if it was absurd, yet he looked damned uncomfortable. Made me think he *had* had a girl in there. Or maybe he liked a nice slow jerk-off on his lunch break. He seemed exactly the sort to film an at-work masturbation video and put it up on Xtube. I stared at him.

"So you basically have no alibi for Tuesday lunch, then," Grady summarized.

"I told you, I was at the park! Maybe someone saw the truck. You could ask around. Isn't that your job?"

"What about Tuesday night, from midnight on?" I asked calmly.

Larry shrugged. "I was here sleeping. I don't go out during the week. I get up butt-fuck early on the milk route. Alarm goes off at five A.M. I'm always on time. You can ask 'em. I don't party on weeknights."

"Was anyone here with you on Tuesday night?"

"No. Shit, I live alone. Who's supposed to be here? Casper the Friendly Ghost?"

"No, no worries," I said, giving him a reassuring smile. "Hey, you don't mind if I take a look around, do you?"

A jolt of panic appeared in his eyes. "No! I mean—hey, man, you can't do that without a warrant or something. Right?"

Goddamned drugs. What I hoped to look for were the boots, but we weren't getting past Mr. Paranoid here. Not today.

"That's all right, Mr. Wannemaker," Grady said. "We'll be in touch."

———————

"I like him for it," Grady said when we got in the car.

I hummed doubtfully. "He was lying. I'm just not sure about what. Seems like we can take our pick of the guy's vices."

"He was nervous as hell and has no alibi for when Jane Doe

was killed or moved on Tuesday. What if he arranged to meet her at the park for a quickie, they argued like you said, he kills her, and then doesn't have time to hide the body? He's got to finish his route. So he stashes her at the park and goes back to take care of her later."

"It works," I said, though I wasn't as convinced as Grady sounded.

"It explains the time lag. And he's the type who'd kill like that, doncha think? Hit her impulsively and then chicken out and cover up her mouth and nose, like you said. Plus, he knows the Millers don't have a dog. He knows those farms."

"I could see him for the murder. Maybe. But what about the way the body was moved? Larry doesn't strike me as having the fortitude to get into that ice-cold water with a dead body and carry her across the field all wet like that, try to be smart and arrange the body. Basically, he's a stoner."

"He's not! He holds down a decent job. Besides, maybe he's playing dumb."

I shook my head. "Not convinced, *kemosabe*."

Grady's cell phone chirped the *Rocky* theme, interrupting our debate. I winced. "You know, there are three decades of movie themes to choose from since then."

He rolled his eyes. "Grady," he answered.

He listened for a moment, then looked at me, his eyes alight. "We have a positive ID on Jane Doe. Her name is Jessica Travis."

"Thank God," I breathed. I couldn't stop a big smile. *There you are, my girl. We've got you now.*

"Hop on 283 toward Harrisburg," Grady said. "We have a home address."

CHAPTER 4

The Naming

Jessica Travis's home was sad. There really wasn't another word for it. It was a small bungalow in a trashy neighborhood of the little town of Manheim. It probably had no more than a thousand square feet inside, the small porch had collapsed on one side, the paint was peeling, and the snow-covered yard looked like it was tangled with weeds. An older Camaro, long overdue for the junkyard, sat in the driveway.

Grady and I shot each other a look as he shoved a piece of cinnamon gum in his mouth. We walked up to the door.

I braced myself. Jessica Travis had been identified thanks to the guidance counselor of Manheim Central High School. He'd recognized the crime-scene photo and confirmed that she hadn't been in school since the day before the murder. Her family hadn't been notified yet. It was a good chance to get a gut reaction from her parents, who had to be considered for the crime. Telling people their child is dead is never fun though.

Grady rang the bell.

It took several tries before anyone answered. The door was pulled open with a yank, and a woman stood there. She looked to be in her forties and she was dressed in a velveteen robe that looked vaguely Christmassy. Her bleached blonde bed head and bleary eyes said she'd just been woken up.

"What do you want?"

"Is this the home of Jessica Travis?" I asked.

Her eyes narrowed. "Yeah."

"Are you LeeAnn Travis? Jessica's mother?"

"Yeah. What's goin' on?" She looked worried as she fumbled in her pocket for a pack of cigarettes.

I showed her my badge. "I'm Detective Harris and this is Detective Grady. We're with the Lancaster police. May we come in?"

She looked at Grady and me as she lit her cigarette and took a deep drag. "Shit." Then she backed away from the door, giving us a silent invitation.

"I haven't had coffee yet. I'll make some," she mumbled, as Grady and I entered and shut the door. The ceiling was so low, it made me feel claustrophobic. The living room sported a tatty couch and a fair amount of old newspapers and trash. "I work nights, so I'm not used to getting up at this hour."

I checked my watch. It was just after eleven in the morning.

"If you don't mind—we'd like to speak to you before you get busy in the kitchen," Grady said firmly. "I'm afraid we have some bad news. You might want to have a seat."

Jessica's mother paused on her way out of the room and took a long drag on her cigarette. "Is Jessica in some kind of trouble? Because I know she ain't eighteen for a few more weeks, but I really can't control her. I ain't even seen her in nearly a week."

Grady glanced at me. I knew what that look meant. Either Jessica's mother really had no clue that her daughter was dead, or she was a very good actress.

"When was the last time you saw Jessica?" I asked.

She thought about it. "Last Tuesday she asked me for some spending money. I make the best tips on weekends, so I usually give her some at the start of the week, but I didn't see her on Monday."

"So she's been missing for a full week? And didn't you report this to the police?" Grady asked evenly.

Mrs. Travis rubbed at her eyebrow with the thumb of the hand that held the cigarette. I winced at the sight of the smoke curling around her eyes, but she didn't seem to mind it. "Look, Jess does her own thing. She's out lots of nights. And she's been telling me for months she was gonna take off for New York. I figured either she done that or she was at some guy's house and she'd show up eventually."

Her voice was hard-edged but there was a hint of fear underneath, like she knew something was terribly wrong.

"Please have a seat on the sofa, Mrs. Travis," Grady said gently.

She moved there, walking stiffly as if resisting it. She sat and looked up at Grady, her jaw set.

"I'm afraid Jessica is dead," he told her.

LeeAnn Travis blinked a few times, took a long drag off her cigarette, and, with no facial expression at all, pulled a large and dirty ashtray toward her and cradled it in her lap like a dog. She stared at nothing. We waited for it to sink in.

"You sure it's Jess?" she said finally.

Grady nodded at me and I spoke up.

"We can go down to the morgue later if you'd like to see her. But I do have a photo." I took out the crime-scene photo we'd been showing around and passed it to her. She looked at it and her hand shook. Her mouth twisted like a cheap dishrag and her eyes got red. "Oh my God." She sat the photo carefully on the coffee table and lit another cigarette off the first. Her hands shook so badly, she could hardly accomplish it.

"Do you have someone you can call? You shouldn't be alone," Grady said.

"My friend Amy, but she's at work right now. I'll call her later."

"We need to ask you some questions, to help with our investigation. Do you feel able to do that now?"

LeeAnn nodded absently. "Yeah."

Grady and I sat. I pulled out my iPad and started the recorder. "This is Detective Elizabeth Harris. I'm with Detective Mike Grady and we're interviewing LeeAnn Travis, the mother of Jessica Travis, on Tuesday, January twenty-eighth, 2014. Can you tell me, in more detail, Mrs. Travis, about the last time you saw Jessica?"

"I work nights at McLeery's. I'm a cocktail waitress. Work six to three. If I see Jess, it's normally in the afternoons between school and when I go off to work. Last Tuesday, she asked me for some spending money and I gave her two twenties. That's it." Her voice was thick.

"Did she mention any plans? Anyone she was going to see? Anyplace she planned to go?"

She huffed. "She didn't tell me shit like that. We'd just fight about it, so we steered clear. Easier that way."

"Fight about it? Why?"

For the first time since I'd told her Jessica was dead, LeeAnn seemed to come to her full senses. She looked me in the eye. "Jess met boys off the Internet. I didn't like it. She said they were nice and cute and everything, but I told her it weren't safe. Is that what happened? Did someone—"

Her voice cracked. She noticed that her cigarette had burned down to nothing, ground it out in the ashtray, and lit another.

"She was murdered, yes," I said as gently as it's possible to say such a thing.

She shut her eyes. "Oh God, no."

"Do you know the names of any of the people she met up with?"

It took her a moment to respond. "No. Like I said, she didn't never give me the details."

"Do you know how she met them? What chat room she was in?"

She shook her head. "My poor baby. I told her. Told her she was gonna get in trouble one day."

"She never mentioned a website or chat room to you?" Grady pushed.

"I'm not big on computers, so it wouldn't have meant anything to me anyhow."

"What about Jessica's father?" I asked.

"Ain't got one," LeeAnn answered crisply.

"Do you have a boyfriend? An ex-husband? Anyone who might have been in Jessica's life?"

She gave me a sharp look then. Her eyes got hard. "Not for the past year."

There was the bite of anger in her voice. A stepfather or Mom's boyfriend would be a good bet, especially if there was bad blood there.

"And before that?"

"There was someone. Charlie Bender. He's a bastard, and you can tell him I said so."

"LeeAnn." I spoke softly and was rewarded when she looked right at me. "Was Charlie inappropriate with Jessica?"

She made a face, tears coming to her eyes for the first time. "She said not. It weren't for lack of interest on his part, that's for damn sure."

Grady gave me a very interested look. "We'll need you to give us any contact info you have for Charlie Bender. And I'd like you to make a list of all of Jessica's friends and boyfriends, current or otherwise, any family she spent time around, and any other friends of yours she met, even if you haven't seen them for a few years. Can you do that?"

"Yeah." She wiped at her eyes. Her whole body was shaking now—just little tremors here and there, like the shudders of a sinking ship. "I have her car, if you wanna see that. Picked it up at that fruit market."

"What fruit market? When was this?" I asked.

She closed her eyes as if fighting to concentrate through her turmoil. "Wednesday last. The man called in the morning and woke me up. Got our number off the registration in the glove compartment. Said the car'd been left there all night and I had to pick it up that day or he'd have it towed. He was nice about it though. I had my friend Amy drop me over there and I drove it home. I had spare keys, thank God."

"The name and location of the market?"

"Oh, something with an 'H,' like Hank's Fruit Market or something. It's on 30 by that antique place."

I knew the place she meant. It was in the town of Paradise. The fact that she'd just blithely picked up her daughter's abandoned car and didn't notify the police seemed to slide from "open parenting" to "criminal negligence." I could feel myself getting angry. This whole scene was a little too familiar. "And you didn't worry that Jessica had apparently abandoned her car there?"

She rubbed a knuckle in her eye, her lip quivering. "I see it now, but I just thought . . . thought she'd had some guy pick her up there and let the car sit. You know how teenagers are. Never think about the trouble they're causin' someone else. And that car ain't worth nothin'. I almost let them tow the damn thing but then I thought, when Jess got back . . ." She trailed off weakly.

Grady gave me a grim look. "We do want to take a look at that car. Is it here?"

"In the garage."

"Did you notice anything unusual about it when you picked it up? Any . . . blood. Signs of a struggle? A suitcase? Anything?" I prompted.

She shook her head. "Nothing like that. And I did look through it," she said defensively. "Thought maybe she'd left a note or somethin', but it just looked like always."

"All right. Did you notice anything unusual in Jessica's

behavior in the past few months—maybe she'd met someone new and was happier than usual, or stressed out or fearful?"

LeeAnn frowned and picked at some lint on her robe with her cigarette-free hand. "She didn't say a whole lot to me most days. She was a teenager. Thought she knew it all." She picked some more, her frown deepening. "A few months ago she was upset about a friend. Asked me what she should do if she thought someone had gone missing. I told her to report it to someone at the school. Never heard if she did. Guess she was pretty upset about that at the time."

"Do you recall the friend's name?"

"She never said. Jess never brought friends here. She was ashamed of this place, I guess. Of me. Kids are, at that age. It's normal." She looked at me pleadingly, as if wanting me to confirm that she was right, that it wasn't about her.

Grady and I exchanged a look. "She never mentioned this missing friend again?" I pushed. *And you didn't bother to ask?*

LeeAnn shook her head.

I left Grady to collect a list of names and went into Jessica's room. I was hoping for a laptop or a computer, maybe some photos.

I'd already been feeling a sense of uneasy familiarity in the living room. Jessica's room brought it forward in a bittersweet rush. The room was small, but I could tell she'd taken pains with it. There were cheery rainbow decals on the window and a bright pink comforter on the bed. There was a bookcase full of young adult books. There was a big poster of the Manhattan skyline at night on one wall. It wasn't the poster of New York I'd had on my wall when I was a girl, but it was close enough.

The house where I'd grown up in nearby Quarryville had been a bit more respectable than this, but not by much. My father was a high school math teacher and my mother a housewife. Dear old dad was also a closet alcoholic who shut himself up in his "office" whenever he was home. My mother was a passive enabler addicted to her soaps and romance novels. Everything was fine with my mother as long as she was left alone. I was the only child of a couple that probably should never have had any children at all.

I stared at Jessica's New York poster with a weird sense of déjà vu. I'd once been a small-town PA girl who'd longed to escape. Fortunately, I had a high IQ like my father and tests came easy to me. I'd gotten into NYU with a partial scholarship. I'd lived my dream and now here I was, back in Pennsylvania in a tiny house in another small town looking at someone else's hopes. Someone who, unlike me, would never live them.

I made myself turn away and keep looking. The room was very tidy, as if Jessica were rebelling against her mother's disorder. There was a mirror and a bag of makeup on the dresser. I unzipped the bag. It was full of newer-looking makeup. It seemed unlikely to me that Jessica would have left it if she'd intended to be gone for long. Her closet too was full of cheap but well-cared-for clothes, including sweaters, skirts, and T-shirts. Jeans were neatly folded over wire hangers. I guessed these were the best clothes Jessica owned. Either her mother hadn't bothered to check to see what Jessica had taken, or LeeAnn didn't know much about her daughter.

There was a book bag inside the closet. It contained three textbooks, a packet of Jessica's senior pictures, and a notebook. I flipped through it but nothing caught my eye. I went out to the living room.

"Where is Jessica's computer?" I asked LeeAnn. She was still working on her list, Grady poised beside her on the sofa.

"Oh. I have it." She put down her pen. "I'm sorry. I can't think of anyone else."

"You have Jessica's computer?" I prompted.

"Yeah. Told her when I bought it we'd have to share. Didn't have the money for two. She used it more than me, but she left it behind. I just figured . . ." She trailed off, perhaps realizing that Jessica would never be hogging the computer again.

"Can you get it please?" I asked quietly.

She got up and went into her bedroom. She came out a moment later carrying a rather clunky Sony laptop. "Here."

I opened it on the coffee table. We waited while it booted.

"What about a cell phone?" I asked.

"She had one. Put a bright pink cover on the thing. Lost it months ago though. Told her I couldn't buy a new one, not till her birthday." She swallowed hard. "Was she . . . hurt bad?" LeeAnn had given up on the cigarettes for the moment and now had her hands buried in the robe's pockets, trying to stop their shaking. Her face looked like a tire someone had let the air out of. I felt sorry for her.

"No," Grady said. "She was struck from behind. She probably didn't feel much of anything."

"Good. That's . . . that's somethin'." She looked like she might be sick. She sank down into a chair again.

The computer had booted. There was a user prompt. I turned it toward her. "Can you log in as Jessica?"

She shook her head. "We had two accounts on there. Don't know her password, just mine."

"Give me yours, then." I wrote it down. "We're going to need to take the computer. If Jessica was meeting men online, we need to see if we can find out who."

LeeAnn looked like she was going to protest for a second, then she nodded. "This guy who hurt her—he kill anyone before?"

"We don't know who killed her, Mrs. Travis, so we really can't say."

She looked me in the eye. "Detective Harris, right? Do you think you can find out? Maybe Jess and I didn't always get along, but she was my only . . . She didn't—"

"I'll find him," I told her, which was more of a promise than I had any right to make, but I meant it. I wasn't really promising LeeAnn Travis though.

I'd find him for Jessica's sake.

CHAPTER 5

A Lesson in Husbandry

"We should show her senior photo around," I said as Grady drove back to the station. "Someone who didn't recognize her from the crime-scene photo might recognize Jessica from that picture. We also have a name."

"Yeah. Good idea."

"It'll go faster if we divide and conquer."

"I'll put Smith and Hernandez on it."

I hedged. "If you don't mind, I'd like to do the farmers on Grimlace Lane myself."

Grady cocked an eyebrow. "Why?"

"I've been wanting to go back over there again. I want to take another look at those woods, get a feel for the place."

Grady smirked. "Like in a movie? You gonna stand in the woods and get into the mind of the killer?" He used a spooky voice.

"Yeah. I have that extrasensory power. Did you miss that bit on my resume?"

Grady didn't laugh. "You still think one of them did it, doncha?"

I tried to look disinterested, though he wasn't far off the mark. "It's possible someone knows more than they're saying. Which wouldn't be hard, since they weren't exactly gushing fonts of information when we interviewed them."

"It's nothing personal. It's just the Amish way to have minimum contact with the English—especially people like state inspectors and the police."

"And uppity women."

"Yes, and uppity women," Grady admitted with a hard look. "Of which you are a prime example. But mostly police. It's that whole 'outside authority' thing."

"Otherwise known as obstructing justice."

Grady frowned. "Harris—"

I did a semi–eye roll, mild enough to be polite because he was my boss, but enough to get my point across. "Not obstructing justice, just reticent, I get it. I greatly admire stoicism. You know, it was my favorite philosophy school in college."

Grady snorted. "Bullshit."

"Anyway, this is just showing them a photo and ascertaining if any of them have ever seen her before. I'll be sensitive. I'll be gentle as the morning dew. But I do want to go out there again. I have a feeling we're missing something in those woods. Okay with you?"

"Yeah," Grady agreed gruffly. "My money's on Larry, the friendly neighborhood dairy man, so I'll go back over there with the new picture. I'll take a uniform with me. You owe me fifty if he does a runner and is in custody by tonight."

I held up my fist for a bump. "You're on, my man."

On my way over to Grimlace Lane, I pulled off at a wide place in the road. Ronks Road climbed a hill here and before me was laid out a view of farmland that stretched for miles. I'd stopped to look at this view several times over the summer, when the fields were green in squares of different textures—corn, soybeans, alfalfa, wheat—and in the fall when you could see Amish farmers out driving teams of horses to harvest crops. It was beautiful and soothing. It was home. Now the snowy fields, houses and barns looked like a folk art painting in the cold light of a winter afternoon.

Unlike most places in America, Lancaster County still had plenty of small farms instead of conglomerate-held thousand-acre empires. The farms here were twenty to two hundred acres, homesteads with farmhouses and barns and dairy cows happily grazing on green pastures. In the view I was looking at now, nearly every farm was Amish, noted by the lack of power poles, the presence of windmills or solar panels, and the ever-present plain-colored washing on the line.

It often surprises tourists how many Amish there are. It's not like you drive out in the country and see their farms dotted here and there. No, there are over fifty thousand Amish in Lancaster County and in many places their farms are back-to-back-to-back. It's not really surprising, considering the fact that they don't practice birth control and they have a retention rate of eight-five percent or more. To be blunt, there are a shitload of Amish.

I found this view helped me clear my head. I'd come back to Lancaster County to find peace, and I guess I had.

It was weird how things worked. When I was growing up here, all I wanted was to escape. But after ten years of being a cop in New York City, I'd longed to come home. I saw too much there, too much violence, too much cruelty and prejudice, too much ugliness. In particular, the events of my last year there were so unbearable, I kept them locked off in an area of my mind I rarely visited. You could say I turned tail and ran, as some of my friends believed. But I preferred to think of it as a choice. It wasn't that I couldn't take it anymore—I chose *not* to take it. I'd wanted to get out while I still had a few unbruised, unwithered pieces of my heart, before the hardened cynic replaced every inch of the girl I'd been, the one who optimistically wanted to help people, to make a difference. I wanted to go somewhere it was green, where there was space between all the buildings and the bodies, someplace where people knew each other, where small-town familiarity meant anonymous hate was not an option, where the darkness was pushed out far enough that I didn't have to stare it in the face every single fucking day.

I wanted a simpler life. I thought I'd gotten it, but this case was stirring currents that disturbed me. It was as if I were seeing another dimension, one below the surface, and I wasn't sure I liked what I sensed there.

———————

What I hadn't told Grady was that, yeah, the woods on Grimlace Lane were calling to me, but Ezra Beiler was calling me too. I had an urge to see him again. I told myself it was because he was the only Amish person we'd spoken to who wasn't surrounded by a huge family as well as an impenetrable wall of otherness. He'd actually looked me in the eye and spoken frankly when I'd interviewed him. And I'd been compiling a list of questions I wanted to ask a local, an Amish who would give me a straight answer.

But bullshit stinks no matter how many kernels of truth there are buried in it. I knew the draw I felt to Ezra wasn't all about the case. Since the first time I laid eyes on him, I'd wanted to know more about him. It was like when you hear a snatch of a song on the radio that you've never heard before but that you're instantly drawn to, and you can't rest until you find out the name and the artist and get a download of it on your phone. I wasn't going to label it or even think about it too hard, but I did want to see Ezra again and test if it was still there, probe around the edges of it like you do a sore tooth.

I left him for last. It was perhaps no surprise that no one at the Millers', either of the Fisher households, or the Kings' recognized Jessica Travis, either by name or by her senior photo. I watched them carefully as they looked at the picture, and if they were acting they were thespian champs. Deacon Aaron Lapp and his wife, Miriam, were out doing some "visitin'" according to their daughter Sarah, age twelve. She was babysitting the two younger children, Job, age ten, and Rebecca, age eight. They were all convincingly uninterested in either the photo or the name.

I pulled up at Ezra's farm about four P.M. At this time of year, there was only an hour of daylight left. I looked toward the woods and quickly made up my mind.

I found Ezra in the workshop in the barn. He was building a rocking chair made out of some synthetic material I didn't recognize. He had on those black pants that rode his hips so effortlessly, black suspenders, and a plain blue shirt rolled up at the cuffs. He looked at me as I came in, then finished what he was doing, screwing the arm of the chair into place manually. He was as attractive as I remembered, unfortunately. I watched the healthy veins in his strong forearms and hands as he worked the screwdriver. I had to look away before I forgot my reason for being there.

After a few minutes, he put down his tools.

"Afternoon, Detective Elizabeth Harris," he said in his broad German accent.

"You remembered."

He considered me and rubbed his chin. "It may surprise ya, but not that many police come by here." There was a trace of amusement in his eyes.

"Hard to believe. I'd think they'd be all over those chairs." I motioned to several that were already done and waiting along the wall.

He took me seriously, or seemed to. He ran a hand over the chair he was working on. "Oh, ja. This is Trex. You know it?"

I shook my head.

"It's a composite. You can leave it sittin' in the rain or snow. It'll never break down, this stuff."

It was also ugly as sin, the furniture equivalent of Crocs. I didn't say it.

"I prefer workin' with pine, but I make these for a local shop. Tourists like 'em. It's easy and it pays good." He headed for the doorway. "Come on."

I wasn't sure where he was taking me, but it ended up being just outside the door of the barn. I half expected him to light up a cigarette, since that's what cops normally do when they "step outside." He didn't. He just took a deep breath, eyes closed and face turned up to the sky, as if appreciating the opportunity to get fresh air. The sun had broken through the murk and it was about 42 degrees out. That was downright balmy for this time of year, but even in my wool coat I was still cold. The drip and squish of melting snow was everywhere, but the temperature was dropping now that it was nearly dark. The runoff would turn to ice overnight.

"So what can I do for ya . . . Detective Harris?" He looked out over the yard, not at me, but the corner of his mouth turned up a bit. It did that funny thing to my stomach.

I shook it off and pulled Jessica's senior photo, encased in a plastic sleeve, from my pocket. "We have a new photo of the girl who was found at Miller's. I'd like you to take a look."

He took the photo and studied it for a long moment. "Still don't know her." His face betrayed no emotion.

"Her name's Jessica Travis. Ever heard it before?"

He shook his head and, with a disquieted frown, passed the photo back to me. "Such a sorrowful thing."

"Yes."

"Hope she didn't suffer." He looked away, back over the yard. His sympathy seemed genuine.

"It was fast," I said. Then thought I probably could have kept that tidbit to myself, Ezra's alibi notwithstanding.

The sun was suddenly way too low on the horizon.

"Listen, I wanted to walk over and take another look at the creek before it gets dark. Would you walk with me? I have more questions."

He hesitated a moment, then nodded. "Lemme grab my coat."

A moment later, he reappeared with a black barn coat and black hat, looking solemn and way more handsome than a man had any right to when putting so little effort into it. I could practically hear the wailing and gnashing of teeth of the metrosexuals of Manhattan. I smiled to myself at the thought as he opened the gate to his pasture.

"Somethin' funny?" he asked as I walked through it.

I shook my head. "Not really."

It hadn't snowed for four days, and with today's warmer weather, the pasture was a slog. At least this time I'd worn wellies, so I had better traction. I kept an eye on the horse trails. The pasture was large—at least ten acres. The mules tended to use defined paths in the snow, much like we would. There were crisscrossing trails where the snow had been beaten down. The ones used most recently were muddy from the snowmelt. I looked back at the barn, where a large horse bay was open onto the pasture.

"Are your animals free to come and go in the pasture all the time, or do you shut them up at night?"

"That bay's open twenty-four hours a day. 'Cept if the weather gets too dangerous for 'em—deep snow or ice. In the spring, if we get too much rain, I have to close them in for days or they'll hurt the sod. And the spring grass can make 'em sick too if they eat too much of it."

"Were they shut in the night the vet was here?"

"No. They ain't been shut in for a good month."

"Do you know if they're in the habit of going down to the creek to drink in the middle of the night or early morning?"

He gave me a funny look. "Can't say what they do at night. It's a little dark out, ya know? But early morning they do. First light."

I thought he was joking a little, despite his absolutely grave delivery.

"What about cows? Are they left free to come and go all the time? Would they typically go to the creek at first light?"

Ezra stopped walking—not because my questions had been so perplexing but because a huge mule was walking straight toward us. Most of the animals in the pasture ignored us and continued to dig through the snow—looking for grass, I assumed. I was just fine with being ignored because, honestly, the mules were damned big animals. But this one was bearing down with a jogging gait and looked like it had no intention of stopping. I just managed not to duck behind Ezra and hide.

He held up his hand. "Whoa."

The mule stopped in front of us and nudged Ezra with its head. Now that they were next to each other, I thought I recognized the mule as the one that had been comforting Ezra the first time I saw him.

"This here is Horse," he said, rubbing the creature's nose. "I'd tell him to get on, 'cept he won't listen, not until he's had enough of a hello."

"You named a mule Horse?"

"Horse has the same sense of humor as me, so I thought he'd appreciate it."

I snorted. Ezra kept walking and Horse walked along behind him, keeping his nose over Ezra's shoulder to be stroked as if that were a natural way of moving along.

"Why do you raise mules?" I asked. "Why not horses?"

"My da bought one to try it out when I was fifteen. This one, in fact. Took to him right away. Liked him so much, I decided to raise 'em. A mule has a lot more personality than a horse, right from the time it falls from its mother's womb. Horse here, for example, he's always thought he was human. And mules're healthier and steadier too. Less fearful on the roads."

"It's a crossbreed, right?"

"Ja. You gotta mate a donkey and a horse. A mule is barren, whether it's a john or a molly." About then Horse had apparently had enough of a hello and went trotting across the pasture toward some equine friends.

"It's an interesting choice, to breed an animal that can't reproduce itself. Must make it challenging."

"One of my best customers calls it 'job security.'" There was a glint of humor in his eyes. "Anyhow, mules are special. Maybe some things the creator makes aren't meant to multiply."

There was a funny tone in his voice, something dark. I wasn't sure what it meant until I remembered what Grady had said about Ezra Beiler losing not only his wife but apparently a child too in a miscarriage. Suddenly my own mourning hit me down low, an undefined pain in my core, and I felt guilty and stupid for the way Ezra made me feel—the way I hadn't felt since Terry died.

I didn't know what to say, so I said nothing. We were nearly at the trees.

"You were askin' about cows. See, mules are smarter than horses by far. And cows make horses look intelligent. Usually cows are milked in the mornin', so farmers will shut 'em up after the evenin' milkin', especially this time of year. Then they let 'em out again once they've been milked in the mornin'."

"What time do they finish the morning milking?"

"Depends on how lazy the farmer is," Ezra said with a gravely serious tone. "But that's just talkin' about milkin' cows. There's also calves and heifers. You need to separate the calves and the heifers from the milkin' cows so they don't steal your milk. They like as not have free access to a separate pasture all the time. Then there's the bulls, if a farm's got 'em. I guess you know why they'd need to have their own acre. And if it's beef cows, well, that's a whole 'nother story. Most farmers with beef cows just leave the herd out all the time cause there's no reason to bring 'em into the barn or keep the bulls apart even."

It was the most information any of the Amish had given me without repeated prompting. We'd reached the creek, and I stopped there and looked at him.

"That's . . . useful. But I'd probably need to take a course in animal husbandry before I'd remember half of it."

"I guess I shoulda just said, 'It all depends.'" He got a wry little quirk in the corner of his mouth and a sparkle in his eyes even as they avoided mine and looked out over the creek. Holy shit. I was beginning to figure out Ezra Beiler's sense of humor, and it was drier than sandpaper in the desert. I liked it.

"What about your neighbor's animals? They're mostly dairy cows, right?"

He shrugged. "I seen 'em down here." He nodded his head toward the chicken wire strung up between his farm and the Millers'. "But can't say I've put much thought into it. Got work enough of my own without worrying about their animals, 'less I see 'em in the road or someplace they're not supposed to be. They get loose in my garden, I'd be real interested in that."

I turned away to hide my smile. "Okay. Do you ever see any hunters or fisherman using the creek?"

"I hear gunshots more than I see 'em, but they're down here for sure."

"It doesn't bother the Amish when hunters trespass on your land?"

"Well, sometimes it's Amish who hunt here. It's allowed, you know, though most Amish farmers don't have the time. But English people do it too. There's a sort of honor system. Hunters keep the deer from getting to be a problem—deer and farmin' don't get along real well. And if they bring somethin' down on your land, usually they'll leave a piece of it at the door. We had a man leave us a forelimb of venison a few times a year when I was a boy."

"I see. So the fact that you have that chicken wire strung up across the creek doesn't stop the hunters?"

"Depends on whether or not they can swim," he said in that ultra serious tone I was beginning to associate with having my leg tugged ever so skillfully. I refrained from rolling my eyes.

"In truth, hunters stay on that far side, beyond the fence." He pointed to the far bank where the woods rose up toward the road and the chicken wire ended up forming a somewhat lazy and lower barrier between the trees. "If they shoot somethin' inside the fence line, they'll sure as heck climb over to get it. Or come 'round from the farms if they have to."

That made sense. Hunters didn't have to be *in* the water to shoot—or to become experts on the lay of the land and the way the animals moved on it. "Right. Do you know anyone who regularly hunts or fishes around here?"

"I'd recognize faces. Can't say as I know their names."

"Fair enough." If we ever had a suspect in hand, being recognized by the locals would help. "But doesn't the chicken wire keep out the deer too?"

"Nah. They jump it easy."

"Then why don't the horses? Or the mules?"

"You ask a lot of questions," he commented with an ironic look. He rubbed his chin. "I suppose a horse could jump it if it was in a passion about it, like if there was a mare in heat on t'other side. But they come down here to drink, and the good grass is behind 'em. They don't particularly care for chicken wire or woods anyhow." He shrugged. "It works. That's good enough for me."

"Okay."

I looked around for a few minutes. Ezra didn't seem to feel the need to fill the space with chatter; he just waited. By then it was getting so dark, I couldn't see anyway. We made our way back up the bank, and I slipped in some mud. Ezra grabbed my elbow and pushed me straight up the bank. Damn, he was strong. My heart beat a little faster all the way back to the farmhouse.

"You look cold. You're welcome to come in for coffee," he said as we went through the gate to the driveway.

I hesitated. I really didn't have anything else I needed to ask Ezra, but I *was* chilled, and I was pleased that he'd asked me in. It felt . . . good to be with him. He was solid and warm and he made me nervous and a little itchy down deep inside. I knew what that itch was, and knew it was best avoided. Ezra was not for me. Even if we weren't from different worlds, even if I was ready to see a man again, he was involved in this case and that was a line you didn't cross. But it had been a long time since I'd felt anything like this, this hot spark of life. It felt lovely, and I was inclined to indulge it—silently and with absolutely no plan of ever acting on it, of course. For his part, Ezra seemed sincere about wanting me to come in. Maybe he was lonely. Or maybe he was fishing for info. Damn my paranoid cop brain.

"I wouldn't mind having your sister take a look at that photograph," I said.

It was a good enough excuse for us both.

Martha was in the kitchen at the stove when we entered. The piquant smell of ham filled the room and made my stomach rumble.

"Hullo," Martha said, turning to stare at me with big round eyes.

"Hi, Martha. How are you?" I asked with a smile.

"Gut." She stared some more. She made me uneasy, I had to admit. I wasn't sure if I was just a freak show to her—being a female cop, being English—or if she disliked me. Or maybe she was just socially inept.

"Ham loaf?" Ezra went to the oven and peeked inside, opening up the door a crack and letting more of that incredible smell out.

"Ja. And beans and cornbread."

"Would it please you to eat with us?" he asked, turning to me. He looked a little nervous.

"Uh . . ." I was taken by surprise. Lord, I'd kill for a hot, home-cooked meal, especially one that smelled like that, but I knew I should refuse. I checked my watch. I'd probably work until at least ten tonight. I had to get back to the station and see what Grady had found out from his rounds. And there were a number of things I wanted to check based on what we'd learned about Jessica Travis.

Then again, I did have to eat sometime. Right?

"If you, uh, really don't mind. I haven't had a chance to stop today. Thank you."

"I'll put coffee on too."

He went to the cupboard and got out some cups. As he did, he looked over at me and met my eyes. He held them, hand paused on the cupboard door. Then he smiled. It was a deliberate smile, a tentative outreach of a smile, warm and personal and a bit timid, like he wasn't sure how it would be received.

It was received like manna from heaven, like the first drops of rain after a killing drought. Something hot and joyful rushed through me like a scouring tide.

Dear God. I smiled back and made myself look away.

———————

The conversation was stilted over dinner because Martha sort of *lurked* in a way that made me self-conscious. I asked about their childhood and learned they'd both grown up in the area, of course. Their parents' farm was only two miles away. There were ten children in their family. Martha was the third and Ezra the fifth. I talked a little about New York but neither of them seemed to be able to relate to it. A lot of the meal was spent in silence. The food was hearty and tasty and just what I needed. I wished I had someone to cook for me like that at home. I rarely made the effort. Even when I had time, it seemed pointless to make a meal for one.

I made a successful bid not to stare at Ezra. In fact, it seemed like the two of us looked everywhere but at each other. Dessert was pound cake with berry syrup and fresh whipped cream—meaning an extra hour at the police gym this week. Totally worth it. Just as we finished, I got a text from Grady. It gave me an excuse to eat and run.

Ezra walked me to the front door and bid me good night. He stood silhouetted in the doorway as I walked to the road. Backlit like that, his body was long and rangy. He stood leaning against the doorjamb with his arms folded on his chest and one boot hooked up on his other calf like some Clint Eastwood poster. Damn it. The girls I'd once hung out with in the city would be spontaneously birthing kittens over this guy.

"Come back again," he said wryly as I stumbled my way to the car.

"I'd like that," I stupidly replied. My tongue felt like it had swollen to three times its size, and I mumbled. *Ahlahtha*. Idiot.

Holy cow, I mused as I drove down Grimlace Lane. I had no freaking idea what this thing with Ezra was. No clue. Or rather, I knew exactly what it was, only it couldn't be that. I had to be wrong.

CHAPTER 6

What She Hid

We caught up with Charlie Bender, LeeAnn Travis's ex-boyfriend, the next morning. He worked at the John Deere store near Mount Joy. The bright green of his button-down uniform shirt looked honest and reliable. Charlie's face, less so. He carried an extra eighty pounds and his face was weathered past his fifty years—by cigarettes, probably. There was a wary set to his eyes. He wasn't thrilled to be called off the showroom floor for a quiet conversation outside, especially in the cold gloom of an overcast winter's day.

"Jessica Travis? Yeah, I know her. So?"

"You were seeing her for a time?" I asked casually.

"Me?" He reacted with a huff of surprise. "Jessica? Nah! I dated her mother. For 'bout a year, I guess. Ain't seen either of them in months."

Grady chewed his cinnamon gum, staring flatly at Charlie. The man shifted uneasily. I kept on my mild face.

"She's a pretty girl, Jessica," I said.

Charlie shrugged. "Yeah."

"A flirt, am I right?"

His eyes narrowed nervously. "What's this about?"

"Where were you last Tuesday, Mr. Bender? Say from ten A.M. to four P.M.?" Grady asked in a not-friendly voice.

Charlie looked taken aback. "Right here. Why? I work Tuesday through Saturday. Ain't been sick in months."

"Lunch too?" I asked.

"I eat in the lunchroom right inside. Only take half an hour so I can go home early."

I nodded, hiding my disappointment. "Can your boss verify that?"

"Hell yeah! Anyone in there can. Say, what's this about?"

I looked at Grady. He took the ball. "Jessica Travis was murdered."

"No shit?" Charlie looked genuinely shocked by the news, and a little nervous.

"What can you tell us about Jessica? Anything at all would help us out." I shifted gears. We'd certainly check his alibi, but it would be pretty stupid to lie about it when it was so easy to verify. And if Charlie Bender was at John Deere all day, he didn't kill Jessica Travis.

"I dunno. I was dating her mother, like I said. Jess was wild. Saw her with lots of men."

"Oh yeah?" Grady looked interested.

"Yeah. I saw her driving around town, always in a different car with a different guy. Sometimes with another couple in the back. Maybe one of those guys did it."

"You recognize any of those guys? The other couple?" I asked.

Charlie shrugged as if to say "Why should I?"

Grady and I both waited, staring at him blankly.

"Pretty sure she was hookin'," he continued bitterly. His lip curled. "But she was still too good for me."

Damn. The thought of Charlie drooling over Jessica made me want to lock him up and call it good. But unfortunately, I was pretty sure he hadn't killed her.

I forced a disinterested smile. "You ever give her a lift? Get a chance to chat with her?"

"Nah. Well . . . whaddya mean? When I was dating LeeAnn, I dropped Jess off at the farmers' market in Paradise sometimes. She worked there over the summer."

Interesting. "Yeah? You haven't chatted with her since then? Anytime in the past year?"

He shook his head. "Ain't been over there. Me and LeeAnn—it didn't end so well."

"Uh-huh. So you saw Jess driving around with these other guys, and you offered to pay up too, but she still wouldn't put out for you. Is that accurate?" I kept my voice neutral.

He grew red with what looked like anger, but he kept his mouth firmly shut. He wasn't stupid.

"Was this before or after you and LeeAnn ended badly?" I pushed. "What age would Jessica have been then, Detective Grady?"

Grady never stopped staring at Charlie. "Well, she wasn't yet eighteen when she died, so she would have been seventeen or sixteen then."

"Sixteen," I repeated with a curious lilt. Huh.

Charlie grew redder. "I never did nothin' with Jess, not at any age or at any time. And I didn't kill her neither. I ain't even seen her in months, I swear."

"I'm going to go talk to your boss, confirm what you said about Tuesday. Detective Grady here will see if you know anything else that could help us out."

"Don't—" he said as I started to walk away. I stopped and looked at him. His face crumpled. "Look, I didn't do anything with or to Jessica Travis. Don't get me in trouble, please. I really need this job."

Damn if I didn't believe him.

His alibi checked out.

———————

When we got back to the police station after our interview with Charlie Bender, I'd only just gotten a cup of coffee and sat down when Grady stuck his head out of his office door. "Harris!"

I went in and closed the door behind me. He sat down and held a paper out to me with an inscrutable look. It was a missing persons report for a person named Katie Yoder. The person filing the report was . . . Jessica Travis.

"Holy shit." I sank down in a chair trying to take in everything on the report at once.

"Filed last October. I did a routine check on Jessica Travis in our system overnight and that came up."

"Anything else come up?"

"Nope. She had no record. Just that."

I still wasn't quite sure why Grady seemed to find the report so important. Okay, yeah, if Jessica's friend disappeared in

October, it was possible her murder in January was connected. But it could also be coincidence, if—

Then I saw the list of relatives: *Father:* Isaac Yoder. *Mother:* Hannah Yoder. A long, long list of siblings. *Home address:* Paradise, PA.

Katie Yoder was Amish.

Grady and I headed over to the Yoder farm right away. By the time we got there, it was eight o'clock at night. We interviewed Katie's parents, Hannah and Isaac, in a tidy living room with plaid-and-oak furniture, white paint and a few religious pictures on the wall. The glow of two low-watt table lamps turned everything as yellow as an old-time daguerreotype.

Hannah Yoder was dark-haired and thin with delicate features. She wore an Amish white cap, a dark blue dress, and an apron that had clearly seen a long day. She wore simple wire spectacles that made her look far too young to have nine children. She was forty-one, she said. Good Lord. Isaac looked older, probably because of the brown-and-gray beard that sent ragged tendrils down to his breastbone. He was a handsome man behind all that hair, with a square jaw and classic nose, but his expression was grim. It wasn't merely the solemn aspect Amish men often invoke. He didn't seem pleased about our visit. Or maybe about me personally. It was hard to tell.

Hannah Yoder kept her eyes on the darning in her lap as her husband spoke.

"We told the officer who came last fall—Katie ain't missin'. She left us to go her own way. We ain't seen her since."

"Yes, we have your statement in the report," I agreed. "But I was hoping you'd tell me about it in your own words. When was the last time you saw Katie?"

"October. A Thursday, I think."

Hannah, who was sewing something white in her lap with an air of utter calm, glanced up at her husband as if in confirmation.

"Ja, a Thursday," he continued. "We seen her in the mornin' and then she never come home for supper."

"And you weren't worried?"

"We knew for some time Katie would leave. She was not content with the Amish way. 'Twas no surprise when it come about already."

"She wasn't content with the Amish way. How so? Mrs. Yoder?"

Hannah looked up at me briefly but didn't answer. She looked at her husband, deferring to him.

He pressed his lips tight as if not wanting to answer. When he spoke, it was haltingly, and he spoke to Grady, even though I was the one asking the questions. I swallowed my irritation. "Katie . . . She was a mite too fair and took vanity in it. Cared more for boys than she ought. We struggled with it, spent a lot of time on our knees in prayer, but it done no good."

"It was as if she had the devil in her," Hannah said sadly. Her voice was so quiet, I barely heard her. Her eyes were still fixed on her work.

I gave Grady a puzzled look.

"The devil? What do you mean?"

Hannah looked up at me briefly but didn't answer.

"She was . . . a temptation to men, from a young age." Isaac's voice was rough. "She had no shame."

"And she goaded jealousy in others." Hannah sighed.

"Our way is humility and righteousness. Katie struggled to follow the path no matter what we did. She could be deceitful, rebellious . . . An unrepentant sinner calls others to sin. It was a blessin' when she finally went her own way. Naturally, if she were to truly have a change of heart, and find her way to God, we'd welcome her home."

"With rejoicing," Hannah added, but the regretful glance she gave her husband seemed to acknowledge this was unlikely to happen.

I knew she was right—that was never going to happen, though not for the reason she thought. I pulled the senior picture of Jessica from my pocket. "Do you recognize this girl?"

I handed it to Hannah, forcing her to put down her sewing and take it. She didn't study it long. "She was a friend of Katie's." Hannah handed it to Isaac and went back to her work.

"Ja. Katie worked at the farmers' market in Paradise last year. Met this one there. She would come by the house to pick Katie up. We asked Katie not to see the girl, then forbade it. But Katie snuck around and done it anyway. People would tell us they seen Katie in Jessica's car." Isaac held the photo out to me like he wanted nothing to do with it.

I took the photo back. "You didn't like Katie associating with a non-Amish?"

"'Keep yourself separate.' That's the law. And that girl was wild. Katie'd come home smelling of smoke and liquor and filled with a rebellious spirit. I'm not sayin' Katie weren't troubled before that. But this English friend made Katie all the worse."

"Did you shun Katie? Is that why she left?" I pushed. Grady shifted uncomfortably beside me. I knew my tone was a bit hard, but there was something here, and I felt the need to dig past the platitudes and the walls they put up to find it.

"She weren't shunned," Isaac said firmly, now looking somewhere between me and Grady. "She was in *rumspringa*. Means she had more freedom for a few years, till she could decide if she would join the church or leave. We didn't like what she was doin', but we hoped and prayed she'd come around. I talked to the deacon. We was gonna give her till her next birthday. She'll be nineteen already. If she didn't straighten out by then, she'd be shunned. And Katie knew it so."

"She always said she would leave," Hannah said, her mouth twisting with what looked like regret and sadness. "She'd tell me right so to my face."

I sat silently for a moment, trying to digest what they were telling me. "The day that Katie vanished, that Thursday in October, do you remember the exact date?"

"'Twas the second Thursday in October," Isaac said firmly.

"Okay. And did she give you any warning? Did she tell you she was leaving that particular day?"

"Ja. She told my cousin Miriam she was going, and to say good-bye." Hannah nodded, putting her work down in her lap.

"Did she say who she was going with? Or how she was leaving?"

"No."

"Do you have any idea who she might have left with? Was there someone she knew with a car? Or perhaps an ex-Amish she was in contact with?"

Hannah frowned and looked over at her husband, troubled.

"The only one we knew of was that Jessica. But Katie didn't go with her," Isaac said.

"No," I agreed. "Jessica seems very adamant in this report that Katie wouldn't have taken off without her. She says they were planning on leaving together, after they'd saved more money. Do you know anything about that? Did Katie tell you about those plans?"

Hannah shook her head.

"No," said Isaac. "She never said it so."

"That Jessica, she come by here a few weeks after Katie left," said Hannah with a frown. "I told her Katie was gone but don't think she believed me. Then she went to the police and they come by, but we told them the same. And that was the end of it."

Hannah was right. The officer who'd followed up on the missing persons report had taken the Yoders' word that Katie had left the area. After one visit with them, he'd closed the file.

"Jessica says in the report that Katie had borrowed her cell phone, and that there's no way Katie would have left without returning it. Did you see Katie with a cell phone? Maybe one with a pink cover?"

Isaac leaned back, his jaw set firmly. "We see her with a phone like that sometimes. It's not forbidden during *rumspringa*. But I wouldn't let her use this in the house."

"Have you seen the phone since Katie left?"

They both agreed that they hadn't.

"And the day Katie left, did she pack a bag? Were any of her things missing?"

"No. But Katie, she wouldn't've taken her Amish clothes. She had no use for 'em," Hannah explained patiently.

"What about personal belongings? A brush?" I struggled to think what else an Amish girl might have owned. "Books? Letters?"

"She walked out on her two feet and all else. That's the way of it when people leave," Isaac insisted.

That didn't sound encouraging. No wonder so few Amish youth left. Talk about being kicked out of the nest with a big boot.

"Why would Katie tell your cousin she was leaving and not you directly? She didn't say good-bye to any of her siblings either?"

"That's the way of it too," said Isaac. "If she'd told us, we'd've been obliged to try and stop her."

"She had no more patience for our prayers and lectures," Hannah said with a resigned sigh and a shake of her head. She pricked her finger with a needle, like something out of a fairy tale. A red dot blossomed on the white fabric. She stuck her fingertip in her mouth.

Grady and I exchanged a silent message. Maybe that was the way of it when an Amish teen left, to just walk out to the road with the clothes on their back and not say good-bye. But there were other, darker explanations. And Jessica turning up dead lent a dire weight to her written statement, her insistence that Katie was *missing*. Grady gave a slight nod to me with his chin. I turned back to the Yoders.

"Jessica Travis was found dead last week. She was murdered and her body was placed in the barn of Amos Miller on Grimlace Lane."

Hannah's face went a putrid color, like that of moldy cheese. She dropped her sewing and put both hands over her mouth. Isaac looked shocked but he wore it better. He put a hand on the back of his wife's chair—whether to comfort her or steady himself wasn't clear.

"We heard about that dead girl that was found. That was Katie's friend Jessica?" he asked with disbelief, looking at Grady for confirmation.

"It was," Grady said.

Hannah and her husband exchanged a look that was part fear, part confusion.

"May the Lord have mercy on her soul," Isaac muttered.

"Did Katie have any particular dealings with any of the families on Grimlace Lane?"

"Not particular," Isaac said.

"She never dated any of the boys? The Millers? Fishers? Kings?" I swallowed and added reluctantly, "Ezra Beiler?"

"No," Isaac said firmly.

I felt relieved. "Right. Well I guess you can understand why this makes us interested in Katie's whereabouts."

They said nothing but they looked genuinely worried for the first time since we'd arrived. I didn't understand how parents could let their daughter go without any expectation of her

return or even news on how she was doing. True, I'd seen plenty
of families with troubled youths, families that were better off
when the black sheep in question—usually a kid badly hooked
on meth or alcohol—simply stayed away. But surely Katie, an
Amish teenage girl, couldn't have been that much trouble. If
liking boys were a crime, I'd have been sentenced to Siberia by
age thirteen.

"Do you have any pictures of Katie?" Grady asked. "We'll
need to check the hospitals and morgues in the area. Hopefully, we won't find anything, but we have to look."

Isaac wiped his face as though he were sweating. He looked
shaken. "No. We don't hold to such like. No photos."

"Katie didn't have any photos of her own that she left behind,
from when she was in *rumspringa*?" I asked.

"No."

"I cleaned out her drawers already," Hannah said with cer-
tainty. "Ruth and Waneta are in Katie's old room now. Didn't find
no photos."

"We can call in a sketch artist," Grady said. "Would you be
willing to help us draw a picture of Katie?"

They exchanged a look and Isaac nodded. "I s'pose that would
be aright."

"Did she have any distinguishing marks?" I asked.

Hannah shook her head. "Not that I can say."

"Here." Isaac gestured to his left front thigh. "A good-sized
mole. Shaped like a butterfly."

Hannah looked at him in surprise. "That's right. I forgot
about that already."

I stared flatly at Isaac. He grew uncomfortable, his face reddening. "I . . . I remember it from when she was a baby."

I said nothing.

Grady cleared his throat. "Can you show Detective Harris Katie's old room, please?"

Grady called for the sketch artist and to get a search started on any bodies matching Katie's age and gender that had been found since October of last year. Meanwhile, Hannah took me up to Katie's room.

"As I said, her clothes and such like were already handed down. Not much to see," she said as she opened the door.

Two girls followed us into the room and stood with their hands behind their backs, regarding me with interest.

"Who's this?" I asked, giving the girls a smile.

"Ruth and Waneta." Hannah pointed them out. Ruth was the older, maybe just on the cusp of puberty. Waneta looked to be seven or eight. They were both quite pretty, petite like their mother, and dark-haired. I wondered if they took after Katie.

"Wanna see some of Katie's clothes?" Ruth volunteered eagerly. She opened the closet and pulled out a typical blue, long-sleeved Amish dress. She held it up to her chest and primped a bit. "This was Katie's. It's mine now, or will be when I grow big enow."

"It's a beautiful color," I said, lightly fingering the soft cotton with a smile. Ruth was certainly not shy. I wondered if that too was a family trait.

"The lady is a policeman. I don't think that's of much help to her now," Hannah said patiently.

"It's all right," I said as warmly as I dared. "Did Katie have this room to herself when she lived at home?"

"Nah, she shared it with Miriam till she got married, then Ruth," said Hannah.

"That's me!" Ruth added in case I was absentminded.

"Hush now," Hannah scolded lightly.

"Actually, if it's all right with you I'd like to ask Ruth some questions, since she roomed with Katie."

Hannah considered the request. "Can I be with her?"

"Of course! I can do it right here."

"Ja, it's fine. Go ahead now."

I turned to Ruth. "Did Katie do or say anything that made you think she was going to leave when she did?"

"She said I'd have the room to myself right soon enow."

I nodded. "But the *day* she left, did you know she was going to leave that very day?"

Ruth shook her head.

"We already asked the children that," Hannah said. "Katie didn't say good-bye to any of them."

"And when Katie was here, did she ever talk to anyone at night, maybe on a phone? She had a phone, didn't she?"

"Vater said she was not to use it in the house." Ruth sounded very firm about that.

"Well, sometimes girls Katie's age don't always do as they're told. Do they?" I smiled.

Ruth looked at me with big eyes. "Vater said not to, and I woulda told."

Well. That explained why Katie didn't confide in Ruth.

"Did Katie ever talk to you about her friend Jessica?"

Ruth shook her head.

"What about a boy she liked? Was she seeing anyone special?"

Ruth shook her head again. I felt a pang of disappointment. Katie must have kept things very close to the chest.

"Was there anything that she was very fond of? Maybe a book or a picture from a magazine, anything you would have thought she'd take with her when she left?"

Ruth shrugged. "I dunno. She liked cats."

"Katie had a small collection of cats. People gave 'em to her for birthdays and whatnot," Hannah clarified.

Ruth ran over to a little wooden hutch on the wall. It was rough, like a birdhouse, with a latched door on the front. She opened it. Inside were four shelves and ten little ceramic cats in different colors and designs. They were the cheap kind you can buy at a roadside stand for a few dollars.

I looked them over, feeling unaccountably hollow. This was the sole treasure of an eighteen-year-old girl?

———

Hannah led the way down the narrow stairs. I started to follow when I felt a tug on the back of my coat. I turned to see an adorable creature—a little girl around five years old. Her fuzzy brown hair burst out from under her cap and her round face still looked a bit tan from the long-lost summer sun. She was a beaut.

"Hey there," I said, bending down a little.

"Shhh," she whispered. "That's not where Katie kept it."

I blinked at her. "Kept what?"

"Her bestest things."

I felt a spark of interest, but I kept my smile calm. "What's your name?"

"Sadie."

"Were you special friends with Katie, Sadie?"

The little girl nodded solemnly.

"Will you show me where she kept her bestest things?"

Sadie shook her head just as seriously. "'Tis secret." Then turned and ran up the stairs.

It took a conversation with Grady, another with Hannah and Isaac Yoder, and then a frontal assault on little Sadie's code of honor—which was considerable for a five-year-old, and put her sister Ruth to shame—but eventually Sadie broke. She led us all into the barn, her lip trembling.

"I promise, we're trying to help Katie," I reassured her.

Sadie wasn't buying it and didn't seem much comforted as she reluctantly led us to the back of the old bank barn. There, a small hidden door that looked like part of the wall pushed inward into a crawl space, maybe four by ten. It appeared long abandoned, maybe part of an original barn that had been built onto over the years.

I stepped into the space while Grady held the door open and Hannah and Isaac stood and watched. The area was dusty, surrounded on three sides by old stone walls and on the fourth by the wooden barn wall. The dirt floor had been wet and re-dried so many times over the decades it had taken on a cracked pattern like a ceramic glaze. The bones of a large bird lay on the ground next to the head of what might have been a rat.

Up against the inside wall was a black plastic garbage bag. The bag was dusty and twist-tied shut. I pulled it up and handed it over the wall to Grady.

"What is it?" Isaac asked as I climbed back over to join them.

"Would you open it, please?" Grady asked Isaac. He sat the bag on a cement ledge.

Isaac undid the twist tie and pulled it open. Grady carefully lifted each item out and placed it on the ledge in turn so that we could all see.

There were neatly stacked clothes—gauzy tank tops, a light sweater, and two short skirts in bright pink and turquoise. There was a chunky silver-colored necklace and clip-on earrings, and a pair of tan high-heeled pumps, cheap and slightly scuffed. Next came a small bag of makeup. Grady unzipped it. Inside was lipstick, mascara, blush, eye shadow, and two foil packets of condoms. At the bottom of the plastic bag was a leather zip wallet. The wallet contained what looked like a few thousand dollars in twenties and fifties and a folded-up piece of newsprint. Grady unfolded the newspaper and we looked at both sides. One side held the small print of staff credits and copyrights and the other side an ad for diet pills. I hadn't gotten the impression that Katie had been overweight, but teenage girls were never happy with their bodies. There was no cell phone in the bag.

Grady met my eyes. The foreboding look on his face matched my own sickening response. Maybe Katie wouldn't have taken her ceramic cats or her Amish clothes, but all this money . . . She never would have left without this.

Grady nodded and I took out my cell phone and started photographing Katie's abandoned belongings.

"Mr. and Mrs. Yoder, is it all right with you if we remove these items to the station to examine them more carefully?" Grady asked. "You'll get everything back. We can count the money together before we take it."

Hannah apparently reached the same conclusion we had, because she let out a sob and turned her back to us, turning into her husband for support though not quite touching him. His eyes too were red and he trembled ever so slightly. He placed a hand on her shoulder. "Take it," he said in a gruff voice. "And may God's will be done."

CHAPTER 7

The Girl in the River

I was driving down Route 30 the next morning toward the police station when I passed Henry's Fruit Market. The name was misleading. It actually carried a full range of groceries as well as locally grown fruit. It was an old-fashioned place of the type Lancaster County excelled in, with a huge '50s retro vintage sign out front complete with painted fruit and lettering.

And Jessica's car had been abandoned here the day she died.

I'd seen the fruit market before, but I'd never shopped there. I did my grocery shopping at odd hours, and frequented the twenty-four-hour, one-stop-shopping gigantic chain stores. Hernandez had done the legwork on the market. He said it had a history running back over a hundred years. It'd been a wooden Amish fruit stand back then. It still employed a lot of Amish workers.

Forensics was examining the car, but our first look confirmed what LeeAnn Travis had said—there was no blood and no signs of a struggle. It was just a teenage girl's fairly filthy car. It was a 1986 Toyota Corolla that had over two hundred thousand miles and looked like a fender bender would cause the whole thing to fall apart, like in some slapstick cartoon. Whatever had happened to Jessica, it hadn't happened in her car. But *where* it had been left—that was extremely interesting. Henry's Fruit Market was in the heart of the town of Paradise, which meant it wasn't far from Grimlace Lane or any number of other Amish homes. Manheim, where Jessica had lived and gone to school, was twenty miles away, and she hadn't been working at the farmers' market over the winter. So what was she doing in Paradise that day?

Hernandez had interviewed the fruit market's manager. It was their policy to tow any car that had been left overnight, but they tried to contact the owner first as a courtesy. Jessica's car had been left unlocked and they had found the registration in the glove box. No one Hernandez questioned recalled seeing Jessica Travis.

There were three buggies and a few dozen cars parked at Henry's as I drove past. I slowed down to take a good look at the place, and Ezra Beiler came out of the market holding grocery bags. I was almost past the last driveway, so I had to decide fast. I jerked the wheel and swung in, earning an annoyed honk from the car behind me.

Ezra went to one of the buggies. He didn't see me until I walked up to him.

"Morning, Ezra."

My heartbeat raced at the sight of him, which was absurd. I was a grown woman, a seasoned cop, not some impressionable schoolgirl. I couldn't deny that I felt a strong attraction to Ezra Beiler, an Amish man. But I certainly could, and would, ignore it.

"Hullo." He looked surprised to see me. He put his bags in the buggy and then turned to give me his attention. There was warmth in his eyes and a hint of a smile on his mouth that looked involuntary, like he was pleased to see me too. At least, I flattered myself that's what it meant.

"Hey," I said. *Duh.* "So . . . you shop here at this market?"

"Looks so," he said drily.

Great. "What I mean is, do you shop here a lot? Sorry. It's early for me."

Ezra looked up to study the position of the sun. It was past eight o'clock and he gave me a look, I swear, that called me a lazy ass. In a wry, Ezra Beiler sort of way.

"Ja. I shop here lots of times."

I bit back a smile. This wasn't *good*, I reminded myself sternly. Shopping here made Ezra more of a suspect. Then again, he did have an airtight alibi for the night Jessica was killed.

"Do you happen to know if your neighbors shop here? The Millers, the Fishers, the Lapps, the Kings?"

Ezra started to answer and then stopped to really think about it. He nodded. "Guess I've seen most of 'em here one time or another. Other Amish I know too. It's close by and it's a good place to shop."

"I see."

As if he couldn't meet my eyes, he looked away toward the road. "Good potato salad. So I hear."

"Good to know."

"Not as good as mine, probably."

"Uh-huh."

He was deadpan but there was no doubt he was being funny. I scratched a nonexistent itch on my nose, trying to collect myself. I hadn't had coffee yet, so my judgment was suspect, but I'd swear to God we were flirting. I reminded myself that one girl was dead and another missing. I needed to keep my head where it belonged.

"You didn't happen to come by here the day before the girl was found in Miller's barn, did you? You mentioned that you delivered some chairs that morning."

Ezra frowned and shook his head. "No, didn't stop for groceries that day."

"Didn't happen to drive by and notice anyone you knew was here? Or maybe a dairy truck, the kind that picks up from your neighbors?"

Ezra cocked his head and met my eyes, curious now. A non-Amish person would probably start asking me questions about the case, but he didn't.

"Guess I must've drove by. But I didn't look to see who was here."

It sounded like automatic pilot worked in buggies too. "Okay."

We were standing between his buggy, with one of his mules attached, and another one with a dark brown horse. That buggy started to move and I stepped closer to Ezra to get out of the way. I noticed the driver was a middle-aged Amish woman. She had a couple of young children with her.

"Do most Amish women drive buggies by themselves?" I asked.

"Most do. Some don't care for it," Ezra said. "My mother don't. She's got lots of sons to take her anyplace she needs to go."

"Is there a legal age? How old does someone have to be to drive a buggy?"

He shrugged. "Big enough to handle the horse. And that depends on the horse."

I looked at Route 30. It was the main route between Philadelphia and Lancaster, and was very busy, especially during tourist season. I'd never envied buggy drivers. Route 30 had a buggy lane in places, but still, traffic on the road drove way too fast. Accidents between buggies and cars happened more often than anyone would like, and the buggy never got the good end of it.

"Sixteen?" I prompted, looking into his brown-green eyes.

He shrugged again. "I was takin' the buggy out alone by thirteen."

"Okay."

"Okay." He crossed his arms against his chest and looked away. His upper lip twitched as if he wanted to say something more, but he didn't.

"I, um, need to go get some coffee," I said by way of ending the conversation.

He nodded his head at the market. "They got some in the bakery. Probably not as good as—"

"Yours." I smiled big. "I'm sure it isn't. Thanks. You have a good day, now."

"Detective Harris." Ezra tipped the brim of his hat at me with his strong, tan fingers, that damned appealing sparkle in his eye. Then he started to untie the mule and I ordered my body to turn and walk to the market. It reluctantly obeyed.

They did have a bakery department inside as well as a deli. All the women behind the counter were Amish, in black or white caps. I resisted the whoopie and shoofly pies and picked up a dozen whole-grain bagels for the office—my contribution to the health and well-being of my fellow officers—and a coffee for me. I looked around the place for a few minutes. The ratio of English to Amish shoppers was probably ten-to-one, but that was still a lot of Amish.

I wondered if anyone in the parking lot that day had seen Jessica Travis, noticed her talking to someone or getting into another car. It was a long shot, but I'd mention it to Grady. We could make up some flyers for the parking area and store, give a number for info.

Sooner or later, someone had to have seen *something*.

It didn't occur to me until I was nearly at the office that I'd forgotten to ask Ezra if he knew Katie Yoder.

––––––––––

The previous evening, Grady had sent the sketch of Katie, along with the information on her birthmark, to every morgue and hospital in the area and out as far as Baltimore, Philadelphia, and Harrisburg. He'd also sent word out to several groups who helped ex-Amish relocate, just in case Katie had really left, but we didn't have a lot of hope there.

I couldn't stop thinking about the phone. If Katie had borrowed Jessica's cell phone, and since it wasn't in her secret stash, where was it? I got the phone number from Jessica's mother, but calling it went immediately to voice mail, indicating the battery was dead. It didn't give off a GPS locator trace either. We managed to get the service provider to talk to us, and they confirmed that the phone had not made any calls or texts out since October 10, 2013, the last day Katie's parents saw her alive.

Had Katie had the phone on her when she vanished? If so, where was it now?

It niggled at me enough that I checked out a metal detector from the precinct and took it over to the Yoder farm. I spent four hours wandering around with the thing—in the barn, around the barn, around the house, down the driveway. It was tedious and ultimately fruitless. I didn't find the phone. I did find Sadie, though, who followed me around like a shy duckling and even enjoyed taking a turn with the metal detector. She had a difficult time with "Detective Harris," which is admittedly a mouthful, so I had her calling me "Lizbess" before long. The rest of the Yoders kept a watchful distance.

It took exactly forty-nine hours from the time Grady put out the APB until we got a response. Katie's body had been found.

———————

Grady and I picked up Hannah Yoder, Katie's mother, and took her with us in the car. Just her—no one else. For having such a large family, I was surprised she hadn't brought along support, but perhaps she wanted to spare the others the pain of it. She was very quiet on the drive into Maryland and often had her eyes closed in prayer. Grady and I didn't disturb her.

The body that matched Katie's description had been washed up in Maryland on Robert Island, a small bump of land surrounded by the Susquehanna River. She'd been found on October 14, 2013. Naked, and with no match on her prints, the body had been remanded to the Maryland State Office of the Chief Medical Examiner in Baltimore, where she was still on ice pending identification.

We arrived at the ME's office around eleven in the morning after a long, solemn drive. Hannah said very little as we sat in the waiting room. There were lots of curious looks at her clothes. Downright staring, in fact, as if we were something from a Lifetime movie.

I tried smiling encouragingly at Hannah but she looked back down at her lap, not accepting the comfort of a stranger. I didn't blame her. We were about to view a dead girl who fit Katie's description and had a butterfly mole on her thigh. What comfort was possible? And a female police officer was as foreign in her world as she was in that Baltimore waiting room.

Normally, a photo or video feed was used for identification, but Hannah insisted, calmly but firmly, on seeing the body in person. The ME's office was accommodating, but it took a while. After about an hour, we were led into a clinical room, the sort of place with drains in the floor and lots of stainless steel where they normally did autopsies. There was a body on a rolling table covered by a sheet. The young man in the white coat who led us in there waited for a nod from Grady and then pulled down the sheet that covered the corpse's face.

The girl had been in cold storage, so there wasn't a lot of deterioration, but the river had had its way with her first. Her dark hair was wraithlike around her head and her dark lashes stark against white cheeks. She'd been young and pretty once and now had the cold, white, plastic look of long-dead things.

Hannah Yoder nodded and swallowed hard. She reached out to find Katie's hand and held it over the sheet. She closed her eyes and prayed over her daughter while tears streamed down her cheeks and her chest shuddered silently. I wanted to put a hand on her shoulder, but I didn't.

Grady collected the autopsy report and I browsed it while he filled out the paperwork to transfer Katie's body to Lancaster. We gave Hannah some private time with her daughter.

The autopsy paperwork indicated that Katie had been hit with a flat, blunt, heavy object on the back center of her head, hard—hard enough to shatter the skull. She probably would have eventually died from that blow, but her airways had been blocked and she'd died of suffocation. She'd been in the water for four days, very likely floating downriver from Pennsylvania, before washing ashore at Robert Island.

I felt sick as I read it. Then I read it again to be sure. Jessica and Katie had died the exact same way.

———

The drive back to Lancaster was solemn, but there was a measure of relief in it too. Katie had lain unidentified in cold storage for months. If we hadn't investigated Jessica's death, if Jessica hadn't filed that missing persons report, we would never have found Katie and her family would never have had any idea of her fate. It's hard to explain the sense of rightness of bringing someone home for a loving burial, but it was one of the sparks of light that made being a cop worthwhile. For some reason the idea of being dead and no one knowing, of being an unidentified corpse in storage or in an unmarked grave, felt like the loneliest thing in the world to me, as if the life that came before hadn't mattered to anyone.

When we pulled up at the Yoder farm, Isaac came out of the house alone. He and his wife exchanged a silent communication and then he took her hand. Just that—no big hug or weeping, just their clasped hands—was filled with as much meaning as anything I'd ever seen. I felt a moment of envy. Their relationship was without question and without end. Whatever came, they faced it together. I suddenly ached for Terry, but in a way that felt remote, as if something inside me knew that we'd never had that solidity. Maybe it didn't exist in the modern world.

"Thank you for finding our Katie," Isaac said to Grady, sounding as stoic as always, "and for arranging to bring her home. We'll pray for her soul and for your safety as you continue your work."

"Thank you," Grady said. "We're so sorry for your loss."

"Very sorry," I added. Then I remembered that the Yoders had been willing to let Katie vanish from their lives forever because she didn't follow their beliefs. In a way, she'd been dead to them for a long time.

"Suppose you'll want to find the person who did this to Katie now?" Isaac asked.

"Of course," said Grady.

Isaac nodded, as if he assumed as much. "Know that, to us, what's done is done. It's in God's hands to punish, not ours."

"If we don't find out who did this, they may hurt someone else," I pointed out firmly.

Isaac nodded, finally meeting my eyes. "That too is in God's hands."

———————

On the way back to the station, Grady said, "You thinking what I'm thinking?"

"That it was the same killer? I'm sure of it."

"So Katie and Jessica met when they were both working at the Paradise Farmers' Market last summer. They became best friends. Katie was planning to leave the Amish, and Jessica dreamed of moving to New York City. Jessica said in her missing persons report that Katie wouldn't have left without her. They were planning to go together."

"I agree. Maybe they were going to wait until Jessica graduated from high school this year. And they were saving up money—Katie's stash."

"Right."

"But how did she get that kind of money? There was over three thousand dollars in that pouch. That's a lot to save from working minimum wage."

"She lived at home and had no expenses. We can go back and interview her folks about what jobs she held."

"Good idea. But what if Charlie Bender was right? What if Jessica was having sex for money? Her mom said she was meeting guys online. What if Katie was part of that?"

"She was Amish," Grady said with a frown.

"Yeah, but you heard what her parents said. They called her a Jezebel, basically. So Katie and Jessica want to run away together, go live in New York, but they need money. Jessica starts meeting men online and soliciting them. Charlie said he saw Jessica riding around town in cars with various men, and sometimes there was another couple in the backseat. That could have been Katie."

"And maybe they met the wrong guy, is that what you're saying? But why are their deaths so far apart? If they'd gotten picked up by a psycho, why didn't he kill both of them at the same time? Jessica lived for months after Katie disappeared. She didn't say anything in the missing persons report about a guy they'd picked up. If she was serious about finding Katie, and she suspected someone specific, she would have said."

"Maybe he met them together, but ended up arranging to see Katie alone. He kills her, and that satisfies him for a while. Then he gets the urge to kill again and reconnects with Jessica. She might have seen him again if she had no idea he killed Katie."

Even as I said it, it didn't feel quite right. Would Katie have agreed to see a man she hardly knew alone and not have told Jessica about it? And would a killer really wait that long before going after Jessica too?

And none of that explained where Jessica had been dumped—Grimlace Lane. *Why there?*

"Katie was Amish, and Jessica was dumped in an Amish barn. There's got to be a tie-in," I said.

Grady was silent for a moment. "Maybe the guy they met online deals with the Amish. He could be a driver or a service provider, like our pal Larry the dairy guy. Maybe he met up with Katie and Jessica with a friend of his, they had sex, then later on he happens to see Katie when she's in her Amish dress and recognizes her. He threatens to tell if she doesn't sneak off with him for a quickie. That's why Jessica didn't know about it. Katie never had a chance to tell her."

"And then he decides to kill Katie?"

"Maybe she was going to tell on him. Or maybe she refused, like you said before, and he was just trying to knock her out to have his way with her and then panicked. Maybe by the time he got to Jessica he had a taste for it, for killing, and reenacted the crime with her."

The whole theory was like a jar of sweet-and-sour vegetables, the kind where you like maybe one veggie in the jar and you have to fish around the stuff you don't want in order to find the one you do.

I kept that opinion to myself.

———

Our daily meeting with the investigation team was more productive in handing out assignments than reeling in information. Smith and Hernandez's interviews at Manheim Central High hadn't yielded anything especially new. The last boy Jessica had dated from there had been involved with her the previous spring and he'd moved on with someone else—and had an alibi. Everyone said Jessica was "wild" but it seemed she'd kept more to herself since her senior year started. She told everyone she was moving to New York as soon as they graduated in May. In truth, it seemed like she was already gone, mentally.

She got average grades, had a 3.2 GPA, and liked art.

The computer was still being processed. Grady lit a bonfire under everyone's asses about that. New assignments were handed out. We now had Smith and Hernandez doing legwork for us full-time. I took on the task of researching Katie's work, and I had a few other tasks for myself that I didn't mention in the meeting.

Back at my desk, I opened up the case file and looked at the photos of the creek on Grimlace Lane and of Jessica's body in the barn. We'd gotten the file on Katie from Maryland, and there were pictures of her body in situ where it was found on Robert Island. She was naked, facedown, and bloated, her head turned to the side, eyes staring sightlessly.

I put Jessica and Katie side by side. Jessica had been taken through the creek by the killer on his way to dumping her in the Millers' barn. Katie had been found in the Susquehanna River.

I stared for a moment, then went to the library and had the clerk pull out a book of detailed maps of the area. I signed it out and took it back to my desk. I found Grimlace Lane and Rockvale Creek. I followed the creek's progression with my finger. It ran into another waterway, Pequea Creek. I followed Pequea Creek as it wound through the borough of Paradise, passed the southern tip of the city of Lancaster, and continued on through farmland.

It dumped out into the Susquehanna River at the little town of Pequea.

Thrumming with excitement, I carried the map book to Grady's office and knocked. When I entered, Smith and Hernandez were there. I placed the open book on Grady's desk with a solid thunk of intent.

"What?" he asked.

"Rockvale Creek. It has a direct line to the Susquehanna. I

don't think Katie was dumped in the river. I think she made her way there from Rockvale Creek."

Grady started to argue on principle, then he shut his mouth. He looked at the map. Smith and Hernandez crowded around too.

Detective Jeff Smith was a real good old boy—fifties, pot-bellied, mentally sharp but physically lazy. At least that was my read. He was the type who I'd look up to find staring at me, but he rarely said more than two words to my face. Manuel Hernandez was still in his twenties and newly promoted to detective. He was quiet, polite, and very eager to please. He'd been in the Army for a few years and was very "Yes, sir. How high, sir?" I liked him. He had something to prove but he was humble about it, not arrogant, like so many of the young cops I'd known in New York. And he treated me with the same respect he gave everyone else.

I showed Grady where Rockvale Creek hit Pequea Creek and then on to the Susquehanna. Where Pequea Creek dumped into the Susquehanna looked like only fifty miles or so upriver from Robert Island. It felt obvious to me. I had the high you get when you finally find that important missing piece.

Katie and Jessica had both been killed at the same place—Grimlace Lane.

But Grady shook his head, his mouth squinched tight in doubt. "I dunno, Harris. That creek is relatively shallow. I mean, even when you were in standing in there, in the middle of it, it barely came up to your . . . um, crotch. And then there's all that chicken-wire fencing up and around. She would have gotten caught on that, if not there, farther downstream. I don't see how her body could have made it all the way to Pequea Creek, much less the Susquehanna. There are rocks and underpasses. . . . And she was en route for what, three or four days, and no one saw the body?"

As soon as he said it, I could see the truth of it. We'd walked up and down Rockvale Creek for a good ways looking for footprints that first day. And yeah, some of the areas downstream from the farms were even more shallow. In fact, I remember thinking that the killer would have had to really wrangle that body to get it very far.

"Hmm." I rubbed my temple, feeling a little foolish. "It was October when Katie was killed. Is it higher then?"

Grady shrugged. "It's highest in spring with the snowmelt. Unless—"

"Wait a minute," Hernandez interrupted. "You said Katie was found October fourteenth of last year, right?"

It was nice to know he'd been paying close attention in the meeting.

"Yeah."

He pulled out his phone and starting googling with a look of triumph. Even before he found it, my own memory was triggered. I'd moved back to Lancaster last August. And shortly thereafter—

Hernandez held out his phone. There was an image of the flooded Susquehanna. It was so high, treetops floated near the newly formed banks.

"October eighth. We got slammed by a couple of fading hurricanes in a row, remember? All the creeks and rivers around here went nuts."

"If the creek had been really high—" Grady began.

"And the water's running fast and muddy, and the weather is crap, so people aren't out," I added. "It's possible no one would have seen a body."

Grady stroked his chin. "Interesting theory. But how would we ever prove it?"

"We don't have to prove it," I said, folding my arms stubbornly. "We just have to know that it's possible Katie was put in Rockvale Creek. If she was, that tells us the killer is even more closely linked to this area than we thought."

For the first time I saw a shadow of an ugly doubt swimming in Grady's eyes. "What the hell? I mean . . . why would the killer have dumped both Katie and Jessica *there*?"

"Once we figure that out," I said, "we'll know who killed them."

CHAPTER 8

Pot of Gold

That night I dreamt I was drowning. I found myself in water so cold I wanted to gasp in shock, only there was no air. It was dark and I fought to find my way out with no sense of where I was or which way the surface was. I panicked, thinking clearly, *I'm going to die.* Then I sensed someone above me, out of the water, waiting. It was Ezra Beiler.

I woke up and sat on the edge of my bed, breathing hard. Putting my bare feet on the floor, wiggling my toes in the carpet, always grounded me, helped the nightmare fade. Nightmares were nothing new, but this one wasn't my usual stock in horror—it wasn't about Terry, it was about the case and . . . Ezra Beiler. I didn't know what to make of that one.

I gave up on sleeping. As dawn broke, I was in my car on the way to Grimlace Lane with the metal detector in the backseat. I parked at the Millers' and told Jacob, who was in the barn, that I'd be leaving my car there for a bit. I headed across the field toward the trees using the metal detector the whole way. Of course, the phone had been lost long before Jessica's body had been carried across that field, but at this point I wasn't sure how many similarities Katie's and Jessica's deaths shared. Honestly? I was shooting in the dark.

I found nothing in the field. It was damn freezing out, and by the time I got to the creek, my hands were cold on the metal detector's handle even with my gloves. The creek was eerie today—either because of the lingering fear of my nightmare or the light wisp of fog that glided above the water like a sea serpent. The trees on either side, bare for the winter, were spindly and black, raising gnarled branches to the gray sky.

It was exactly the sort of place you'd expect to find a clue, if real life worked like a Hollywood film, which it doesn't. I worked the metal detector up and down on this side of the creek. I found a coin and a very old, rusted horseshoe. I didn't find Jessica's cell phone.

I was just contemplating how unlikely the phone was to be here, and thus how stupid it would be to get my pants wet wading to the other side of the creek, when a voice startled me.

"Mornin'."

I nearly jumped out of my skin. That's not something you want to be seen doing as a cop, much less as a homicide detective. My embarrassment only grew as I saw Ezra Beiler leaning over the fence to his property. I felt my face heat, which was quite a contrast from the glacial state my skin had taken on in the frigid air.

"What are you doing down here?" I went for suspicious and shrewd—it was a good cover for jumpy and scared of my own shadow.

Ezra looked unfazed. He tugged his hat down a bit. "Horse told me you were here."

I narrowed my eyes at him. "Oh, really? Did he call me Detective Harris or Elizabeth? Just curious about how familiar mules are."

A smile tugged at the side of his mouth. "Don't recall him sayin' either one. He just looked a bit too excited about getting his morning drink."

"I see."

I did see too. I saw a man slouching against a fence who looked way too damn gorgeous in a rustic, just-rolled-out-of-bed kind of way. It hurt my stomach to look at him, the way tragedy hurt. It made me wish for things that I thought I'd given up dreaming about long ago and, tragically, that would never happen.

I grumbled in disgust at myself. "I'm working."

"Uh-huh. Wanna check my land next? Maybe you can find me a pot of gold."

I scowled. I'd rather find a cell phone or, barring that, a cup of coffee. "Yeah, I was planning on it. Have to go back and get my car first."

"Nope. There's a shortcut." He tilted his head to the right in a "follow me" and walked up the bank toward the field on his side of the fence. I went up on mine. About midway up the property line there was a wooden step stool, five feet tall, perched over the fence. It was like a two-sided ladder with a seat at the top. I'd seen these before, that first day we were following the tracks, but I'd been mostly focused on the creek.

"Is this for Amish step aerobics?" I asked.

"What?"

"Never mind."

I passed the metal detector over the top of the fence to Ezra, then started up myself. Anything that would get me to coffee sooner—no mountain too high, etc. I should have stopped to get some on my drive out. I was a grumpy ass without caffeine, or maybe it was the nightmare.

Or maybe it's wanting what you can never have.

I was distracted and not paying the best attention. My rubber boots were slick from the ice and mud of the creek. The combination was a disaster. As I swung my second leg over the fence and turned my body on the ladder, my anchoring foot slipped and I fell awkwardly down the wooden rungs.

It wasn't far enough that I would have hurt myself too badly, maybe banged up my shins and hands on the rough wood of the ladder. But the damage was far worse that that, because Ezra caught me in his arms. There we were in the winter chill and weak morning light, in an empty field, my back pressed to his chest, only the wool of our coats between us, my feet tangled in the ladder so that my full weight was against him. *Christ.*

We froze. I was afraid to move. I was afraid I'd unbalance us both, and afraid too that the moment would end. Ezra just held on solidly, his forearms like the roots of a tree wrapped around my ribs. His breath was as hot as a furnace on my neck. I understood that if my hips had not been canted up, with my feet tangled in the ladder, my butt would have been to his groin, a fate that I was grateful to have escaped, if only because of the sheer embarrassment of it.

"Pull your right foot out slow," he said, his voice rough and close to my ear.

Dear God.

I did as he suggested, pulling my boot out of the rung slowly and placing it on the ground. The other leg followed of its own accord, and then he was stepping back, letting me go. I looked at the ground and frowned, not sure how to look him in the eyes after that.

"Well. That was graceful. Sorry."

"No harm done," he said evenly. "I forgot you English were so ungainly."

I huffed a laugh.

"Gonna put on some coffee. Come up to the house when you're done."

"Thanks. I'll make an effort not to break a leg on the way there." I retrieved the metal device from where he'd leaned it up against the fence and headed for the creek.

———————

I had no luck in my search along Ezra's creek bank, except that it gave me plenty of opportunity to cool off, both physically and mentally. Nothing had happened, after all, other than the fact that I'd slipped and he'd helped me out. There was no reason to be self-conscious—except for the way his arms had felt solid and strong around me and the way it had warmed me like a roaring fire. That truth was in my head and mine alone. I didn't have to admit it to anyone.

And, I wanted some damn coffee.

I knocked on Ezra's front door and he opened it with slight smile. "Pot of gold?"

"Not today. Anyhow, I thought you Amish were above avarice."

"I just wanted the pot," he deadpanned.

I laughed as I followed him into the kitchen, where he already had two cups and plates, jam and butter on the table.

He brought a pot of coffee and set it on a hot pad. "I'll put the toast down."

"Toast?"

"You have to try Martha's preserves."

Well, I wasn't going to argue with that, especially since the little homemade jar on the table looked like blueberry, my favorite.

"How come you always make me coffee?" I asked.

"Seemed to like it the first time."

Logical. "Guess I did."

"If I made you some, would you ever not want it?"

"Not gonna happen."

"Well, then."

That settled, he brought back a plate of toasted bread, which I swore was a homemade whole grain. The butter was in a little crock—real, fresh butter. Dear Lord. Between that and the homemade blueberry jam, my mouth thought it had died and gone to heaven. I tried very hard not to groan. There were definitely perks to Ezra's lifestyle.

"This is the best jam in the world," I enthused with conviction and a full mouth.

"I like it well enough. We raise them—those—blueberries."

I found it interesting that Ezra corrected himself around me. I wasn't sure if that was because he didn't want me to think he was ignorant, or if it was something he was trying to do with his speech all the time, and if so, what the impetus for it was. Most Amish spoke both German and English, and English was not their priority. "Aren't you eating?"

"Had breakfast a while ago already."

"Hmmm."

It was a bit weird that he would make me toast without planning to eat himself, but then the cop in me was a cynical bastard. I kept my mouth shut and ate. Homemade bread, fresh butter, and real blueberry preserves. I'd take those over tiramisu or crème brûlée—two of Terry's favorites—any day. When I'd consumed enough to think about something else, I decided to put some purpose to my visit.

"Did you know Katie Yoder?"

He'd been watching me eat with a slightly amused tolerance, like a parent might a child, but at that his face went slack and his back tensed.

"I heard. It's terrible news."

"What did you hear exactly?"

He gave me a wary glance and looked down at his coffee. "Heard she was found dead down in Maryland. They're plannin' a service for her."

"Is that all you heard?"

"Ja." He looked at me with a slight frown, like he wanted to ask me what I meant, but he didn't.

I considered telling him about Katie's relationship to the dead girl who had been found next door, but I decided I'd better not. I had to keep my cop hat on or at least barely clinging to the back of my head, no matter how much I liked Ezra. I sighed.

"You knew Katie? What was she like?"

He titled his head to the side, considering. "Young. A bit foolish. More English than most."

"What do you mean by that?"

"Just seemed that way to me. Katie Yoder . . . she didn't have a modest way about her."

"Meaning . . . ?"

He looked troubled. "Didn't know her real well. I came up a few years before her. I was married already when Katie started going to the sing-alongs and such."

"Hmmm." I poured myself a bit more coffee. The fresh cream made me want to weep with pleasure, though it was probably going straight to my thighs.

"Did she have a reputation? Among the boys?"

Ezra stroked his bare chin, looking uncomfortable. "Maybe so. I don't listen to such gossip."

"She was pretty?"

He nodded. "I'd say so. I'd say she thought so too, but I'm no judge."

"Was she friends with Martha?"

Ezra looked at me sharply. "Not hardly. Martha . . . No."

I wondering what he'd almost said. *Didn't like her? Was too godly for a girl like that? Hated her on sight? Was jealous?* I didn't ask, but apparently my cop stare worked on him too.

"Katie . . . was a little wild. Too wild for the likes of Martha," he finally said with great reluctance. "I don't care to speak ill of the dead. God rest her soul."

"Okay." I let him off the hook seeing as how he'd fed me coffee and blueberry jam and all. "What about the farmers' market where Katie worked, in Paradise. Do you know it?"

"Ja." He looked at me with sudden interest. "I was gonna take some rockers over to Hennie's this morning. That farmers' market is on the way. Want to go with?"

I *had* planned on checking out Katie's employment today. "Yeah. I can follow you in my car."

"Can ride in the buggy if you like." He shrugged, like it didn't matter.

"Okay."

After all, I'd never ridden in a buggy, and it might be good for me to get a better feeling for Amish life. I still believed this case had more to do with being Amish than Grady wanted to believe. Immersion, it was called.

And I was in deep.

———

I got into the buggy next to Ezra. There was plenty of room on the hard bench, and I kept to my side, holding the door handle to remind myself to stay there. I was wearing my usual suit with a wool trench coat over it, my hair pulled back in its cop bun. I was glad I was at least dressed modestly, because it felt immodest to be there for some reason. The buggy was enclosed for the winter and the front window was a bit small. It smelled of leather and pine and Ezra inside. Two of his Trex rockers were carefully wedged in the back.

"S'posed to snow," Ezra said as the mule pulled us out onto the lane.

"That's not Horse," I noted, looking at the darker-coated mule in front.

"That's Sandy. Gotta get the younger ones trained, though Horse would love to come every time."

"I bet." An idea occurred to me. "Do you take the mules out often just to train them? Like around the neighborhood?"

"Sometimes."

"Ever notice anything unusual?"

He glanced over at me. "Like what?"

I didn't know where I was going with this line of questioning, honestly. If I had the right questions, maybe I would already know the answers. "I don't know. Someone walking that you don't know. A parked car. Anything."

"Not that comes to mind."

We trotted past the Millers' and the Fishers' and then the Lapps'. Aaron Lapp was out by his mailbox repairing the post. He looked up as the buggy approached. I saw the moment he recognized my face through the window. I was surprised by the look of anger and condemnation that came over him. He didn't hide it either, but watched us pass with that thunderous look.

Was he angry at Ezra for having an English in his buggy? An unchaperoned woman? Was that not allowed? Or was his anger directed at me for being too familiar with one of his flock? Had he noticed the other times I'd stopped by Ezra's? Or was this about the investigation?

Ezra stared out the windshield as if he hadn't noticed, but I could tell by the color staining his cheek and his tensed posture that he had.

"Is this going to get you in trouble?" I asked.

He let out a held breath. "No more'n I am already."

"Want to talk about it?"

He shook his head firmly. "It's nice *not* to talk about it."

So I was an escape for Ezra too. If that's the way he was treated by his neighbors, he was probably in need of a friend. I could live with that. "Okay."

Nevertheless, I was a cop, which made me nosy by training, and I was getting to the point where I really wanted to know more about Ezra Beiler. I was working my way around an approach in my head when he saved me the trouble.

"You have family here?"

"Not really. I grew up in Quarryville, but I was an only child. My parents died in a car crash a few years ago." I didn't mention that the police thought Dad had been drinking. "I have some cousins around, but I haven't seen them in a long time."

"Oh. Sorry about your parents. Can't imagine."

Given how large the Amish families were, I thought it probably would be hard for Ezra to imagine not being surrounded by relatives.

"How did you come to work for the police, then?"

It was a fair question, one I got from just about anyone I met for the first time. "I was studying criminal justice in college. I thought about being a lawyer. But then I witnessed an accident. It was in the city. A girl was hit by a car. There was a female police officer who was there, held the girl's hand and kept her calm while they were waiting for an ambulance. She was so"—*strong, calm, warm*—"professional. Helpful, you know? And school was so expensive. I decided to quit and go to the police academy." *Where I could actually be useful right away and earn money rather than burning it.*

I'd eventually finished up my criminal justice BA taking classes part-time, with financial help from the NYPD. But that felt like boasting, and Ezra didn't need to know that.

Ezra digested the information. Unlike most people, he didn't seem to feel the need to pass judgment on my choices.

"You married?" he asked after several minutes of silence. His tone was neutral and he kept his eyes on the road, though we weren't exactly breaking land-speed records with the mule and buggy.

There was a low tingle in my belly. If he asked that, he was interested, right? Unless, of course, he was simply making conversation. "I was."

"Divorced?"

"Widowed," I said, hoping to draw him out about his own past. He looked a little surprised but didn't glance at me and said nothing.

"You?" I prompted, though I knew.

"Same."

"What happened?"

He appeared to wrestle with what to say. "She was hit by a car."

"Oh God, Ezra. I'm so sorry."

"Yeah." Then: "Sorry about your husband too."

"So am I."

I was still more than sorry about Terry, the man who had been my husband.

Ezra Beiler was the polar opposite of Terry Leblanc.

When we'd met, I was a beat cop and Terry was the victim of an armed mugging. He hadn't been hurt, just shaken. We never did find the perp, but Terry canceled all his credit cards and he got me in the bargain. He always said he was the luckiest mugging victim in the city's history.

Terry was urbane, sophisticated. Compared to him, I always felt like a rube. When we met, he was forty-nine and I was twenty-four. He was a man who always had been, and always would be, very handsome, a silver fox, as my friends called him. He had a strong, noble face and brown hair with a lot of gray that was long enough to hit his shoulders. He was a dapper dresser, the kind of man who still wore vests and ties. He had a beautifully decorated apartment and a reasonably successful career as a literary novelist. And I—I was a girl from small-town Pennsylvania who'd become a New York cop, chugged beer with the guys, and had girls' nights out with other female cops who talked like dockworkers. Despite my bit of higher education, I was from a blue-collar world.

I often felt like Terry's arm candy, particularly around his friends, though Terry pooh-poohed those feelings. There were times when I wondered if Terry's main attraction to me was my looks. Well, honestly, he wasn't shy to admit that he thought I was beautiful, that he was proud to be seen with me. He liked to see me in a dress. Like my mother used to say, I "cleaned up well." But if Terry was a bit of a seducer at the start, if I was a bit awestruck, we ended up with a genuine love. We were together for two years before we got married, and I had him for four years after that.

It wasn't perfect. There were times when Terry could make me feel small. He had a sharp brain and a wicked tongue. But he doted on me, was proud of me, and encouraged me. He exposed me to so many things I never would have experienced without him. He encouraged me to finish my degree and go for the promotion to detective. If I was still a rube deep down inside, Terry had helped me polish off the rough edges. He helped me be *more* of what I inherently was—a strong and confident woman, a public servant, a righter of wrongs.

But as much as I had stars in my eyes about his suave lifestyle initially, by the end I merely tolerated it. The literary parties bored me out of my skull—a lot of pretentious posturing as far as I was concerned. And his love of beautiful things and expensive food and wine got to me sometimes. He had a fairly modest income as a writer and so did I. I was uncomfortable with his extravagances. I was a simple girl at heart. I could be happy in a cabin in the woods with a single bedroom and a woodstove. Especially with my job being as stressful as it was, I had a craving for the clean and basic and safe; Terry needed more. When we traveled, he wanted fine dining in Paris whereas I would have been happy going hiking in Vermont. We did what Terry wanted, of course, and I always enjoyed it. As I said, I experienced a lot of things with Terry that I never would have done on my own. I mean, what's not to love about Paris? I was grateful.

I loved him. I respected his talent. He was my first and only real love. And I was devastated when he was murdered.

I sat in that buggy watching the rural winter landscape go by, hearing the *clop clop* of the mule's hooves on the asphalt, and I felt that pang of hunger for the simple that had driven me back to Pennsylvania. I'd wanted to escape from the ugliness I'd seen in my ten years on the force—the gang shootings, the domestic violence, the terrorist threats. . . . It had all accumulated into a pile of shit weighing on my soul that had been bearable on some days, unbearable more and more often, and ultimately was topped off with the big, oozing cherry of Terry's senseless and horrific death. I wanted . . .

"Detective Harris?" Ezra said quietly. It sounded so formal.

"Call me E." I sat up straighter, coming back to the here and now.

"E?"

"Short for Elizabeth. People call me E when they're not calling me Detective Harris," I explained with a smile.

He pursed his lips thoughtfully. "May I call you Elizabeth?"

No one had ever called me that. It was too feminine and old-fashioned a name for a modern woman, a police officer. I'd been Liz in high school, but my friends in New York had started calling me E, and it was infinitely more hip. But the way Ezra said it—*Elizabeth*—made me feel all warm inside. Maybe I liked feeling feminine and old-fashioned around him. Which was something to contemplate—later. "If you prefer. Hey. See those houses over there?"

We were approaching town. I pointed across a mile or so of empty fields to a distant cluster of prefab houses. If it had been summer, there would have been a million cornstalks blocking the view.

"Ja."

"I live in the blue one on the far right. If you ever need anything."

I turned to look at him with a smile, because I needed right then to reach out. He glanced at me and smiled back, and my mood got a little lighter.

"I'll remember." I thought he sounded pleased. I made up my mind that he was.

"The market's just up here on the right. I'll leave ya and stop back by after I drop the chairs off."

"An Amish taxi service. This could be a thing."

Ezra snorted. "I'll text ya when I'm back. That way I don't have to tie Sandy up."

"Oh," I said in surprise. Of course, I'd known he had a cell phone. "You need my number?"

He looked away, a slight flush rising on his cheekbones. "You gave me your card once already."

And you still have it? Maybe even put my number in your phone? That was interesting.

"So . . . you're going to text me to say you're outside waiting with the horse and buggy?" I teased.

The corner of his mouth tugged up ever so slightly. "Not at all." He turned his head and looked me in the eye, his face serious. "It's a mule."

I barely made it back to the station house before our noon meeting. It was a Saturday, but we were all working. We'd taken to grabbing a conference room—Grady, me, Smith, and Hernandez—with bagged lunches to go over our progress on the case. As I headed over there, Grady caught up with me.

"Where were you all morning, Harris?"

"I got up early and took a metal detector over to Grimlace Lane. I checked along the creek for that missing cell phone of Jessica's."

Grady looked dubious. "The cell phone we think Katie had on her when she died?"

"That's the one."

"And?"

"Nothing. Then I went over and talked to the guy who runs the stall where Katie worked at the Paradise Farmers' Market."

"Good!" Grady clapped his hand on my back in a rather paternal way as we went into the conference room. "I've got some things to fill you in on too."

I brought the team up to speed on what I'd learned from Katie's old boss, which wasn't all that much. Mr. Dearling was a man in his sixties, and he and his wife ran the stall. They sold organic salads—pasta salads and the like—which his wife made. Having a "true Amish" in the stall was good for business, Mr. Dearling said. Katie was a good worker, had a pleasant disposition, and the customers liked her. She'd made minimum wage and, as far as he'd seen, never spent a dime of it at the market.

As for Jessica, she'd worked in the baked-goods shop next door and she and Katie had become friends quickly. They went off together every day at the end of their shift. Mr. Dearling admitted that he'd been worried about what Katie's parents would say about Katie spending so much time with Jessica, but he'd not interfered. Jessica had quit her job when school started after Labor Day and Katie had worked through September. They always laid off the summer help after the last weekend in September because the tourists dried up and they didn't need the help.

Mr. Dearling and his wife were not suspects as far as I was concerned. They were truly surprised and saddened at the news of Katie's death, and neither of them had the physical strength to carry Jessica's body. Mr. Dearling said both of the girls got plenty of attention from the boys who wandered by, but there was no one in particular who stalked or harassed them that he could recall.

As I recounted this to Grady and the others, I skipped the part about my riding to and from the market in Ezra Beiler's buggy and about Deacon Lapp's thunderous look. The blueberry jam did not come up.

Any more interest in what might or might not have gone on at the farmers' market was quickly put aside by Grady's news. The computer people had given Grady a report on the contents of Jessica's computer.

"Jessica had an e-mail account, lcbaybee@tmailer.com. She used it for soliciting on Craigslist." He passed out a sheet of paper with a screenshot of a Craigslist page. There was an ad circled.

2 young girls looking for sugar daddies to love. Beautiful and willing. Only serious gentlemen please. Pic available on request.

"That gets right to the point," I said.

"'Young' and 'willing' probably would have done it," Smith grumbled.

"And there was a folder of photos too. These were probably used for setting up appointments with their johns."

He showed them to us on his own laptop. There were a half dozen of the selfie variety, Jessica and Katie made-up and blowing kisses or smiling at the camera. I moved closer to get a good look. I'd seen Katie's corpse but never a picture of the living girl. God, they looked young. And very pretty, both of them. Katie was in makeup and in her English clothes—I recognized them from her hidden stash. But there was something different about her all the same, sweet and a bit unworldly yet with eyes full of invitation. Jessica was a pretty blonde, but she was a girl who existed a dozen times over in every small town in America. She couldn't hold a candle to Katie.

The idea that these two put themselves out there for anyone who could log on to a computer sent a chill of horror down my spine. They must have been so, so desperate to get out of here.

"Do we know for sure they took money for sex?" I asked.

"Apparently 'sugar daddy' is understood to mean there would be money involved," Grady said. "We didn't find her e-mails on the laptop. It looks like she only accessed them in a browser, and tmailer has a rep for being difficult and slow. But we may have luck with Craigslist. All the responses to Jessica's ad had to go through them and there's precedent that they'll open their records, particularly in a murder case. They don't want to become known as a place to get victimized."

"That's fantastic!" I was already laying it out in my mind. "If we can find someone who contacted Jessica around last October—"

"Yeah," Grady said, smiling broadly. "That tmailer account was set up August twenty-eighth, so the killer had to contact them sometime between then and October tenth, when Katie Yoder was murdered."

It was the hottest lead we'd had yet, and everyone knew it. You could feel the energy in the room move from frustrated to full-out excitement. There's nothing like being on a murder case when it breaks, particularly when it's a difficult one. I could feel the rabid joy in the base of my spine. *Get this guy. Gonna get this guy now.* Maybe it was something like a prizefighter feels as he enters the ring to win a title, or a Rottweiler the moment the front door gives way while the mailman is standing at the curb.

"Hopefully, we'll get the records today. There'll be a lot of grunt work going through the e-mails and, hopefully, IP addresses. We might even get lucky and find someone with a prior on the list. Smith and Hernandez, you'll be on that."

"Yes, boss! I'm there." Hernandez looked as enthusiastic as I felt. Smith just nodded with a you-bet-your-ass grimace on his face.

Grady looked at me then, and there was something worried in his eyes. Suddenly, I remembered the creek at Grimlace Lane. *Why there?* The sense of cracking the case faded a little.

"I'm gonna stay on Legal to make sure we get those records. Harris, I was thinking you might go back out to the Yoders. I want to know if Katie's mother and father had any idea what she was doing, if they might have argued with her about it." He said the last bit reluctantly, like it wasn't likely, but I understood. This wasn't over.

"Sure thing."

I didn't ask why he wanted *me* to do it. Maybe he thought Hannah Yoder would be more open talking to a woman. Then again, maybe he'd decided it was time to push the Amish after all, and I was the stick with which to do it.

CHAPTER 9

Broken Fences

Hannah Yoder was busy making a voluminous potato salad when I interrupted her day. Isaac had taken the boys to a cattle auction, she said. I offered to talk to her in the kitchen while she continued her work, and she took me up on it gratefully. Unfortunately, Ruth, Waneta, and Sadie were also in the kitchen. I watched them all bustling around for a few minutes. Hannah gave them brief instructions—chop the onion, get the eggs on—but Ruth and Waneta were already old hands at cooking. Adorable Sadie, the five-year-old, sat on a stool and calmly shelled what looked like dried pea pods into a bowl.

"You know how to shell peas, Lizbess?" Sadie asked me as if it were a very important question.

"I used to do it when I was little," I said with a smile. "Is it fun?"

Sadie shrugged with an "eh" of a sigh. Apparently shelling peas was just okay.

The picture they made was so appealing, I felt a pang of longing. I would never be a traditional woman—never wanted to be. Still, the sense of family; the beauty of cooking good food together; the cozy, unpretentious home; three lovely daughters . . . It made my own empty house and work-centered life feel like a hollow shell by comparison. And I felt self-loathing for bringing the ugliness of my questions into their idyllic world. Then I remembered that Katie Yoder had been part of this domestic scene and was now dead. Whatever foul doings had happened in her life, they possibly threatened more girls like these.

"It would be best if we could talk alone," I suggested to Hannah.

"Oh." She stopped dead in her work, as if the reality of the situation had just occurred to her—no doubt for the hundredth time. "Ruth, Waneta, go and strip the beds for the washin'. Sadie, help your sisters now."

Ruth had been struggling to get a heavy iron skillet out from a bottom cupboard, and Hannah took over, lifting the thing with one hand and placing it gently on the stove. She was stronger than she looked.

The girls left and Hannah, probably for something to do except look at me, scooped some butter from a crock into the skillet, stirring it around with a large wooden spoon as it melted.

"Mrs. Yoder, we've found out that Katie and Jessica were arranging to meet men through an Internet service." I hesitated. I didn't relish giving up Katie's secrets to her mother, especially not when Katie was dead, but I had no choice. "We believe they were having sex for money."

Hannah's face didn't change, but she flipped off the burner

with a twist of her wrist and came to the table. She sank into a chair as if too weak to stand, and put her face in her hands.

I waited.

"And one of these men killed her?" she asked, taking her hands down to look at me. Her face was pale and her eyes puffy and red. She'd probably been crying on and off since we found Katie, maybe even since we found the money pouch. Her eyes were wet again now.

"It's very possible."

She shut her eyes as a wave of pain crossed her features. "If you lay down with serpents, you get bit."

She sounded mournful rather than harsh, and, well, she wasn't exactly wrong.

"Can you think of a reason why Katie would have needed money that badly?"

She wiped her face and shook her head in resignation. "She wanted to leave. I had the idea she was savin' for it. She never spent, you know? On candy and such like. Even though she worked hard, always."

"Why did she want to leave so badly?" I asked gently. "Was there something troubling her? Maybe she wanted to get away from a boy she had an unrequited crush on? Or she was having difficulties with you and her father or maybe a friend? Was anyone cruel to her? Other girls?"

Hannah stared off at the wall, her face tense with thought. Finally she spoke haltingly. "She had friends when she was younger, but then more 'n' more the Amish boys and girls her age stopped bein' friendly. There was something . . . off with Katie. From a young age. She'd act inappropriate. Like she wanted to make men . . . lust after her. Older men. It didn't matter who. She craved attention, I guess. Maybe she was one who couldn't thrive in a big family. We don't have time for coddles and such like. Or maybe she liked bein' able to bend men to her will. I don't know, but it was plain as day and . . . shameful."

I wasn't sure what to say. It seemed so unlikely, here in this home, and seeing Katie's sisters, to imagine a girl raised in this environment just deciding to act wantonly. Was Hannah right? Had Katie been born that way? Was she a nymphomaniac? Or just a girl easily infatuated? Had she craved affection? Or was she rebelling against such a structured life in the one way she knew would drive her parents batty?

"I'm sorry to hear that," I said.

"Don't get me wrong, there was much to love about Katie." Hannah gave me a troubled glance. "She could light the sky with her smile. She was a hard and willin' worker. Affectionate. She was the perfect child when she was younger."

"I'm sure she was." I smiled.

"That made it all the worse for us. We prayed with her night after night."

I shifted in my seat. That didn't sound like much fun, especially for a teenage girl. "So you're not surprised to hear that Katie was meeting men for money? Did Isaac know?"

Hannah got a wistful look. "Course we didn't know. I was always taken by surprise by her ways." She paused, then looked down. "One time, she was only twelve years old, I come into the room where one of the good church brethren had come to visit, and Katie was reaching out to touch him *there*." She blushed, looking extremely uncomfortable. "The poor man was embarrassed near to death, and so was I." She looked up at me. "I only tell you this story just so's you understand—Katie was driven to these things from a young age. It's as if she had some devil in her. We prayed for God to free her from it, and many a time I saw her repent, truly repent. But she always backslid. And it led her to death, my poor, poor girl."

The tears came copiously then. I waited, fairly certain she didn't want comforting. Even though she'd been honest with me, there was still this sense that she could never understand me, a female who wore suits and carried a gun, and she didn't want to. I was an outsider. At last she cleaned herself up with a handkerchief from her apron pocket and stood. "Was that all you come to tell me?"

I stood too. "Yes. Is there anything else you can tell me? Any man or boy Katie was seeing that you knew about? Or someone who maybe liked Katie and could have been jealous over what she was doing?"

Her face drew tight. "I told you, Katie didn't take to the Amish boys, nor they to her. We knew she was seein' men outside, English men, but she never told me about it. I can't help you."

"All right."

"Please—" She stopped herself, as if she knew she shouldn't say what she wanted to say, then bit her lip and continued. "Just let Katie rest in peace now. It was God's will and it's done."

Anger rose in my throat like bile. But I smiled at her tightly. "Oh no, Mrs. Yoder. It is not done. I will find out what happened to Katie and Jessica. You can be sure of that."

———

When I got in on Monday morning, Grady was waiting for me. "I talked to Sharon about Katie."

"Oh yeah? Did your wife solve the case for us?" I teased.

He snorted. "Yeah, so take the day off. Have a massage and a manicure."

"Don't tempt me."

"No, Sharon didn't solve the case, smart ass, but she did make a good point."

"Thank God. We need one of those." I flopped into my desk chair.

"She thought we should talk to a psychiatrist, someone used to dealing with youth and sexual issues. What Mrs. Yoder told you about Katie, it didn't seem right."

"It sure as hell didn't. So you're not on board with the 'possessed by a devil' theory?"

Grady tossed a paper clip at me. "Seeing as you're feeling your oats today, *E*, maybe you should stay here while I go talk to the nice psychiatrist in Harrisburg. You can help Hernandez follow up on IP addresses."

"You've got an appointment?" I was excited.

"Yup. With a woman psychiatrist Sharon's met a few times in her work for the LGBT center. The appointment's for nine."

"I'm going. I think it's a great idea. Tell Sharon I owe her lunch."

"Yeah, that's the last thing I need. You and Sharon trading stories about me."

I waggled my eyebrows as if to say, "We already have." He snorted, but behind the bluff he looked ever so slightly afraid.

Dr. Emma Foster worked with the state interviewing and treating victims of sex offenders. She was in her early forties, slender, and wore a navy suit that was so thick and practical, it looked like it could survive a nuclear holocaust. She was scary bright and would have fit in well in New York. She even had a slight Jersey accent.

Grady and I sat in her office and filled Dr. Foster in on our case—Katie's death, the girls' soliciting, and my interview with Katie's mother. Dr. Foster took a few notes and when we were done she nodded. "Okay. Well, when I hear something like that, about Katie being so precocious sexually and particularly the incident where she touched a grown man's genitals at the age of twelve, I have one question."

"What's that?" Grady asked.

"Who was her abuser?" She looked at us with a tight, angry frown. "You're talking about an Amish girl. She didn't learn that behavior at home or at school. I doubt very much that her parents displayed any sexuality around their kids."

"No," I agreed. I'd been around Hannah and Isaac Yoder enough to know they weren't the type for PDAs of any sort.

"So? She learned it somewhere. And if she was bold enough to try to touch a grown man's penis, she hadn't just heard it talked about, she'd done it before. Someone, some male, was having sex with Katie by then, and maybe had been since she was much younger."

Grady and I looked at each other. I felt sick. It wasn't as

though the idea had never crossed my mind, but I hadn't taken it very seriously. Everyone had put the blame on Katie. She was a wanton, a temptress. She liked to wield her power over men. She was overly affectionate. She was soliciting for money. But Dr. Foster was so sure about it. And she was right, of course. Someone had sexualized Katie when she was young, far too young to have given reasonable consent. But who?

"It's likely someone in the family, right?" I asked, making an effort to remain calm and professional.

Dr. Foster nodded and leaned forward. "Listen. I'm working with the state right now to open up an abuse program specifically for Amish and Mennonite. There are already programs they can use, but getting the word out there is challenging. We want to put posters up in their stores and along Route 30. I want these women and girls to know there's someplace they can turn." This was clearly a cause of passion for Dr. Foster.

"Is that really . . ." Grady began doubtfully.

"Necessary? Absolutely. This is a patriarchal culture in which kids are taught from a young age not to trust outsiders. You obey your parents without question. You accept bad things that happen as God's will. So if they're abused, who are they going to tell? Does a girl that age even know what's going on? There's certainly no sex education in their schoolrooms, so it's up to the mother what she tells her girls. And she was raised in the same sheltered way."

Grady got red in the face. He was not amused. "I know a lot of Amish, Dr. Foster. It's hard for me to believe there's much of that going on in their communities. They're good, moral people."

Dr. Foster had clearly run up against this sentiment before.

She dug in her heels. "Of course, Detective Grady. I'm not saying it's in every home. In fact, it may well occur in a lower percentage than it does in the general population. But it does happen.

"A woman named Saloma Furlong wrote an autobiography called *Why I Left the Amish*, in which she writes about the sexual abuse she faced as a child at her brother's hands. And there was a court case four years ago in which a young Amish woman went to the police about her two brothers, who'd been sexually abusing her several times a day from the time she was eight years old."

Grady shook his head, his brow furrowed.

"Detective, this is a repressive, isolated culture where sex is forbidden outside of marriage, submission and forbearing are the highest virtues, and men have absolute authority. It happens. And the worst of it is, when it does, they don't alert outside authorities. If a man beats his wife or has sex with his daughters and repents, the church leaders forgive him. His slate is 'wiped clean.' That's admirable, but it also means he's still at large and is free to reoffend."

"I believe you that it happens in extreme cases," Grady admitted reluctantly. "Hell, we're seeing more trouble these days from Amish kids in *rumspringa*—drinking, drugs. But I just can't imagine it with most of the Amish I know, and not with this family. Harris, you've met the Yoders."

"They didn't seem to be hiding something like that," I admitted. "But you know as well as I do that you can't always tell. And Isaac Yoder did know about Katie's birthmark."

"Any father would know that."

"Maybe. Anyway, we haven't met all the family yet. Two of her older brothers married and moved out. It might have been one of them when they still lived at home, or a cousin, or even someone in the church. Maybe they even know they have a pe- dophile in their midst but he repented, as Dr. Foster said, and they're keeping it quiet."

I was fixed on that idea. Any Amish man in the area could know that part of Rockvale Creek well. Of course, Katie's sex offender wasn't necessarily her and Jessica's murderer, but I wanted to find him regardless. It was an important piece of the puzzle.

Dr. Foster nodded. "That's correct. It doesn't have to be someone in the home, just someone who had the opportunity to get Katie alone now and then. Look, you wanted to hear my expert opinion, and that's what I've got. Katie may well have been promiscuous. Coming from a large family, with a stoic father, some girls will do anything to be held and appreciated, and they consider sex a fair trade. But if she was acting out sexu- ally that young, she was abused by someone in her life. That's my opinion."

Some girls will do anything to be held and appreciated. I knew whereof she spoke. My own upbringing had been so devoid of physical affection that I'd gotten into sex young. I'd lost my vir- ginity to a boy my own age when I was fourteen. I'd even been the aggressor—I was curious. But after two weeks of panick- ing over whether I might be pregnant, I swore off sex until I was much older. I didn't want anything to trap me in my parents' lives. I wanted the attention all right—I just wanted other things more.

Still, I thought I understood girls like Jessica and Katie, what drove them to seek out boys, sex. But then, I'd never been sexually abused. That was a whole other level of pain and need and plain fucked-upness. So maybe I didn't understand at all.

"Thank you, doctor," Grady said with a reluctant smile.

———————

Grady was quiet on our drive back to Lancaster.

"It really bothers you to suspect the Amish of something like this, doesn't it?" I probed.

He grunted. "Look, I know they're just regular people. And Sharon has had to deal with more than a few Amish youth that have been put out of their homes. I just . . . I don't want to see this turn into a witch hunt."

"I agree."

He huffed.

"No, I get it. We want to believe in a perfect world, don't we?" I mused, looking out at the farmland we were driving through. "Even if we know damned well we can never achieve it ourselves, even if we don't *want* to. This picture-perfect scene. We want to believe it's the way it was with our grandparents and that it was all so much more pure and good than the way things are now. It's like a treasured fantasy."

"Fuck you," Grady sighed. "I'm not romantic about the Amish."

"I'm talking about myself," I said firmly. "And all the tourists who flock here. It's like we want to believe in them."

"Well, I grew up here and I've worked in this community ever since, and I don't have those illusions. The Amish have their issues and they don't have things easy. Living in the nineteenth century isn't all it's cracked up to be. They work their asses off and they're at the mercy of bad weather, bugs. No matter how sick you are, the cows have to be milked. No thank you. I'll take my microbrewed beer and my Sunday football on TV, and you can pry it out of my cold, dead hands."

I laughed. "I don't think any of us could really give up our comforts. I sure as hell couldn't. Forget it. I don't know what I'm saying."

"I know what you're saying." Grady shot me a look. "And you're right. People do want to believe, and it would be bad as anything for the local tourist trade if we find out we have an Amish murderer. And yeah, you've convinced me it's possible. Happy? I just hope to God that isn't the way it turns out."

"Me too," I said.

But honestly? At this point I was like a hound on the scent. All I really cared about was finding Katie and Jessica's killer. And if he *was* Amish, then I wanted to rip off the mask and expose him with a vicious repugnance that was, maybe, not entirely professional.

Did the killer put on a righteous face? Was that why Katie, and then Jessica, had not struggled, but had turned their backs on him and been struck down? Was he the same man who'd abused Katie since she was Ruth's age? Or Waneta's? Or, God forbid, even little Sadie's? Was he someone who could go after one of them?

I wanted to find that man with everything inside me.

———

Instead of going back to the station, we drove over to Deacon Aaron Lapp's farm. I'd only had the chance to speak to the man once, the day after Jessica's death. He came across as a hard man, foreboding as a brick wall. He wasn't old—maybe late thirties—but his demeanor gave him a much older vibe. I still remembered vividly the look he'd given Ezra and me when we'd driven past him in the buggy. It didn't dispose me to like the man. He had dark hair, almost black, including a long, untrimmed beard. His eyes were piercingly blue, and he looked strong and capable.

The Lapps owned twenty acres on Grimlace Lane and they had two dairy cows and a few horses. They also had a baked-good stand on the premises in the summer—supplied by Miriam Lapp and run by their kids, I assumed. And they farmed on about fifteen acres. What else they did for money, or if the church paid their deacons, I didn't know.

Part of me wasn't looking forward to this interview and part of me—the argumentative part—really was.

Miriam Lapp opened the door. She was in her thirties, a plain-faced woman, my height and big boned, with a large nose and heavy chin. She'd been nearly silent during our first interview with the Lapps after Jessica's death, letting her husband, Aaron, do the talking. She seemed shy of strangers like many Amish women. Today she took one look at us, told us politely to wait, and closed the door again.

Aaron Lapp came out on the porch a few seconds later dressed in a warm coat. "What can I do for youse?"

"We need to speak with you about something rather sensitive involving Katie Yoder," Grady said. "Is there someplace quiet we can talk?"

"This is good," Aaron said stubbornly. He looked only at Grady, not at me.

I saw Grady was a little annoyed at being kept on the porch. It was damned cold out, overcast and grim, and after the heat in the car, it wasn't pleasant to stand outside. I tried hard not to visibly shiver.

"Very well," Grady said flatly. "I'll get right to the point. I need to ask you if you're aware of any sexual abuse happening in your church, specifically anything that might have happened to Katie Yoder."

Aaron's face grew red, his brow thunderous, and his eyes darkening to a deep blue. If I'd seen that look on his face when I was a child, it would have terrified me. "I will not discuss this," he told Grady.

"I'd advise you to talk to us here," I said firmly. "Or we'll have to take you in for questioning, and there will be a lot more people present at the station."

"That's right," Grady said, backing me up. "So what's say we just get this over with?"

"You can't make me speak," Aaron insisted, still looking only at Grady.

"This is a case of murder," I insisted, sounding calmer than I felt. "Double homicide. Even if you insist on waiting for the trial, you'll have to speak then, under oath and in front of the press. And people will wonder what you had to hide, why you wouldn't speak to us earlier."

"This is for the good of the community, Mr. Lapp," Grady said, more cajolingly. "We have two dead girls and we know Katie was sexually abused. There's a problem here, and you need to let us help you take care of it."

Lapp studied Grady's face for a moment before looking away. "We will deal with it. It's our way."

"I'm afraid the state doesn't see it like that. You'll have to talk to us one way or the other."

I saw Aaron's shoulders slump in resignation. He knew we were right.

I pressed the advantage. "As deacon, you must know what goes on in most homes in your community. Were you aware of any sexual misconduct going on in Katie Yoder's home?"

"No," he said firmly, his back straightening. He finally looked me in the eye. "Isaac Yoder . . . no. *Verlick* not. Never."

"What about Katie's brothers? Or cousins?"

He pursed his lips, hesitating. "Katie Yoder was a harlot. If she lured a man to her bed, it was a sin on his part, to be sure, but it was purely willful on her part."

I bit back a retort on how young Katie had likely been when this had started, about how he flung the word "harlot" out very liberally about a child. But I could see it wouldn't do me any good to argue head-on with a man like Deacon Lapp. It was smarter to play along for now. "That may be true," I agreed, nodding my head for good measure. "We've heard others say things like that about Katie. We'll need the names of any man she convinced to sin in that way. We'll need to speak with them personally."

"We'll be as discreet as possible," Grady added in a lowered voice. "Unless it turns out to be directly related to the murder, no one needs to know."

Lapp considered it for a long moment. I thought he might even have prayed, silently. We waited. Finally he nodded, as if making up his mind. "No one in Katie's household did anything they need ask forgiveness for when it comes to Katie. Her brothers are fine men. As for others, most Amish boys thought Katie too wild, too mature. She was seen around with English men. You should look into that."

"Yeah, we know she was seeing English men," Grady agreed, still placating the man.

But I sensed something more. Aaron Lapp was withholding on us—I could smell it.

"There *was* someone, though," I said, letting my voice go hard. "Some older Amish man Katie saw now and then. Maybe a married man. Who was it?"

Aaron looked away, his mouth in a line. "She was seen going to Ezra Beiler's house," he said with reluctance. "After his wife died. Katie had no business there. That's all I'm sayin' on the matter."

Without another word, he went inside and shut the door hard.

CHAPTER 10

Pulling Up Roots

Grady wanted to go over and talk to Ezra right away. We were close by, and I had no reason to put it off. I couldn't exactly confess that Ezra had fed me ham loaf and blueberry preserves on previous solo visits, that we'd maybe become a little friendly with each other, and that I had secret, irrational crush on the young Amish widower. I couldn't admit that I'd lain in bed and thought about Ezra holding me the way he'd held me that time I'd fallen off the ladder, only next time preferably someplace warm—and private. How could I explain that it was the first time any man had stirred those feelings in me since Terry's death, and that I'd indulged said feelings, not bitten off the first shoots as I should have done.

Therefore, I also couldn't admit how epically pissed off and disappointed I was right now that Ezra Beiler had lied to me.

So we went over there. Together.

We found Ezra in the barn, cleaning out horse stalls. When

he caught sight of me, a smile took over his face that was warm and wide. It bounced off my anger like a boomerang. He noticed Grady, and my icy expression, and his smile vanished as if it had never been.

Ezra leaned the pitchfork carefully against the wall of the empty stall, stripped off heavy gloves, and came over. "Detective Harris," he said, his face neutral. He nodded at Grady too. "Detective."

I felt a moment's satisfaction that he'd remembered my name from that first visit but not, apparently, Grady's. I squashed any remotely favorable feelings though, hanging on to my anger.

"Mr. Beiler," Grady said flatly. "If you have a few minutes, we have some questions."

Ezra looked at me, as if seeking some cue. I stared back blankly. "All right. Do you want to—"

"Right here will be fine," I interrupted him. "I'm recording this."

I didn't want to be invited into his house. I didn't want to be distracted by his pleasant demeanor this time, and I wanted him to goddamn well know I was not happy. I turned on the recorder on my cell phone. "This Detective Elizabeth Harris interviewing Ezra Beiler, February third, 2014. With me is Detective Mike Grady."

Ezra's back stiffened and he looked at my collar instead of my eyes. He was clearly picking up on my tension.

"Mr. Beiler," I began firmly, "two days ago, on February first, I questioned you about Katie Yoder. Do you recall that conversation?"

He shot me a confused look. "Ja."

"Yes, you do remember that conversation about Katie Yoder?"

"Yes."

Out of the corner of my eye I saw Grady shift, apparently surprised by my hard-assed tone. I didn't care.

"At that time, you indicated to me that you didn't know Katie Yoder all that well."

He blinked. "I said she was younger than me. We didn't come up at the same time. 'Tis true."

I gave him a hard stare, and he looked away. There was hurt lurking in his brown-green eyes that made me feel sick inside, but I pushed forward. "You neglected to mention the fact that Katie visited your house on more than one occasion after your wife's death."

His expression didn't change, but I saw his Adam's apple bob with a heavy swallow.

"Well? Can you explain the purpose of those visits?"

His cheeks colored and he dropped his eyes. He looked away, toward the door, and I could feel him turning away in that moment in a sense that ran far deeper than physical. I had a spike of regret, but it was too late now for a softer approach. And he had lied to me, damn it. And maybe played me too. I hated the idea that I'd been hoodwinked by a pretty face. *Me.*

"Come inside," he said and, without looking at us for agreement, he went to the door of the barn and left.

———

Ezra was entering the house as we came out of the barn, not waiting for us. I followed, Grady behind me. He stopped me with a hand on my arm. "What was that about?"

"Just tired of being jerked around," I said, downplaying it with a sigh. I pulled my arm away.

I opened the front door to Ezra's house remembering the sense of anticipation with which I'd passed through it the last time I was here. I didn't know if I'd been more of a fool then or if I was being more of a fool now.

Ezra came down the stairs in the front hall as we entered, Martha behind him.

"Asked Martha down," Ezra said, looking deliberately at Grady and not at me.

"Good idea, Mr. Beiler," Grady said.

Ezra led the way to the kitchen and waved at the chairs around the table. There was no mention of coffee or cake this time.

We sat as Ezra went to a pine sideboard and opened a cupboard door. Grady tensed, putting his hand near his hip, but as mad as I was at Ezra, I couldn't imagine him pulling a gun on us. He didn't. He brought out a pile of books and workbooks and brought them over. He thunked them down in the center of the table more heavily than was necessary. They were textbooks—math, English, history, science. There were two thick workbooks labeled *GED*.

Oh.

"This is why Katie come by," Ezra said flatly. "She wanted to talk about leavin' the Amish. Ain't so, Martha?"

Martha looked a little confused about what was going on, but she nodded. "'Tis so."

Damn. I took the GED workbook off the stack and flipped through it. Nearly every page was filled with cramped writing. I looked up at Ezra. "Whose workbook is this?"

"Mine."

Grady sighed heavily next to me, though whether in relief or surprise I didn't know.

"You're trying to get your GED?" I asked, unable to look him in the eye.

"Got it last month," he said stiffly.

"And this?" I picked up the other workbook. Only a few pages had been done.

"Mine," said Martha meekly, as if she was ashamed of it.

"Katie was studying for the GED with the pair of you?"

"No, nothin' like that." Ezra was still standing and he folded his arms over his chest defensively. "She just . . . heard gossip I might be leavin' and she wanted to ask about it—what she had to do to get a social security number and about the GED and such like. It ain't easy to leave. She come by a few times to talk about it is all."

His accent had grown broader, his speech rougher. I wasn't sure if that was because he was upset or if he just no longer cared about trying to impress me. I knew what he was saying was true. Amish children were only educated through the eighth grade, and even that took place in their own one-room schoolhouses. Most of them were born at home and didn't have things like birth certificates and social security numbers. That made it very difficult to get a job or an apartment or a credit card if they ever wanted to leave.

"You're planning to leave the Amish, Mr. Beiler?" Grady asked.

Ezra looked at the wall, the color still high on his face. "I am."

"And you, Ms. Beiler?"

Martha shrugged. "Maybe so."

Part of me was glad to hear what Ezra was planning. I wanted him to be happy, and, selfishly, I wanted him free. I hated that judgmental scowl he'd gotten from Aaron Lapp just for riding in a buggy with me. But I was still upset that he'd lied. I put the workbook down. "Why didn't you tell me this when I asked you about Katie Yoder?"

"Wasn't my business to tell. 'Twas Katie's business."

"She's dead," I said pointedly.

Ezra pressed his lips tight but didn't answer.

I sighed and looked at Grady. I'd been so angry when we got here. I realized now that a good part of that anger was fear—fear that Ezra had been involved with Katie in some way, a way that could incriminate him in pedophilia or murder. And even if not that, even if he'd had sex with her when she was older and more than willing, it would have underscored the fact that he belonged with his own kind, and maybe that he was less discriminating and more manipulative than I'd thought he was. And maybe there was some green-eyed jealousy in there as well. Now those emotions dissipated like a foul vapor, leaving a dark hollow in their wake.

"Did Katie say anything to you when she visited? About what her plans were? Where she was going?" Grady asked Ezra and Martha.

Martha looked down at her pudgy fingertips and chewed fingernails, her face pink with discomfort.

"Said she was going to New York next summer," Ezra reluctantly admitted.

"And that wasn't relevant to a murder investigation?" I asked in disbelief.

He looked me in the eye, frowning. "Murder? But Katie . . . She was murdered?"

"We can't really talk about that," Grady said, giving me a subtle nudge with his knee.

Damn it. I rubbed my forehead. I'd forgotten that Ezra might not know Katie was murdered or that her case was tied to the dead girl they'd found next door. Apparently that wasn't the sort of information the Yoders wanted to share with anyone.

I felt like an idiot, and not just then, but like I'd been an idiot with Ezra from the start, operating with half a brain. I looked up at him again, and at the sight of him standing there stiff and hurt I wanted him all over again and, equally and contrarily, I was determined to pull my head out of my ass and behave like the disinterested professional I was supposed to be.

"One more question, Mr. Beiler," I said. "When Katie came to visit you, how did she get here? Her parents' farm is on the other side of Paradise."

He shrugged. "She walked down from the Lapps'."

"The Lapps'?" I blinked at him. "Aaron and Miriam Lapp? A few farms down?"

"Yes."

"Did she visit them often?"

He looked confused at the question. "Katie Yoder cleaned house for 'em. Always did so."

I heard Grady's mumbled groan beside me, but I was in no frame of mind to be that subtle. I stood up, slamming both palms on the table and leaned over it toward Ezra.

"Kindly repeat that?" I said quietly.

His face paled but he stood firm. "Katie Yoder cleaned house for the Lapps. Ya didn't know?"

"For God's sake!" I yelled, throwing my hands up.

"Harris . . ." Grady warned, standing up.

I turned to him, ready to tear out my hair in frustration. "Am I speaking a foreign language? Am I insane? Why did not one out of the fifty people we've interviewed mention this?"

Grady struggled to respond to my outburst. I could see he wanted to laugh, the way you do when someone makes an idiot of themselves, like splitting a seam or slipping on a banana peel, even though he knew he should admonish me. But goddamn it, it wasn't funny!

"Seriously!" I insisted.

"Let's go, Detective Harris," he managed, finding an appropriately reprimanding glower. "I think we've got what we need here."

As we left the house, I turned to look back at Ezra, hoping to give him a final it's-not-you-I'm-just-frustrated look. Even in my hubris, I felt bad for being so angry with him. But he'd already shut the door.

We pulled out of Ezra's place. It was late afternoon by then, and there was a red haze over the fields that was not, strangely, due to my anger. No, it was real enough, the first death throes of the setting sun filtering through a low-lying mist—beautiful and cold.

"Stop at the Lapps'," I said stiffly.

Grady pulled over on Grimlace Lane and put the car in park. "Only if you calm down first."

"I'm fucking calm!" I shouted, which made Grady laugh and me too, damn it.

"Sorry," I muttered. "Obviously not calm."

"Look, don't take it personally," Grady said. "It's like . . . I dunno. Like you said, they're not forthcoming. If we don't ask the question specifically, we're not going to be told a damn thing, apparently."

"But we asked Hannah and Isaac Yoder—*Did Katie have any particular dealings with anyone on Grimlace Lane?* They said no."

"I know." Grady shook his head in a "go figure." "I was there, remember?"

"And we're standing there asking Aaron Lapp about Katie Yoder, and he doesn't mention she cleaned house for them?"

"It's a tight-knit community. I guess to them that was just normal to be in and out of each other's houses so they didn't think to mention it."

I growled. "I feel like Hannah Yoder was deliberately hiding it."

"I don't think she was hiding it," Grady said patiently. "She just didn't think to mention it, the way she didn't mention Katie brushed her teeth or went to church on Sundays. Maybe she has a different idea of what 'particular dealings' means."

"It's like we're speaking two different languages."

"We are. Don't let it make you nuts. We're just gonna have to be even more specific."

"No problem there," I grumbled. If I had to use neon flashcards, I was going to get answers.

"Okay?" Grady asked, placing his hand on the keys. "Let's go talk to the Lapps, but acting pissed isn't going to help. You were a little rough on Ezra back there."

Goddamned Pennsylvanians were so nice. "He lied to me!" But Grady's words caused another twinge of guilt. "Never mind. I'm fine now. I've got it under control. Do you see it though? Katie *cleaned houses here on Grimlace Lane.*"

"I see it," he said, frowning worriedly. He started the car and drove the short distance to the Lapps'.

When we arrived, the door was answered by Sarah Lapp, the oldest daughter. She was twelve, tall for her age, and rail thin, with a face so narrow it was almost sharp. Her tightly pulled-back dark hair and white cap made her features look even sharper.

"Can I help youse?"

"We need to speak with your parents," Grady said.

Sarah looked doubtful. "Wait here already."

After several long minutes, the door opened again and Miriam Lapp stood there looking at us with pressed lips that said she wasn't happy to see us. "I'm sorry, but my husband went to town."

I glanced at Grady. Maybe this was a stroke of good fortune. We might get more out of Miriam Lapp if Aaron wasn't around.

"That's fine. We'd like to speak with you in that case," I said firmly but politely.

"Oh, I mustn't, with my husband out." Miriam made no move to open the door farther.

"It will only take a moment," Grady said with a conciliatory smile. "If you'd be so kind."

Apparently she wasn't used to being outright defiant. She reluctantly let us in.

"I must make supper in a bit," she hedged as we sat down in the living room. She looked like she didn't want either one of us to be there.

"This won't take long," Grady said, still smiling.

I got out my iPad and started the recorder. A clock ticked loudly on the wall. Like the Yoders' home, the living room was clean and neat, with traditional furniture in oak and plaid. There was the smell of just-baked sugar cookies in the house.

"This is Detective Elizabeth Harris interviewing Miriam Lapp, Deacon Aaron Lapp's wife, February third, 2014. With me is Detective Mike Grady."

Miriam's hands anxiously twisted a handkerchief, but her face was unreadable.

"We have some questions about Katie Yoder," I began. "We understand she worked for you?"

"'Tis so."

"And what did she do for you exactly?"

"She come to help clean. She don't work here no more though."

"No," I said coolly. "We're aware of that. When did Katie start working for you?"

"Just after my daughter Rebecca was born. I was laid low for a bit. Had a surgery. Katie started comin' to help."

"What year was that?"

Miriam had to think about it. Her fingers moved as if she were counting on them. "Would have been . . . 2006."

I did a quick mental calculation. Katie started cleaning house for the Lapps at eleven years old. In my world, that was still young enough to be babysat. "And you paid her a wage?"

"Course we did!" Her back stiffened. "She didn't do it for charity."

"How often was she here?"

"She come Mondays and Thursdays."

"And when was the last time you saw Katie?"

"Last October." Miriam didn't flinch but her mouth took on that hard line again.

"So she worked for you up until the time she disappeared?"

"'Tis so."

Grady and I exchanged a look. I had a million questions, but the challenge was to find the right ones.

I gave Miriam my best sympathetic, womanly look. "I'm so sorry for your loss. Were you and Katie close? Was she a friend or perhaps more of a daughter?"

Miriam frowned, as if confused. "She was a third cousin. Her mother, Hannah, is my second cousin."

"What I meant was, did Katie discuss things with you? For example, boys she liked, her friends, or any trouble she might have had at home?"

Miriam glanced at the clock. Her forehead and cheeks blushed pink, but she spoke firmly. "We would never discuss such like, not Katie and me. She was much younger. She did housework, that's all. We didn't gossip."

I thought her blush indicated she was aware of Katie's reputation though.

Grady broke in gently. "Did you ever discuss Katie with Hannah?"

Miriam looked down into her lap where her large hands were

wringing the handkerchief to within an inch of its life. It if had been a chicken, it would have been decapitated by now.

"Hannah and me prayed over Katie many times."

"What did you pray about?" I asked softly.

She used the handkerchief to wipe at her brow and eyes, which were dry as far as I could see. "Hannah worried that Katie was so man hungry. We prayed for God to give her modesty. We prayed for her soul. Now I *must* get to supper. It's late." She stood, clearly willing the interview to end. But Grady didn't move and I didn't either.

"Did Katie tell you she was leaving?" I asked, deliberately sitting back in the chair to show I wasn't going anywhere.

"Yes."

Now that surprised me. I sat up straighter. I recalled that Hannah Yoder had mentioned that Katie had told a cousin Miriam she was leaving. Damn, had it been Miriam Lapp? I'd met at least three other Miriams since this case began and a dozen cousins. All these common names were confusing.

"What exactly did Katie say to you?"

Miriam stuffed the handkerchief into a pocket of her apron and kept her hands in there. I could practically taste her desire to get to the kitchen.

"She come for work as usual. Said she was leavin' and wouldn't be back again. She asked me to say good-bye to her mother. Now I must get on."

"This is very important, Mrs. Lapp," Grady put in gently. "If you could just spare us another five minutes."

With extreme reluctance, Miriam sat back down. She seemed

calm enough but very interested in getting rid of us. I wondered if Aaron Lapp was the type to get angry if supper was late or if she spoke to us alone. I wondered if he was the type to hit her for such transgressions. He didn't come across as a tolerant man, and Dr. Foster had me seeing potential trouble when I hadn't seen it before. I felt sorry for Miriam, but I didn't want to leave without the answers we needed.

"Did she say she was planning to leave that same day? The day she told you this?" I asked.

"Didn't say so. I weren't surprised to hear she'd gone though."

"So Katie told you that she was leaving the community?" I reiterated, looking at her hard.

"She did."

"You said the two of you weren't close, and you didn't gossip with Katie. So why would she tell you she was leaving when she didn't tell her own family?" I heard the chill in my voice, the frustrated anger that had been lurking resurfacing once again.

"Well, she wanted me to pay her, not so?" Miriam blinked innocently, as if it were obvious. "Said she was quittin' and wanted what we owed. Fifty-six dollars, I think it was. 'N' I give it to her and wished her luck." Her hands twisted in the pocket of her apron anxiously. "In truth, I weren't sorry. 'Tween Sarah and me, we didn't need the help no more, but I hated to fire her."

I sighed and looked at Grady. "Did she tell you how she was planning to go? If someone was picking her up?" I asked.

Miriam shook her head. "Didn't say."

"And when did you tell Hannah and Isaac about Katie's good-bye?"

"Next day, Isaac come around lookin' for Katie since she never come home that night, and I told him what Katie said."

"How did Katie get here, when she came to work?"

"She rode a bike."

"And that last day she was here, she left on the bike?"

Miriam thought about it. "S'pose so. Didn't watch her, but after she left the bike was gone. Now I really must make supper. I'm sorry, but if you have more questions, you'll have to talk to my husband." She stood up once again, very determined this time.

I stood up too and took a step into Miriam Lapp's space. "Just one more thing, Mrs. Lapp." I took a breath and tried to connect with her, looking her in the eyes, but her gaze darted away from mine as if it made her uncomfortable. I spoke softly. "We have reason to believe Katie was sexually abused from the time she was young. Do you have any idea who might have been her abuser?"

I felt Grady tense beside me. Miriam looked like I'd slapped her in the face, her cheeks going pale and slack with shock.

"'Tis a lie," she said in a soft, mortified voice.

I pressed on doggedly. "Katie spent time here. Maybe you heard or saw something—"

"No! I don't believe it," Miriam said with utter determination, her lips pulled tight in anger. "'Tis a sin to spread such filthy lies!"

She looked at Grady as if for support, her cheeks splashed with the blush of outrage. His fingers closed on my elbow.

"Thank you for your time, Mrs. Lapp," he said. "Please, if you can think of anything further, contact us." He tossed a card onto the coffee table and all but pulled me out the door.

We were quiet on the way back to the station. My mind was churning.

Katie's bike. Where was the bike now? Had it ever turned up? If Katie did intend to leave the community that day, or shortly thereafter, had she actually done so? Had someone agreed to help Katie get out and then killed her after she was under his control? Or was it possible that she'd told someone other than Miriam Lapp that she was leaving, and this *other* person had a real problem with that?

"I still think it's someone who picked them up on Craigslist," Grady said at last.

"Maybe," I agreed.

"The guy could have known this area. Maybe he'd even picked Katie up here before, after work. He could have put her bike in the back of his car or truck and that would have given them some extra time to fool around for an hour or two."

"Uh-huh." I tapped my fingers on the door handle.

Grady sighed. "Maybe Katie told him about the animal trails. And if he was used to picking her up around here, he'd know the area."

"Interesting idea," I said, and it was. It didn't strike me as terribly likely though. At this point we weren't just grasping at straws, we were working a double shift in a goddamned straw factory.

Grady pulled out his phone and made a call. I heard him

talking to Hernandez. He shut the phone. "We got the IP addresses of people who responded to Jessica's ad from Craigslist. Finally. Smith and Hernandez are going to work late, and I told him to recruit Anderson and Levine. You in?"

"Sure. But I really want to check up on Katie's bike. I'd call the Yoders if they had a phone, but *not*. It won't take me long to drive over there."

Grady sighed. "I want to get back to the station and get the IP address check rolling. You can grab your car and go from there. Don't be long?"

"It'll take forty minutes, and I'll bring back food."

"My hero," Grady said.

When I got out of my car at the Yoders', Sadie was swinging on the porch swing with one of her brothers, who was maybe a year older than her, both of them bundled up in their winter coats. Sadie jumped from the swing with an uncaring thwack and ran toward me. Her brother eyed me warily but stayed where he was as the swing twisted in Sadie's wake.

"Hey, Sadie. How are you?" A big smile hijacked my cheeks as I bent down to greet the little girl.

I thought she was going to throw herself into my arms, but she stopped short of that and, with great decorum, patted my cheek instead with her cold little hand. I could see the tips of mittens tucked into her pockets. Apparently she didn't like wearing them.

"Lizbess! You missed supper."

"Oh, darn! Well, that's okay. I'm not hungry." That was a total lie. "It's nice to see you. You look very pretty today." I tugged on her black wool coat teasingly. She had a streak of dirt on her nose and her end-of-day hair had all but broken free of her black bonnet. She was so damn cute.

Her face got even more serious than usual and her lower lip trembled. "Katie is dead," she told me.

I felt horrible. I remembered the day I'd cajoled Sadie into giving up the whereabouts of Katie's "bestest things" with the promise that we were trying to help. I also felt pain at Sadie's wording. There was no attempt to soften the blow. It wasn't "Katie isn't coming back." Or "Katie's with Jesus" but "Katie is dead." Did Sadie even know what that meant? Living on a farm, perhaps she'd already seen death up close and personal.

"I know, honey. I'm so sorry."

Maybe I shouldn't have done it. There was a warning voice in my head telling me to proceed with caution. But when the heavy drops fell from Sadie's eyes, her face still so quiet and solemn, I didn't have it in me to resist pulling her into a hug. She didn't fight me, but put her little arms around me with enthusiasm and, with a soft wail, cried into my shirt.

It felt sweet to have the little girl in my arms, even though her grief was hard to bear. We were like that for maybe thirty seconds before Hannah Yoder came charging out of the house. She was drying her hands on a dishcloth and her face was worried. "Sadie! Come in the house now."

Sadie pulled away and ran to her mother before I could say good-bye. With a pat on the little girl's shoulder, Hannah sent her on into the house.

I got to my feet, feeling a little uneasy about what had just transpired. It was clear my attention to Sadie wasn't welcome, but I hadn't meant any harm. It made me wonder if Hannah was overprotective of having people touch her children. It made me wonder if she had a good reason for that. I wanted to find out.

"Good evening, Mrs. Yoder," I said, pulling myself back into police mode and walking slowly closer. "Sorry to disturb you after supper, but I needed to check on Katie's bike."

Hannah folded her arms across her chest, not smiling. "Haven't seen the bike. Thought Katie took it with her."

"So the bike went missing the same time Katie did?" I asked, to be sure.

Hannah shrugged. "Course. Katie rode that bike everywhere. Figured she rode it to meet up with whoever was . . ." There was a pause, her breath hitching. "Back when it happened, we thought whoever she was leavin' with. Figured she took it with her in their car. She couldn't drive, so she'd need it to get around still."

The bike was another thing it would have been helpful for them to have mentioned from the start. In fact, I recalled Isaac specifically using the words "walking away." He must have meant that metaphorically.

If you don't ask the question specifically, they're not going to tell you.

I felt the start of a headache. I took a deep breath for patience. "Mrs. Yoder. You said Katie had told a cousin of yours that she was leaving."

"Ja."

"Can you give me the full name of that person?"

Hannah looked uneasy. "My cousin, Miriam Lapp."

"I see. This is Deacon Aaron Lapp's wife? Residing on Grimlace Lane?"

"That's her." Hannah folded her arms more tightly and spread her feet, in black athletic shoes, a bit apart, as if steeling herself. Her face was completely neutral.

"And Katie worked for the same Lapps cleaning house, is that correct?"

"Sure." Hannah said it like it was something everyone knew. Somewhere deep inside my head, I screamed.

"You didn't mention it when we asked about Katie's work or about Grimlace Lane," I pointed out, smiling tightly.

Hannah shrugged. "Guess I didn't think much of it."

I scratched my forehead with my thumb, trying to figure out what to say next. I supposed I'd learned what I'd come out here to learn about the bike, and I should have been on my way. But I could hear Dr. Foster's stern words. *Someone abused Katie from a young age.* Did her mother know? It was possible she didn't. Children are often reluctant to admit abuse to their parents, either because they're ashamed of it, think they'll get in trouble, or their abuser threatens them if they tell. Still, it bothered me that Hannah remembered Katie as some Jezebel without knowing that Katie had been victimized. Besides, Hannah surely had to know *something*.

"Hannah," I said quietly, switching to her first name in a bid to gain her confidence. I took a step closer and tried to impress upon her, with my expression and tone, that I wanted to help. "There's something I want to ask you. You remember that story you told me, about Katie touching a guest to your home inappropriately at age twelve?"

Hurt came into Hannah's eyes. She gave a slight nod.

"Well, we spoke to a psychiatrist. She believes Katie was

sexually abused, starting from when she was quite young. There's no reason a girl her age would—"

Hannah took a step back, as if disgusted by me. Her hand flew to her mouth but she didn't speak.

"Please," I urged. "I believe that you didn't know about it. And I know it's difficult to think about something like this happening in your own family. But maybe you had a slight suspicion. Or maybe you noticed Katie going off with someone, or there was someone who paid her a little too much attention, or someone she seemed nervous around."

Hannah lowered her hand, her face stony. I could see it come over her, as if she'd decided I was not to be trusted.

I cut off the questioning with a sigh. "I'm only trying to do my job."

"Your job? Our Katie is dead and you want to defile her memory in this way? Bring these dirty lies, suspicions into our home? Accuse us of—"

"I'm not accusing anyone of anything. I'm just trying to find out what happened to Katie." I'd hoped, as Katie's mother, she would understand, that ultimately she and I had the same goal. But all I saw on Hannah's face was fierce protectiveness—against me. Maybe Hannah cared about Katie, but she cared about her living family more.

"Please go now," she said firmly. And without another word, she turned and went into the house.

———

I sat in the deli waiting for the to-go bags of sandwiches for another long night at the station. I twiddled with my phone. I felt uneasy about my visit with Hannah Yoder. Should I have put things more delicately? *Was* there a way to delicately ask if Hannah suspected that her husband or sons had sexually molested her young daughter?

Also, I couldn't stop thinking about Ezra. I felt supremely shitty for the way things had been left with him. It was true that he'd withheld information from me, but I no longer thought he'd done it with any sort of evil intent. Nor did I believe he'd fooled around with Katie Yoder.

Unless he was still lying. Unless he'd been messing around with her after all, and I was too mesmerized by him to think objectively.

No. I didn't believe that.

Cursing myself, I looked at his photo on my phone, the one I'd taken the day we'd interviewed all the farmers. I'd moved all the others to my PC at the station and deleted them off the iPad, but not this one. I hadn't been able to resist keeping it in the cloud.

I scrolled through my received texts. I still had the one he'd sent me when he picked me up from the farmers' market. My thumb hovered over it uncertainly.

I was absolutely not going to call him.

I did, however, type out a text.

> Sorry about earlier. I was frustrated about the
> case. Hope I didn't offend you and Martha.

I stared at it. As a detective, I had nothing to apologize for. But as a friend, I did. I argued with myself for a good five minutes over whether or not to send it. A young single woman, a police detective, could not be *friends* with a hot young Amish guy. And certainly not anything more.

But he's leaving the Amish. He was leaving even before you showed up. That did put things in a slightly more hopeful light. After all, if Romeo had willingly renounced the Montagues, if Tony had quit the Jets . . .

I laughed at my own ludicrousness and pressed Send. And then I sweat.

The sandwiches and drinks came out and I was nearly back at the station when my phone pinged. I parked and fought to get it out of my pocket.

Ya did a bit.

Well that was honest. I typed in a response.

Sorry.

He replied. Ok.

The man was succinct, I had to give him that. I tapped the phone on my leg, trying to think of what to say. "Can we still be friends" sounded absurd. And I certainly couldn't write something like "I'm glad you're not still offended because I like you." Geez, this was nuts. I finally went with:

Ok then.

Alright came back quickly. I smiled, hearing Ezra's laconic tone.

Very good, I typed.

Settled came back. I laughed, joy and anxiety bubbling up in my chest. Holy cow, I was in so much trouble.

Good night, Ezra, I typed. Send.

Good night, Elizabeth.

CHAPTER 11

Germination

We worked late, and then I hit the gym at the station for an hour to relieve some stress. By the time I had a snack, took a shower, and went to bed, it was after one A.M. My alarm failed—probably because I hadn't remembered to set it—and I woke up late. I arrived at the station the next morning at nine A.M.

I turned into the parking lot and rolled to a confused stop. Tied up in front of the station house were eight buggies with their horses. My phone pinged. It was Grady.

Where are you? Need you here now.

I had a very bad feeling about this. I parked and hurried inside.

Grady met me in the hall and pulled me toward the chief's office.

"What's going on?" I asked.

"There's a delegation here from the Amish church. They asked to speak to the chief and they want you and me present."

I wondered if this could be a good thing—maybe they'd come to give up Katie's abuser? The firm set of Grady's jaw told me nothing.

The office of Chief Lumbaker, our chief of police, was filled with Amish men in their black clothes and long beards. As we entered, they were speaking among themselves in German, but they stopped as soon as they saw us, their demeanors going blank. I noticed Aaron Lapp was front and center of the group. The look he gave me was hard enough to make me shiver. I straightened my spine and gave him a friendly smile, mostly because I figured it would annoy the hell out of him.

Chief Lumbaker was in his fifties. He looked like the picture of a conservative businessman in his suit, but from my few dealings with him, I thought he was fair and open-minded. Still, I didn't know him all that well.

"Now that we're all here," he said, "why don't you proceed, Mr. Lapp?"

Aaron Lapp took a step forward and clasped his hands in front of him gravely. His blue eyes were cold. "We have come to a decision amongst ourselves. We've tried to cooperate with the police on this matter, but it's now at the point where we are being unfairly harassed."

I clenched my jaw, feeling queasy. My heart started beating too hard. This was not good.

"Mr. Lapp—" Grady began, but Lapp held up a hand and went on.

"In particular, Detective Harris is no longer welcome." He

pointed at me accusingly. "This woman wears a gun and uses foul language—"

I was *going* to use some foul language in a minute.

"—she goes against all our beliefs, yet she has made no effort to maintain the distance we desire, but has made overtures to befriend our children and seduce our young men. This will not be tolerated!"

Geez, the guy had a voice like Abraham thundering down the Ten Commandments from on high. He made me squirm inside, made me feel guilty, and worried about what my bosses would think. And then—then I felt angry.

Everyone was looking at me. Chief Lumbaker and Grady too.

Grady tried to defend me. "I don't believe that, Mr. Lapp. I have never seen Detective Harris act disrespectfully or do anything inappropriate." Despite his words, there was a hint of doubt in his eyes. Maybe he was wondering about the way Ezra had smiled at me the day we'd walked into that barn. Hell, I would have if I were in his shoes right now.

"You are not always there," Lapp said pointedly.

Grady blinked. "Detective Harris?"

I folded my arms. "I've done nothing wrong." I gave Grady and Chief Lumbaker my silent assurance with a hard look.

"We will not argue the point," Lapp said. "We sincerely request that Detective Harris be removed from any dealings with our community. And the truth is, we have answered your questions several times over. We want no more badgering of our people, especially not our women and children, having their heads filled with unwarranted and inappropriate allegations." He gave me an ugly look. "From here on, any more questions you have for one of ours, you must come to the elders first. If we agree the question has value, we will go with you to do the questioning. We will work with Detective Grady in those things."

Grady broke in. He sounded calm but his hands were fisted at his side. "Detective Harris is the most experienced homicide detective we have. We need her expertise on this case."

Chief Lumbaker grunted. "I thought you were pursuing other angles. Is there any reason to believe the Amish are more deeply involved? Do you have proof they haven't already told you everything you need to know from them?"

I looked at the chief in disbelief. "Sir, with all due respect, we should not discuss the details of the case in front of . . . of civilians."

The chief frowned at me. "These men are not suspects, Detective Harris. If you have something to say, say it now."

Holy hell. He said it so flatly, so indisputably. I couldn't believe what I was hearing.

"No, sir. I think we have all we need from the Amish for the moment," Grady said tightly. "Is there anything else?"

I shut my mouth, which had been hanging open, with a snap.

"You and Detective Harris are excused," Chief Lumbaker said. He and Grady exchanged a look I didn't like, a look that said they'd be talking about this later. Probably without me in the room.

Grady took my elbow and steered my numb body out the door.

I paced in the break room. Grady had shut the door behind us so we'd have privacy. At least until the next cop had a caffeine crisis.

"But this is sexism, pure and simple!" I all but shouted.

"Of course it is," Grady admitted. "But it's not on the department's side, it's on our constituency's side. Unfortunately, we can't afford to ignore what the Amish elders want."

"Why not? They don't run the police department, do they?"

"Of course not!" Grady snapped. "But they're a large and important part of this community. And they have a point, Harris. It's not our job nor our place to try to influence their beliefs."

"I never—!" I was too flabbergasted to even finish that sentence.

"I know that," Grady said in an almost-pleading voice. "But you are a role model, whether you try to be or not."

I rolled my eyes.

"Come on, Harris. You're beautiful and you're smart and you exude competence."

"If you're trying to butter me up . . . !"

"So, *yes,* you do influence the people who you come into contact with. That's not a bad thing. But I can see why the Amish don't necessarily want you spending a lot of time around their young girls and, yes, young men."

He eyed me pointedly. He had to suspect something about Ezra Beiler. But at least he wasn't going to ask about it. I hoped.

"But . . . that's ridiculous! This isn't high school! They can't just ask me to not sit at their lunch table! I'm a homicide detective. Whether they like me or not, I have to do my job!"

Grady rubbed his forehead as if a construction crane were moving blocks around in there. He sighed. "Okay, look, no one is saying you'll be taken off this investigation. But Lapp has a point.

We don't have any direct evidence tying the killer to the Amish—"

"That's bullshit!" I started counting off my fingers. "There's the sexual abuse—"

"Which is Dr. Foster's assumption that we haven't proved—"

"—there's the fact that Katie worked for the Amish family two doors down from where Jessica's body was found, there's the fact that both were likely placed in Rockvale Creek—"

"Also unproven. We don't know for sure that Katie wasn't dumped in the Susquehanna."

"—and the fact that the killer knows the area. Come on!"

Grady took a deep breath. "I know all that. But, in fact, we don't have any *irrefutable* evidence that cannot be *explained another way*. Now, I know you've had a hard-on for this being a member of that neighborhood since day one, and I was willing to give you some space on that. But in all honesty—"

I'd turned sideways to Grady, huffily closing him off, and he pulled me back by my arm and made me look at him. He spoke intently. "I'm talking as your supervisor here, Harris. In all honesty, our best lead on this case right now is those Craigslist responders. We already have a few names and addresses that need to be checked out. That's where I need you to focus. And that doesn't require you to interview the Amish, does it?"

I was still angry, but doubt started to trickle in like rainwater down the cellar walls. As much as I wanted to kick and flail about being told I couldn't talk to anyone I goddamn well wanted to, there was some logic to what he was saying. We had followed up with the Amish quite a bit without much progress, and from any objective point of view, the Craigslist angle was the most promising. We needed to find the men who had actually spent time with Jessica and Katie, who had paid for their nubile young bodies. Even if Katie's past abuse was very real, it might have no direct relation to these murders—that is, to my ultimate objective of finding the killer. Katie might have been sexualized when she was young, that might have led to her willingness to trade her body for money, and some john may have killed her for that. Sometimes you don't learn everything you want to know on a case. Sometimes you have to let go of the details to make progress on the bigger picture.

Why *was* I so fixated on the Amish? Was it really gut intuition about the murder? Or had some wrong switch gotten flipped in my head? Was I just enamored by them, wanting to spend time among them and dig into their world? Or did I have some desire, hidden even to myself, to despoil? Did I *want* to be an influence for another way of life?

I had to admit that when I'd spent time with Sadie and Waneta, seen them look at me with such curiosity and admiration, I'd hoped I could maybe open up some other potential paths in their minds. My intentions were nothing but good—what woman wouldn't want to give a hand to a girl she suspected was being forced down a narrow path without much real choice? But who was I to make such a judgment? Was my life so incredible that I wanted everyone else to live like I did? A lonely workaholic with a perpetual psychosomatic chill and nightmares of her beloved's murder? God forbid.

And then there was Ezra. I was guilty as charged there, even if only in my own heart. He liked me, I was pretty sure of that. Had I led him on?

"Fine. I'll focus on the Craigslist angle," I said abruptly.

Grady looked relieved. "I appreciate your cooperation, Harris. We'll get through this." He put a hand on my shoulder.

Requisite boss pep talk. I forced a smile. "Yeah."

"We'll find this guy."

I nodded, pretending enthusiasm.

"And, you know, if you have any more questions for the Amish, just tell me and I'll talk to them. I can even record the conversations, so it'll be like you were there."

Virtual detective work. Because I was a pariah. Perfect. I forced a smile. "I'll go check with Hernandez on the Craigslist stuff now."

"Good."

Grady looked relieved that I wasn't going to throw some emotional scene. Well, maybe I had thrown a teensy one, but I'd pulled myself out of it. The last thing I needed was to be labeled an emotional female who had to be tiptoed around. Not Elizabeth Harris. I was a pro. I did what was best for the team.

That didn't stop me from resenting the hell out of it.

———

For the next week I worked on the Craigslist angle with twelve-hour days and no break for the weekend. A lot of people had responded to Jessica's ad. Here's an analogy: Place two large prime ribs with all the trimmings on a silver platter in the middle of a wolf preserve. We had hundreds of responses to check out.

Unfortunately, all we had were the user names, e-mails, and IP addresses of the people who had responded to the ad, because they'd done so through Craigslist. Jessica's computer didn't have a record of her old e-mails, because apparently she'd done all her e-mailing in the cloud, and we didn't have her password. Our tech team had tried to break it without success. The mail service, tmailer, had an aggressive privacy clause in their terms of service, and they weren't being helpful. Grady was working to get a subpoena, but none of us wanted to wait around for that. So we went down the list we had one by one, going to see them in person if they were anywhere nearby—and most were. We were looking for men who had at least met up with the girls. So far, we hadn't found any who admitted to doing so. Jessica was apparently very picky about who they accepted "dates" with. If not for Charlie Bender's testimony about seeing her driving around with strange men, I would have wondered if she'd accepted any at all.

I focused on the work and tried not to think about that scene with the Amish delegation. Still, at odd times it wafted through my brain like a bad odor, making me angry all over again. I also tried not to think about Ezra Beiler. Grimlace Lane was off limits to me now. And, in no uncertain terms, Ezra was too. It wasn't that I was so obedient that I couldn't rebel a time or two—or twelve. But I thought it best to let things ride, focus on work, and let the juices settle—sort of like resting a roast when you take it out of the oven.

Ezra threw me for a loop, and right now, I needed my sanity intact. And, yes, the idea of driving up to his house with Lapp's eyes watching me didn't seem like a good idea.

I didn't text him either. He didn't text me.

———

It was almost two weeks before I saw Ezra again. It was a Saturday in mid-February and the weather forecast was for four to six inches of new snow and high winds. I didn't miss my days in a uniform, when that sort of weather would have meant extra hours on slick roads trying to keep senseless people from killing themselves. As a homicide detective, it was something of a snow day. Grady came by to shoo us out about noon.

"You're not going to be able to do any house calls in this weather. Go home before the roads get crazy. You've been hitting it hard for a long time, Harris. Take a break," Grady told me.

I leaned back in my chair and stretched my shoulders, which ached from too many hours hunched over either a computer or a steering wheel. The thought of going home while it was still daylight—or at least overcast storm light—and having a long hot bath, maybe a relaxing, self-administered pedicure while watching bad TV . . . It sounded like heaven.

"Let's pretend I argued with you vehemently, but in the end you convinced me," I sighed.

"Done," Grady said with a chuckle. "Now, stop wasting my time with your hardheaded arguments and go home. That's an order."

"Yes, boss."

I thought there might have been an insult in there somewhere, but who cared?

―――――――――

By the time I got out of the bath, it had started snowing in earnest. I peeked out the curtains I hardly ever bothered to draw and saw big, fat flakes and a leaden gray sky. I found a flashlight in a kitchen cupboard, brought it into the living room, and plopped it on the coffee table in case the power went out. Wearing flannel pj's, I put on *Four Weddings and a Funeral* and started taking the old paint off my toes.

I wasn't fussy by nature. I didn't do a lot of things my girl-friends in New York had considered high living, but once in a while a pedicure was a wonderful thing. Even though no one ever saw my feet, it was a nice feeling when I remembered the red polish on them while I was at work, and I liked seeing them propped up like a rising fleet of tiny dragons from the other end of the tub.

Of course, just as I got settled in, the doorbell rang.

Grumbling, I got up and peeked out the security hole. Ezra Beiler stood on my doorstep.

"Oh shit!" I muttered to myself, suddenly painfully aware of my pink flannel pajamas with little white sheep on them. How embarrassing.

"Just a minute!" I hollered through the door. And then, for good measure, "Hang on, I need to change."

I turned off the TV and raced into my bedroom. I frantically pulled on a pair of jeans and a slouchy old boatneck sweater that I'd always thought was flattering. Its light cocoa color went well with my dark hair and pale skin.

Why was I thinking about that?

My hair was still up in a dry bun from the bath, and I pulled out the clamp and fluffed it ruthlessly. It would have to do. I wore no makeup, but then Ezra was used to women without it, so maybe less was more. I opened the door.

Ezra seemed happy to see me, but he was pink-cheeked with shyness or embarrassment. "Hullo, Elizabeth."

"Hi! It's nice to see you," I said, which was a monumental understatement. He looked gorgeous and solid and real standing there on my doorstep, and warm despite the swirls of snow behind him, like he had the sun in his chest and it just radiated out. The mere sight of him relieved some ugly tension I'd been carrying around for days without realizing it.

He was staring at me too. He blinked and looked away. "Brought you some things." He held up a wicker basket that had flaps, picnic basket–style.

"Oh? 'Tis so?" I teased, but my stomach rumbled in anticipation. I hoped it was edible, whatever it was.

"'Tis so," he replied in a bone-dry voice. He studied the front of my house, perhaps for construction ideas.

I bit back a smile. Then I noticed there was a car idling in my driveway, an old Ford sedan with an equally old man behind the wheel. "Did you get a ride?"

"Ja. I called a driver. Didn't know if it would be a good idea to bring Horse to your neighborhood."

"Probably for the best. I'm still waiting on that hitching post I ordered online."

He gave me a strange look, like he wasn't sure if I was making fun of him. I hurried to say something nice to assure him I was not.

"So . . . can you come in for a bit?"

He glanced behind him at the driver. "I wouldn't mind a visit if you're up for it. I can call Ben when I'm ready to go, 'n' he'll come back."

I frowned. "Well, with the snow—" I cut myself off abruptly. Ezra studied his shoes.

Stupid mouth. If I pointed out the incipient blizzard, he might feel obliged to leave right away because it would be hard for the driver to get back.

Ezra looked up at the sky. "Not so bad," he lied as the sky fell on his head.

I was pretty sure I didn't have to tell an Amish man, a local, about the fact that this snow would soon make the roads impassable. The idea that Ezra might get stuck here for hours, *that he knew that and didn't mind*, made my insides turn into hot jelly. My knees suddenly felt weak. I clutched at the handle of the door.

"Yeah, it's fine. Call him later," I said without a trace of facetiousness. I grabbed the wrist that wasn't holding the basket and, with a breezy wave at the driver, pulled Ezra into the house and shut the door.

The basket contained the food of the gods. That was a large jar of Martha's blueberry preserves, a loaf of fresh-baked bread, a container of homemade butter, a glass bottle of cream, and a quart of potato salad.

"I love you," I said with wide eyes as I unpacked the box and placed the treasures carefully on the kitchen counter.

Ezra snorted, but he blushed a little too. "You seemed to like them—those things. So I figured I'd bring some by."

"My hero." I gave him a big smile. "Can I make you some coffee? I'm afraid mine will be a pathetic specimen compared to yours, but the fresh cream will help."

"I'd like that," Ezra said.

I fumbled around with the coffeepot, grounds, and filters, feeling thoroughly discombobulated. Ezra freaking Beiler was standing in my kitchen. He'd called a driver to bring him over here. In a snowstorm. And he'd brought me a basket of home-made food. That was like courting, wasn't it? The girlish butter-flies in my stomach flipped out, doing a victory dance. Some small voice in my head reminded me that I had reasons to avoid Ezra—professional reasons. I shut that bitch down.

I managed to start the coffee percolating with half a brain.

"I heard what happened," Ezra said seriously. "'Bout the el-ders goin' to the police station and askin' that you stop talkin' to us. So I figured I wouldn't see you over at my farm again."

"No. I—" Damn. "I didn't want to get you in trouble with your deacon. And I've been busy with work." I shrugged like it was no big deal. But the idea of Ezra having heard about that scene in the police station made me feel a little humiliated. That had not been one of my career highlights.

I looked out the window at the snow while the coffeemaker went through its groans of despair. The snow was thick and heavy enough that I could see only a few feet from the window. The lit-tle bird feeder hanging right outside was topped with a few inches of fluff and getting fluffier by the minute. Ezra would not be going anywhere soon. I felt way happier about that than I should have.

I made some toast to go with the coffee—mainly because I was dying to try the goodies Ezra had brought. I asked after Martha and Horse while I fiddled—they were "gut" according to Ezra. By the time we were seated at the kitchen table with our coffee, plates, toast, butter, and jam, I'd run out of small talk.

I finally asked the question I'd been dying to ask. "So. When did you decide to leave the Amish?"

Ezra's jaw clenched and he looked down into his coffee. After doing countless interviews, I knew the signs. He was struggling with himself about what to tell me. I hadn't meant to turn the conversation to such a heavy topic, but I kept my mouth shut and let him work out what he wanted to say.

He spoke haltingly. "My wife lost our son when she was six months along. He was so small. . . ." Ezra held up both his palms together. It was only for a moment before he dropped them, but I knew he was seeing the baby there. "They said it was God's will. And when my wife . . . died. They said that too was God's will. I knew then that the trust I had, the way I'd tried so hard to fit in . . . it was over. I made up my mind to go. And I had nothing to keep me there no more."

"I'm sorry."

"I'm sorry" is a funny phrase. Whenever those words are really needed, they're useless, and yet, they have to be said. I slid my hand over and put it on his larger one on the table. I squeezed and he squeezed my hand back. But then he frowned and pulled away.

"Don't deserve your pity."

"Why not?"

He glanced up at me, his eyes haunted. "I wasn't without blame in it all."

I waited, but he just stared at me, as if he wanted to say more but was afraid to.

"Tell me," I said quietly.

He took a long drink of coffee and looked out the window.

"I hadn't joined the church yet. Had it in my mind I wasn't gonna. I had plans, plans to go live somewheres else. Always knew I didn't have it in me to be a good Amish. I'm the one who always has to ask 'why.' Then I started seein' a girl. Her name was Mary. I tried not to get in too deep, cause I knew I was leavin', but . . . she wanted to, and . . . I didn't stop her. Next thing I knew, her da was at my house tellin' everyone I'd ruined her."

He swallowed hard, still staring out the window.

Crap. That sucked. "How old were you?"

"Seventeen."

"Was she pregnant?"

He shook his head once, his mouth pursed. "Didn't know for sure at the time 'cause it had just happened, but no. Didn't matter though. Her da spoke so loud about it, her reputation was broke."

"So you got married?"

He nodded and looked at me as if pleading for me to understand. "When it was in front of me, when I had to make a choice to either do what everyone thought was right, or walk away from the Amish *right then*, from my family and . . . and everything I'd worked for, everything I knew . . . I couldn't do it. I was afraid to make a mistake I could never take back. And then there was another person who would be hurt by it too. Mary. Didn't think I could live with that. So I joined the church after all. Had to, to get married."

The emotion in his voice was raw. I'd never heard such a painful speech. I thought I got a glimpse of what that had been like for him at the time—agreeing to a life sentence of being tied to a church he didn't believe in, of being married to a woman he didn't love. And why?

She wanted to, and I didn't stop her. Ezra's voice was loaded with self-recrimination, but how many seventeen-year-old boys would stop a girl if she really wanted sex? Ezra was a seriously good-looking man. And it struck me as odd that Mary's father found out immediately what had happened if he hadn't caught them at it. I smelled entrapment. Maybe Mary had been madly in love. Maybe she had a sense Ezra was going to leave and she was desperate to hang on to him. That didn't excuse the manipulation.

"What happened to Mary?" I asked, avoiding adding in my opinion of her.

Ezra stood up and went to the window over the sink. He stared out at the snow. "Didn't know her all that well before we married. After, I found out she had problems. She was so low all the time, down on herself. Some days she couldn't even get out of bed. I guess her family thought gettin' married would make her feel better, just like I thought having a baby would make her happy. But then she lost him."

"That must have been awful."

"About a month after she lost the baby, Mary was hit by a car while fetchin' the mail out to the road. The driver told me . . ." Ezra put both hands on the edge of the sink and closed his eyes. The last of it came out as a whisper. "He said she looked right at him."

"Oh my God."

I couldn't stand it. I got up and went to him and wrapped my arms around him from behind. I had been as tall as many of the men I'd dated, including Terry, but Ezra was a good head taller. With his broader shoulders he was so much bigger than me, it felt a bit silly trying to comfort him. Silly in a wonderful way. I pressed my face into his shoulders. The core of him was solid muscle. He didn't touch me back but he didn't pull away. His voice was muffled and thick as he went on.

"I like to think she didn't plan it, that it was just . . . she went out for the mail, the car was there, and she was feeling real low. She thought it was her fault, you know? That the baby was born too soon. Said she couldn't even have a baby right. She never thought she was worth anythin' no matter how much I told her elsewise. She could tell that I didn't . . . sometimes I resented bein' there."

"I'm sure you did the best you could," I murmured.

He pulled away and faced me, still upset. "No. I won't lie. I didn't do all I should have. I should have gotten her help. They come to see her every week, her family and mine and the deacon and others in the church. We all prayed, but it didn't help. I should have taken her to a doctor. I let her down. I felt sorry for her, but I didn't want to be married. A lot of times I just escaped into my work and ignored what was goin' on. And that's the truth."

His guilt was palpable. I knew there was no easy way to take that from him, though I wished to God I could. "Listen, Ezra. You were so young. You were forced into a marriage you didn't want—"

"I wasn't forced," he insisted, unwilling to avoid the blame.

"Okay, you were *goaded* into a marriage you didn't want. You did the best you could. It sounds like Mary was severely depressed, *clinically* depressed. I was a cop in the city. I saw what depression can do. Lots of times the person can hide it—the family has no idea how bad it is until it's too late. Add in losing a baby . . ."

"They said—" He swallowed. "They said it was God's will that the baby died. And I think . . . they never said it, but I think some of the men—my father, Deacon Lapp—thought it was punishment for our sins. That the baby died because we had sex before we were married or because I didn't have the faith I should. I know it's wrong to hate, but I hated them for that. I done everything they asked but it wasn't enough. I guess that was the last straw that broke me, when I stopped caring what they said. When Mary died I shaved my beard. That was my promise to myself that I was leavin' as soon as I could, and this time, nothin' would stop me."

His eyes were troubled and a bit wild. He was strung with tension, like he was holding some giant weight. I remembered the story I'd heard as a child about Atlas holding up the world. For some reason, Ezra struck me like that. I wanted to take that crushing weight away.

"I'm sorry I made you talk about this."

"*No,*" Ezra insisted with a firm shake of his head. "I meant to tell ya. Thought you should know."

We stared at each other. He thought I should know?

It certainly had nothing to do with the case. Together with his visit and the goodie basket, I only knew one way to interpret that. He wanted me to know the worst about his past because he liked me. He thought I had a right to know about his disastrous marriage so I could make an informed choice about being with him.

There was absolutely no doubt in my heart about my answer. I put my hands on his face, went up on my tiptoes, and kissed him.

As incredibly attracted as I'd been to Ezra from the start, and as long as it had been since I'd had sex with someone, I hadn't intended to pounce on the man. I only intended a brief meeting of mouths, a response to his unasked query, an invitation for him to proceed. So after brushing my lips against his, I rested my forehead on his cheek.

I breathed in his expelled breath. He smelled of the earth, even in the dead of winter, and of horses and wood smoke and soap. I bit back a flood of want, determined not to push this moment.

His hands touched my waist and his head tilted down, his mouth nudging into mine, seeking, trembling, yearning.

Gone. There was a moment in which my brain shut off and when it came back I was flush against him, his arms were around me, and he was kissing me deeply. Or maybe I was kissing him. Whoever was responsible, the kiss was all heat and friction and glide. At first he seemed unsure of what to do, as if he'd never kissed quite like this before, but he threw himself into it with desperation and a greedy hunger. It was as if this could be pulled away from him at any second, and he had to take it all *now*. He pushed into me as if he was trying to go *through* me, all muscle and will and hardness, and maybe defiance too.

"Ezra," I soothed, pulling my mouth away to speak.

"Don't. Don't, don't, don't," he mumbled, his hands pulling me closer.

"Shhh. I'm not going anywhere."

"You can't want me."

I laughed. "Now you really are confused."

I kissed his neck, unable to resist tasting the place below his ear. He made a throaty sound and held me tighter. He was so strong, I swore he was going to crush the life out of me. I heard his heart thumping fast and felt the trembling of want in his hands. I was tempted. It had been a long time for me. But I forced myself to push away.

"I'm not going anywhere," I said again, to reassure him. But I didn't want to be like Mary. I didn't want to seduce him into bed and then have him regret it later.

He started to reach for me and stopped himself. He swallowed. We stared at each other for a long moment, both wanting more and both making a conscious decision not to take it.

"Sorry if I disrespected you," he said at last.

I couldn't stop a smile from spreading over my face. "I thought I came on to you."

A spark of humor lit in his eyes but he answered solemnly. "Pretty sure it was t'other way around."

"You rebel," I said. "Driving cars in the snow and kissing loose women."

"I wasn't the one driving the car," he said laconically.

I nudged his shoulder for that, teasingly. Then I decided I was in control of myself enough to lean into him again. He put his arms around me lightly this time, the fire banked. "You feel good," I whispered.

"You feel right to me too." He sounded a little surprised. He hugged me closer with one arm.

We stood there like that for a bit, him leaning against the kitchen counter and me leaning against him. I was just about to suggest we move into the living room when he said, "I don't have much. When I leave the Amish, I'll be starting from nothing again."

I pulled back and looked up at him, puzzled.

"I hope to keep my customers. For the mules and the furniture. But I'm not sure where I'll have to move to. Gonna sell the farm. I can't stay where I am."

"Okay."

His brow knit in a puzzled frown. "You know I have to find a place to rent where I can keep the mules. I make pretty good money off 'em and I hope to build the business. It won't be anything like this house, probably."

I shrugged. "As long as it's not so far away that I never see you."

"You want to see me?"

"Ezra." I pushed a lock of hair off his forehead. "The last man I cared for was murdered. Compared to that, none of these are big problems. We'll figure it out. If we both want to."

"I want to," he said without hesitation. "You're the first person in my life who's ever made sense to me, Elizabeth Harris. I may not know much, but I know that it feels good to be with you. You see me as I am, and you . . . like it. My whole life everyone only saw me as an Amish man and I wasn't very good at being one."

My chest burned. "You're perfect just the way you are." How could he not know this?

He said nothing for a moment. Then: "What happened to your husband?"

Well. Ezra had been open with me. I supposed I owed him the same courtesy. But if we were going to get into that, I definitely needed to sit down. I refilled our coffee cups and led him out to the living room couch. This was a difficult story, and, needing some distance to tell it, I sat at the end of the sofa and curled my feet up under me. He sat in the middle and put an arm across the back but made no move to touch me.

"We lived in New York City. I was a detective by then and I was working late, as usual. Terry went out to the drugstore down the block from our apartment to pick up a few things. While he was there, two armed robbers came in. They ended up killing three customers and two people who worked there."

Ezra was perfectly still, but his eyes reflected a pain I knew wasn't all for me.

"The stupid thing was, Terry didn't even try to fight the robbers. He wouldn't have played hero. He just stood there in his trench coat in the aspirin aisle, hands up, and they shot him."

I'd seen the security footage from the store. It was the absolute cold senselessness of it that got to me. No one was trying to stop those two young ex-cons from taking the cash in the store's register, or anything else they wanted, and their faces had been covered in ski masks so no one could have identified them. Yet still they'd gunned down my husband and the others for no reason.

I realized I was shaking. Ezra put one large hand on my calf. "There's so much I don't know about the world out there. It scares me sometimes. The elders say there's so much wickedness and murder."

"It's not all like that. There are a lot of good people out there. No place is all good or all bad." I sighed. "Not even Grimlace Lane."

"True enough. Even heaven can be hell when you don't belong there."

I thought about that. "God, that's profound."

"Ancient Amish wisdom," Ezra said solemnly. I knew he was trying to lighten the mood.

I snorted. "It is not."

He growled and pulled my legs onto his lap, pinning me down. "Are you callin' me a liar?"

"I think you spin more yarn than a knitting factory, Ezra Beiler."

"Take that back!"

He tickled me so I tickled him. We wrestled and kissed and wrestled some more. It made my heart *hurt*, in a good way, to see him playful. It was a moment of joy for him, like something had been set free inside him for the first time in his life, and I had given him that.

As we wrestled, the kissing began to outpace the horseplay. By a lot.

Now that the floodgates had opened and Ezra was here with me, it was impossible to turn off wanting him in every way. I'd never expected to feel this way after Terry. And I did feel a little guilty about that. But finding Ezra was such a miracle, and I knew he needed me too.

It wasn't going to be easy. We were from different worlds. And, as happy as he was right now, I knew his process of separating from the Amish was far from over and would be painful. And then there was me. What would Grady say? Ezra wasn't really a suspect, but it still was dicey territory, especially after that visit from the Amish delegation.

But I had a hard time assimilating anything like logic where Ezra was concerned. My heart was like, *Screw that. Just gimme.* Maybe that was the definition of the word "faith." Maybe faith isn't something you choose to believe. Maybe it's something your heart believes in for you.

CHAPTER 12

In Custody

The following Tuesday, our slow work with the IP addresses finally struck the jugular. We traced one to an address that was all too familiar. Grady called a quick war council in his office with Smith, Hernandez, and me.

"I've been in touch with Klein's. Larry is due back from his pickup route at three. We're going to arrest him at the dairy. I'd rather not have a four-thousand-gallon milk truck in the middle of this."

"Where do you want us?" I asked, buzzing with adrenaline.

"Harris, you'll be with me at the dairy. Smith and Hernandez, you'll tail Larry in an unmarked and report on his whereabouts until he ends his route. Make sure he doesn't get a whiff of this and take off. And he *won't see you*. Got it?"

Hernandez grinned. He kissed the tips of his fingers and blew them out in a "vanish" gesture. "Like ghosts."

The guy had been watching too much *Godfather*, but he was enthusiastic. I had to give him that. They took off.

"You're going to actually arrest him? Not just bring him in for questioning?" I asked Grady.

"He lied, Harris," Grady said angrily. "He denied that he knew Jessica from her crime-scene photo, and he denied it again when I went back there with her high school picture. Yet he obviously knew her. He responded to her Craigslist ad. His IP is on the list!"

"Right," I agreed firmly. "So let's haul his ass in and question him. But we don't even know that he actually hooked up with them. Jessica might not have responded."

"You're the one who started this line of investigation," Grady huffed. "'The killer has to know the area,' you said. Well, Larry Wannemaker knows the area. He doesn't have an alibi, he was in the park on his lunch break at the time Jessica was killed, and he'd been in contact with her through the Craigslist ad."

It did add up to a shitload of trouble for our friendly neighborhood milkman.

"When did he contact her?"

"Last September!" Grady said, his eyes glowing. "He must have hooked up with them last fall. He's not a bad-looking guy, right? So maybe Jessica sets it up. Then he meets Katie separately—hell, maybe he just happened to see her biking to the Lapps' while he was picking up from the Millers'. He tries to get her to give him a freebie and she won't, so he hits her and accidentally kills her. In January, he hooks up with Jessica again, arranging to meet her at the park. Now he's got a taste for it, so he does her too."

It was plausible but it didn't quite fit inside my head. The way Katie was killed was opportunistic. If Larry then called up Jessica months later—if he *intended* to kill her—why was it the same MO with the blow to the head and then suffocation? Was he trying to relive what had been a thrilling experience? But if he met up with Jessica intending to kill her, why do it on his lunch break when he knew he wouldn't have time to deal with a body? Why go back and discard her hours later? And why *there*? That was the sticking point that just wouldn't budge in my mind. What was the point of dragging her through the creek and putting her in an Amish barn on Grimlace Lane? Yes, Larry knew the area from his milk pickup route. But that didn't explain why he would go to all that trouble. Surely he didn't think he could pin it on Amos Miller or his boys.

"Harris," Grady said sharply, drawing my attention. His stare said it all—*Are you with me or not?*

"Hell, yeah! Let's go get the son of a bitch," I responded enthusiastically.

I pushed my doubts down for now. It was showtime.

———————

Larry's dairy truck rumbled into the parking lot at the Klein's dairy processing facility. Grady, myself, and two uniformed policemen were waiting inside the lobby where he couldn't see us. Grady spoke into his walkie-talkie, and as Larry hopped out of the truck, two black-and-whites pulled around from the back, caging in the truck so it couldn't move.

"Let's go!" Grady said. We went flying out the door.

Larry looked at the police cars in befuddlement, then he

looked straight at me as we strode quickly toward him across the parking lot. The look in his eyes was pure "oh shit" along with a heavy dose of terror.

"Larry Wannemaker, put your hands in the air!" Grady said loudly as we approached. He put his hand on his holster so that Larry could see it.

Larry did the least intelligent thing he could possibly do—he turned and ran. He dodged around a black-and-white and headed for the road. I knew he was going to bolt a second before he did by the tensing on his face, and I was after him at a dead run before any of the others. He could have been armed, but I was betting he wasn't, not while working his job. He was lean and fast though, and I cursed him inside my head as I gave chase, hoping this wouldn't end with Larry being dead and our questions left unanswered.

Dumb shit. Did he really think he could get away from us on foot? Maybe he was guilty. Either that or he had a real problem with impulse control.

He reached the road, a two-lane blacktop that was not heavily traveled. The recent snow was piled on the shoulder, but the blacktop was clear. He turned right and ran hell-bent for leather. I chased after him. I wasn't catching up but I wasn't falling behind either, and when an unmarked sedan pulled up in front of him and cut him off and Smith and Hernandez emerged, screaming orders and holding their guns, Larry stopped and put his hands on his knees, wheezing and out of breath.

Thank God for pot.

"Larry Wannemaker," I huffed, as I got up to him, "you are under arrest for suspicion of murder. You have the right to remain silent. Anything you say can and will be used against you in a court of law. You have the right to an attorney. If you cannot afford an attorney, one will be provided for you. Do you understand?" I slipped the cuffs over his hands and listened to them click. It was a satisfying sound.

"I didn't do it. I didn't kill anyone," he pleaded, looking up at me through his long and not entirely clean curtain of hair.

I said nothing.

We spent hours with Larry in the interrogation room back at the station. He'd declined an attorney, said he had nothing to hide. And then he said the same things over and over and over.

Questioning a suspect for hours is a way to shake them down, wear away their defenses so you can spot the lies underneath, catch them in inconsistencies. But as exhausting as it is for the suspect, it's not a hell of a lot of fun for the detectives either. I am not a brute by nature, and my whole being was in a sort of euphoria over my new relationship with Ezra. I had to focus on my memories of Jessica's and Katie's dead bodies and how young they'd been, how undeserved their brutal ends, in order to be the hard-ass I needed to be.

"I told you and told you, I did see the Craigslist ad and I did e-mail her! I met up with 'em once, back in the fall. Haven't seen 'em since. I'm tellin' the truth."

"When in 'the fall' did you meet up with them?" Grady asked coldly.

"Like I said, I think it was early October. I don't remember exactly, but I know it took about three weeks from the time I saw the ad to when we got together. I dunno, she wanted to e-mail back and forth, asking a lot of dumb questions. She wanted pictures. Then it took some time to work out everyone's schedule, you know?"

I knew it was important to establish the timeline. I gave Grady a nod with my chin. "I'll be right back."

I went to the coffee station. I'd noticed before that the previous year's calendar was underneath the current one, either due to laziness or, in this case, amazing forethought. I grabbed it, spoke to Hernandez briefly, and took it back to the interrogation room.

I plopped it on the table. "Here." I pointed to a circle over September 23. "This is the day you first contacted Jessica via Craigslist. So tell us when you met up with her and Katie."

He looked over the calendar carefully, paging between September and October.

"It was a Tuesday night. I think it was this one," he pointed to October 8. "But it coulda been a week later."

Katie had disappeared October 10.

"So you contact Jessica and she sent you photos. Then you sent her a photo," I said.

"Yes."

"Therefore, you knew when we came to your house that very first time that we were talking about Jessica Travis, the girl you had sex with."

He shut his eyes tight. "I had sex with *Katie*. Already told you that! My buddy John, he was with Jessica. It was a double date, like. And I didn't tell you because I knew there'd be bullshit like this!"

"Did you know Katie was Amish, despite how she was dressed?"

He pressed his lips tight. "I really want a cigarette."

"Maybe when you've actually answered our questions," Grady said.

Larry sighed. "This is so bogus. Yes, I knew Katie was Amish. Jessica said so in her e-mails. And I had first dibs, right? Because I answered the ads. So I got Katie. The Amish thing . . . you know how it is."

I stared at him blankly. He shifted uncomfortably.

"It was just . . . hot. Forbidden, you know? I didn't believe she was Amish at first, the way she looked. Thought it was a scam. Didn't care, because she was real pretty anyway. But when she talked I could tell she was Amish all right."

"How could you tell?" I asked.

He shrugged. "She had that accent. And you could tell she wasn't educated or anything."

"Where'd you pick them up?"

He spoke in that impatient tone guys have when they've said something fifty times already. "We picked Jessica up in downtown Manheim. It was about eleven at night. She directed us to drive out in the country, where we picked up Katie. She was just walkin' down the road."

"And then?"

"And then Jessica told us how to get to a little dirt road that ran in the woods. It was only like five minutes away. We parked there and had sex."

"How much did they charge?"

He swallowed. "Seventy-five each, just like I told you."

"Were you aware they were underage?"

Larry shook his head, looking defeated. "I didn't ask, okay? I really didn't think about it. I mean, they put themselves on Craigslist. It's not like I picked her up at the playground."

"Describe exactly what you did with Katie Yoder," I said.

He rubbed his eyes. "We were in the backseat. We kissed a couple times. I felt her up. Then she wanted to put a condom on me. I had my own and I used that one instead. I put it on. She laid down and pulled her skirt up and that was it, we were fucking. That's all."

Grady and I just looked at him.

"Look, you want to know the truth?" Larry exclaimed. "It wasn't that good. I mean, she obviously wasn't into it. She just laid there. John, he liked Jessica, but he really didn't want to pay for sex. Me, I just didn't feel right about the whole thing. So I never contacted them again. I mean, I can get women, you know? Maybe not that young and maybe not that pretty, but I'd rather have a chick who's into it. You get what I'm sayin'?"

He gave Grady a come-on-man-you-know-how-it-is look. I tapped my pen on the table, face blank.

"Anyway, it sounded like they weren't going to keep doing it." He shrugged.

That was the first time he'd said that. My antenna pinged. "What do you mean?"

He scratched his head. "I was just remembering. So after we, you know . . . Jessica and John were still busy for a while, so I talked to Katie." He fiddled with his jacket zipper.

"Go on."

He looked torn about whether or not he should.

I leaned forward and spoke sympathetically. "If you didn't kill them, Larry, the best thing you can do is come clean about everything. If you withhold anything, it's going to make you look guilty. Just be honest."

Larry rubbed his nose, looking very uncomfortable. "Fine. So I asked Katie if she was really Amish, even though I'd already figured she was. She said yes. Then I asked her why she was doing what she was doing. You know, meeting up with strange men. She laughed at me. I told her, you know, that she shouldn't be doing it. That it wasn't safe. I mean, I felt kind of bad for her, you know? She said she wasn't gonna be doing it much longer, that she had a way to make some real money. Big money. She was bragging about it." He looked at me nervously. "I don't know what she was talking about, honest, I don't. I said something like 'Okay, good.' And that was it. We dropped Katie off where we picked her up and then took Jessica back to Manheim. I didn't see them again. I didn't hurt either one of them, I swear! John wouldn't have either. He's a good guy."

I sat contemplating Larry. If what he said was true, that was an interesting conversation. Had Larry really just remembered it? Or did he think Katie talking about "big money" would make him an even more likely suspect, that we'd think he killed her for it?

"She say where she was getting this big money?" Grady asked, sounding like he didn't believe Larry for a minute.

"No. She never said and I never saw her again. Jesus, how many times do I have to repeat myself?"

"It'll be interesting to see what John has to say about all this when he gets in, don't you think, Harris?" Grady asked me.

"Sure will," I said flatly.

We'd already gotten John's details from Larry and were tracking him down. According to Larry, John was married. His wife was unlikely to be pleased to hear what he'd been up to, but I had a hard time dredging up any sympathy for him.

Grady sighed. "Start from the beginning. You saw the ad on Craigslist when?"

CHAPTER 13

Wheat from Chaff

During the rest of the week, things stalled out again. John Stanza, the friend who had "double-dated" with Larry, was a big, bearish guy who was humiliated by the whole thing. He had a solid alibi for the time of Jessica's death. He'd been working at a mechanic garage in Harrisburg and had been home all that night as well—according to him and his exceedingly unamused wife. He had no priors.

Larry's dairy truck and his own car were gone over by the forensics team. They found nothing—no trace of blood, no blonde hairs. If he'd killed or moved Jessica in either one of them, he'd done a hell of a cleanup job. There were no records of a rental car or anything else suspicious on his credit cards. Grady got a court order and we searched his house. We found a bit of cocaine, nearly a pound of pot, and some suspicious prescription drugs. We didn't find the boots that had made those prints in the snow or anything else to link Larry Wannemaker to the murders of Katie Yoder and Jessica Travis.

Grady kept Larry in jail for the drugs. He still had a real jones on for Larry having done the murders and wanted me to figure out how he'd done it. I told him I didn't think Larry was our guy. Grady got pissed off with me, but I was pretty sure he suspected I was right. Hernandez and Smith brought in four more responders to the Craigslist ad and Grady and I grilled them. I didn't consider any of them good suspects, and none of them had any ties to Grimlace Lane that we could find.

It was roadblocks all the way around.

Except with Ezra. That was more or less full steam ahead. Every few nights I texted him as I left work and he walked down Grimlace Lane to meet me. I picked him up where Grimlace met Clearview Road. Because it was risky going out for both of us, I'd take him back to my place.

He was like a comforting drug. When I wasn't with him, the world just didn't turn right, like it was slightly off its axis, and the stress of the case sat on my chest like an ugly little gargoyle. But when I was in his arms, all of that went away. He didn't push to go any further, and I didn't either, but just being with him was enough. It was like ripping off a Band-Aid every time I had to drop him back off at Grimlace Lane.

I didn't like the situation. It felt underhanded, furtive, picking up this beautiful Amish man on a dark country road. It reminded me of the way Larry had described them picking up Katie. I didn't like the comparison at all. I didn't want to hide my relationship with Ezra Beiler. But he wasn't ready to walk away from his farm quite yet, and I had no idea how Grady and Chief

Lumbaker would respond to the news of our relationship. So we snuck around.

———————

"Did you like livin' in New York City?" Ezra asked me on a Friday night. We were curled up on my couch. I was getting no sleep whatsoever, and I really didn't care.

"It was exciting at first," I admitted. "But after a while the lack of green got to me. And the crowds. I was happy to come home." I kissed his fingers.

"This is home?"

I looked around at the blank walls of my living room. "This . . . this is a rental. Just a place to be until I can make a real home. Hopefully with someone."

I felt a flush of nerves as I said it, and I looked away from those brown-green eyes.

"Someone? Will there be a lottery?" he asked seriously.

I laughed.

"'Cause I'd like to buy a ticket."

I looked at him slyly. "You already have a whole bunch of tickets."

His lips quirked. "Anybody else have tickets?"

"No. But . . . you're just getting ready to leave the Amish. You should have some time to be free for a while. Figure out what you really want."

He thought about that for a long moment, his mouth pursed. "I'm startin' over. I'd just as soon do it with you. No point in startin' over twice. That's a plain waste of energy."

His voice had that laconic irony, but I knew there was vulnerable truth in there too. I nestled closer to him on the couch and stroked the blond fuzz on his chest where I had opened his shirt. My heart skipped along with a happy "tra-la-la." "Yeah?"

"Ja. Horse is good company and all, but he makes a mess when I let him in the house."

I rolled my eyes. "What about Martha. She's leaving with you, isn't she?"

He frowned. "Not sure she will in the end. She doesn't really wanna leave the Amish, but she knows if she stays, she'll be an old maid. She's past courtin' age, and we have a small community. It's unlikely she'll find a husband now. And she wants to get married more'n anything."

"That's too bad." I wasn't really surprised given Martha's plainness and, at least around me, her oddity. There probably wasn't a lot of joy in life for an Amish woman if she didn't marry and have children. Though having been in the dating pool in "real life," I wasn't sure Martha would fare all that much better out here.

Ezra nodded. "That's why she come—came to live with me once Mary died. She knew I was preparin' to go. Martha hasn't had an easy life. She had a beau once, or thought she did, but he turned out to favor someone else."

I sat up, something tickling my brain. "Who?"

Ezra blinked at me. "She never said. Why?"

I looked up at the ceiling, pondering.

"You have that look," Ezra said.

"What look?"

"That I'm-gonna-fix-everything-in-the-whole-world-because-I'm-so-smart look."

I poked him in the ribs. "I do not. And that's far too much to glean from a single look anyway."

"Nope, that's your look," Ezra said with absolute, solemn certitude.

I sighed and wrapped my arm around his chest. "If you say so."

He turned his head away and swallowed. "It means a lot to me, Elizabeth, that you're so . . . I respect you. You care about people. You care about what happened to those girls and you want to make it right. You're a good person but you're your own person too. Just means a lot is all."

God. I gently turned his face to look at me. "That so? Well, I can't fix the whole world, but maybe I can fix you."

"Maybe so." There was something hot in Ezra's eyes. It stole my breath away.

"Maybe you can fix me too."

"All right," he said grimly.

"Good, then."

"Good."

I kissed him.

I'd been waiting for Ezra to take the lead, not wanting to coax anything from him he didn't want to give. And maybe he'd been doing the same. But after a rough week, I felt an itching need for him, for closeness, and maybe he did too. He led the way further into the dance, waiting for me each step, and I followed him all the way. Joyfully.

In bed, Ezra Beiler showed an unlimited work ethic and an unaccountable lack of mercy for someone who'd been raised a pacifist. When I showed him how to please me, he learned quickly and was determined to repeat it until he got it right.

Dear *Lord*.

Afterward, as we caught our breath in my queen-sized bed under a down comforter, Ezra proved to be a cuddler as well as a talker.

"I like that you're not shy about taking your pleasure," he told me, acting shy himself.

"Didn't, um, didn't Mary 'take pleasure'?"

"Don't think so," he said quietly. "Seemed like it was just for me. She liked to be held though."

"That's a shame."

He picked up my hand and nuzzled my wrist. "You act so tough, but here"—a kiss—"you're delicate as a china cup."

"Mmmm." My pride said I should argue the point, but I was too pleasantly sleepy.

"And here . . . so soft." He stroked my belly with lazy fingers.

I moved onto my side and we stared into each other's eyes as he ghosted his fingertips over my skin, not with passion this time but with gentle affection. It felt intimate—so, so intimate. I could feel our two hearts lying open and unguarded between us.

I thought about how my path had twisted about. I'd come back to Pennsylvania to find peace, to remember there was goodness in the world, and I'd found Ezra Beiler. He was nothing at all like Terry, but I knew that I could love him just the same.

Maybe there wasn't just one person who could fit you in life. Maybe people were more complicated than that. Terry fit certain facets of me and strengthened them. The side of me Ezra fit was a different Elizabeth Harris. I liked that person. I felt comfortable being her, and I felt good about a future between her and Ezra. Life was strange and, for the first time in a long time, I felt that it was capable of being . . . marvelous.

"You make me feel real good," Ezra whispered.

I smiled. "I like you too."

Hernandez came into the break room, where I was making yet another cup of coffee. Ezra and I had seen each other almost every night for the past few weeks, and it was starting to catch up with me. It was six P.M. and I felt like if I didn't hit a pillow soon, I'd pass out at my desk.

"Hey, Harris." Hernandez smiled at me. He had a good smile—big, white teeth.

"Hey."

"You look tired." He got close to me and tilted his head to study my face, apparently checking out the purple accents under my eyes. His eyes were warm and . . . sexy. "The case keeping you up?"

I refrained from taking a step backward and/or spilling hot coffee down my shirt. Hernandez was flirting with me. Not that I wasn't used to a lot of guys at the station making it clear I had an open invitation—oh, boy—but Hernandez had never done it before. He was a good cop and a nice guy. Pretty cute as well. I liked him. I didn't want to lose his friendship.

I hesitated. I wanted to defuse but not offend. "Actually, I'm sort of in a new relationship. Haven't been getting a lot of sleep."

"Ah." His smile faltered, then came back strong. "Good for you." He hit my shoulder good-naturedly. "Being kept up having hot sex beats the hell outta being worried about a case."

"Well, that keeps me up nights too."

Hernandez got his coffee and leaned against the break table. "Any new ideas?"

I tapped my cup. "I keep thinking about something Larry said when we interviewed him. He said Katie told him she was expecting to come into some money soon—big money."

"Hmmm."

"Assuming she wasn't lying to Larry, and Larry wasn't lying to us, where was this money supposed to come from? There was only so much money she was going to earn prostituting herself on Craigslist. And her parents weren't about to give her any. . . ."

"Right." Hernandez thought about it. "You found some stuff of hers, didn't you? That bag in the barn? Anything in there?"

I started to say no, because I remembered clearly what had been in that bag—clothes, shoes, makeup, a little jewelry, condoms, the money pouch. . . . Maybe it was worth another look.

"I'll go get it," I told him. "Meet me in the conference room."

I retrieved the bag from Evidence. The money had been returned to Katie's parents, but the pouch was there along with everything else. I took it into the conference room and spread the stuff on the table.

Hernandez went through her clothing, checking pockets, but of course that had already been done.

I carefully unfolded the single page of newsprint that had

been in Katie's money pouch along with the money. I'd looked at it when we found it of course, but it hadn't seemed relevant at the time. I smoothed it out on the table.

"What is it?" Hernandez asked, giving up on the clothing.

"Not sure. It's just a page from some tabloid. The *National Tattler*."

It was an inside page dated Saturday, September 7, 2013. There was an ad for diet pills on one side. But nothing like that had been found among Katie's possessions. I turned it over. The other side showed a table of contents with articles about the death of a soap star, a celebrity feud, a murderous cheerleader, and a pair of conjoined twins. The rest of the page was taken up with an information directory—a list of the tabloid's editors and contact information.

I turned it so Hernandez could get a good look. He met my eyes.

"It's a long shot," I said.

"Hey, it's been a whole day since I've been stuck on the phones. I'm on it."

"Thanks," I said sincerely. "I'll take half if you will." I made a Xerox of the page, tore the list of names down the middle, and handed him a strip.

"No problem, E." Hernandez held out his fist for a bump. I looked at it. Maybe that was taking the one-of-the-guys thing a bit too far, but I wasn't going to complain. I bumped it. *Yo.*

Hell. Maybe the Amish elders didn't want me on their turf, but things were going to be okay here in the Lancaster police department.

It took thirty minutes. I was on the phone at my desk when Hernandez called my name. He stood at his desk, receiver at his ear, and gave me a thumbs-up. He motioned that he was going to transfer the call. I got off mine quickly and picked up line two.

"Detective Elizabeth Harris. Who am I speaking with?"

"This is Jim Johnson. I'm the crime editor for the *National Tattler*." The man sounded confused and more than a little interested.

I looked up. Hernandez was standing at my desk looking pleased with himself. He mouthed, *Katie*.

"Were you in touch with an Amish girl named Katie Yoder last September?" I asked.

"Yes, I was. We talked several times and I made her an offer for a story, but then she vanished. I thought maybe she wasn't able to get proof or she changed her mind. Now I have some questions for you, if you don't mind, Detective."

"Hang on," I said. I covered the phone. "Get Grady," I told Hernandez. "And meet me in the conference room. I'll transfer the call."

Jim Johnson was a hard-assed reporter. He tried to get out of us what had happened to Katie Yoder and why we were involved. But it wasn't the first time I'd dealt with the press, or Grady's either. We ended up telling him it was a murder investigation—and not disputing the fact that it was *Katie's* murder but not confirming it either. We promised him he'd be the first reporter we talked to when the time came. That opened up Jim Johnson's sealed lips.

Katie Yoder had contacted the tabloid and eventually been forwarded to Jim. She claimed to have a story about sex abuse among the Amish, and sent him photos of herself, probably taken with Jessica's phone. Jim had been interested but wary. He told her he'd need proof. And if she could get something like an incriminating video, get the guy to confess on camera, preferably with a little kissing and groping, he thought he could get her ten to twenty-five thousand dollars.

"A story like hers, with her face and personal testimony along with an authentic video? It would have been worth some money," Jim claimed. "Amish stories always do well for us. Add in sexual abuse of a young girl and that's the kind of story you can bleed for weeks to sell papers. I have some contacts in reality TV that might have been interested too. I offered to agent her. If, you know, she could really get the goods."

I just bet he had.

"So, what was the story she told you?" Grady asked. He watched me over the conference table with an unreadable expression.

"She wouldn't give me a name. Said she'd do that once we had a firm deal. She wasn't stupid, Katie Yoder." Jim sounded sad.

"She must have said something," I pushed. "Was it a family member? Any indications it was her father or brothers? Her abuser was Amish, right?"

"Yeah, he was Amish. It started when she was only eleven and it went on for years, so he must have been considerably older than her. That's what I know for sure."

I stroked my chin, my gaze locked with Grady's.

"No names?" Grady asked again, just to be sure. "Not even an initial?"

"Nope. She just called him 'this man.' She was very wary. She wanted the money, that much was clear, and she was going to make sure no one took the story away from her until she'd gotten her fair share. Like I said, she wasn't stupid."

"Did she tell you what kind of proof she had or was going to get?"

"When I told her the kind of money we could get if she had video, she said she'd *get* video, just like that. I told you, she wanted as much money as she could get from the story." He paused. "Do you think this guy killed her?"

We hadn't even verbally told him the victim was Katie yet. I wasn't going to play that game with him.

"As we said, this case is ongoing and we can't discuss anything that might hurt our chances of finding the killer. But Detective Harris here will be in touch when we *can* talk," Grady said.

"I certainly hope so." Jim Johnson had an edge to his voice. "I went out on a limb for you guys."

"And we appreciate that. You're been enormously helpful. We'll be in touch."

Grady disconnected the call.

I knew Johnson would sniff out something. With some digging he could even find out that Katie Yoder's body had been found in the Susquehanna and had sat in the cooler in Maryland until claimed by her Amish parents. That stuff was public record. But there was nothing we could do about that now.

"Fuck." Grady rubbed his heavy face. "Great work, Harris, Hernandez."

I was bubbling over with energy. This was a huge lead. "That's two sources now that say Katie was abused—the psychiatrist and now a reporter who talked to Katie herself. We have to find that guy, Grady. If he got a whiff of what Katie was planning . . . Talk about a motive for murder."

Grady nodded grimly. "Yeah. I'll ask for an urgent meeting with the elders of the local district. I'll impress upon them the importance of giving this guy up. Someone has to know something." He stood. He must have seen the frustration on my face, because he added, "Go write up a list of questions you want me to ask them and e-mail it to me."

I just glared at him.

"This is the way it's gotta be, Harris. Do it," he barked.

I went to type up my damn list.

———

Grady arranged the meeting with the Amish elders, which wasn't going to happen till after supper. So I was still at the station, waiting anxiously, at nine P.M. when he returned. Everyone else had left for the day. Grady nodded at me and I followed him into his office.

"Well?" I asked, before he even sat down.

"I got the whole thing on audio, so you can crawl over it at your leisure but, bottom line, they still claim they don't know."

"Goddamn it!" I paced. "They have to know!"

"Closed doors, Harris. I dunno. I don't think they'd outright lie to me. Maybe they really had no idea Katie was being abused."

I growled.

"I did impress upon them the importance of finding out. They promised me they'd do their own inquiry. Maybe they'll turn something up. They have a better shot of getting their own people to talk than we do."

I wanted to say: *Bullshit! They're the very people who aren't talking.* But I kept it to myself.

"There's . . . something else, Harris. Have a seat."

The tone of Grady's voice was worrying. The dark look on his face was downright stomach-dropping. I sat down in his guest chair.

"Okay."

He leaned forward, putting his forearms on his desk and folding his hands neatly. He pinned me with a stare and suddenly I felt like I was sitting across the interrogation table from him. That was not a place I wanted to be.

"Tell me the truth—are you seeing Ezra Beiler? Because Aaron Lapp says you are."

Shit. Did the guy have eyes in the back of his head or what? I licked my lips, my heart racing. I considered lying. I didn't.

"Yes, I am seeing Ezra Beiler."

Grady let out a groan and fell back in his chair, hand over his eyes.

"It's not the department's business who I date after hours. The man is not a suspect."

"Everyone involved in this case is a suspect!" Grady shouted angrily. He lowered his hand and glared at me.

"Calm down. It's not that bad."

"Of course it's that bad! One of my homicide detectives

is having sex with an Amish man, a murder suspect! What could be worse than that?"

I couldn't resist. "I could be the killer," I deadpanned.

"Damn it, this is not funny!" Grady slammed his hands down on his desk. I winced internally, but managed to keep from showing it on the outside.

"You're right. The situation is . . . somewhat labyrinthine."

"Labyrinthine? Maybe while you were getting that hundred-thousand-dollar education, you should have learned some fancy words for 'no' and 'hell no.'"

I knew a few fancy words for those, but I figured he wasn't literally asking me.

"Listen, Grady, it's not what you think."

I fought to stay calm, even though I was getting a sick, horrible feeling I was about to be fired. After the meeting with the Amish delegation, I already felt like I was on shaky ground. I should have followed orders and laid off. And I did—to a point.

I spoke low. "First of all, Ezra Beiler is one of the only people in this entire thing who has an ironclad alibi for when Jessica was moved that night. You know that. He is *not* a murder suspect."

Grady's nostrils flared with his heavy breathing as he glared at me. "He *is* a person of interest, though. That puts him off limits. Jesus, I shouldn't have to tell you that!"

"Okay," I agreed. "He's a person of interest. But he's only tangential to the case. He's also an Amish man who's struggling to find his way to a new life. Did you know he was married to a suicidally depressed girl, and that when she lost their baby and then stepped out in front of a car and killed herself, the Amish made Ezra feel like it was his fault?"

Grady gave a very annoyed, very grumpy huff, as if he didn't want me to stir his sympathy.

"You heard him yourself. He's trying to get up the resources to leave, and he's *alone*, Grady. I befriended him, and I'm not ashamed of that."

"And then?" Grady's hard look said, *Don't tell me that's all there is to it.*

"And then . . . well . . . stuff happened. It does sometimes between little boys and little girls. See, there's this stork. . . ."

Grady made an exasperated noise and got to his feet, too angry to sit.

"No, I need to hear it all, Harris, whether I want to or not. Who started what? And when? Did you—"

"Seduce him? Come on! Don't treat me like a predator."

Grady's eyes swept up and down me in annoyance. His look seemed to acknowledge the fact that a lot of effort probably wouldn't have been required on my part.

He sighed and tapped the desk with his pen. "Jesus. Wait till Sharon hears about this. So you 'befriended' Ezra, and you ended up sleeping together?"

I thought about giving another smart answer, but I knew Grady deserved my full honesty. Plus, I really hoped not to lose my job. "I went to see him a few times, asking him questions about the Amish. He was the only person who would talk to me! And the only one I believed for sure wasn't a suspect. We enjoyed spending time together, but that was all. Then he . . . he came to my house a week or so after I'd been banned from Grimlace Lane."

Grady stared at me.

"He brought me blueberry jam!"

He rolled his eyes. "You must have *indicated* that you were interested."

"I knew there was an attraction there, yes. But I thought I could manage it, at least until the case was over. I thought that right up until the moment when I couldn't. He told me about his wife and I . . . He needed me, Grady. And I didn't have it in me to reject him."

"You're saying he came on to you?" Grady pushed, looking doubtful.

I ruffled my hair in frustration. "I'm saying I opened the door, but he walked through it on his own two feet. It was mutual. Mutual-of-Omaha mutual. All right? I'm not trying to justify myself, only—"

"What's going to happen if Ezra turns out to be more than *tangentially* linked to this case, huh? We don't have all the facts yet. We don't *know* what happened out there on Grimlace Lane. And even if he's got nothing to do with it, how do you think it's going to look when this story breaks? And it will, Harris. Via Jim Johnson or someone else, this story is going to break, and if the killer turns out to be Amish, it's going to be ugly."

I had no response.

"We found the body of a gorgeous young girl in an Amish barn," he reminded me. "Then a beautiful young Amish girl who'd been sexually abused turned up naked in the Susquehanna. I send in my female detective to investigate, and she starts having an affair with the hunky widowed Amish guy who lives next door. What do you think the *National Tattler* would do with that story?"

For a moment, I had a mental image of Ezra's face plastered on the *National Tattler* with a stark headline: "Detective's Hot Amish Lover." No, we didn't want to go there. I couldn't do that to Ezra, and not to Grady either. Crap. Lancaster County was so small and remote. I'd forgotten that nothing was really secret in this world anymore. Viruses could spread from a province in China to the backwoods of Canada in just a few days, and news moved even faster.

"I'm sorry," I said, and with the horror of what could be crawling inside me, I damn well meant it. "I had no intention of bringing harm to this department. I didn't think of it like that."

"You thought with your . . . your . . ."

I raised my eyebrow at him.

"*Lady bits*, is what you did," Grady sighed.

I laughed, but I thought that analysis was a bit unfair. Well, maybe not entirely unfair.

Grady ran a hand through his hair. "Jesus, Harris. Sharon likes you. I like you. A lot of people here like you. But you don't make it easy for me to support you."

That made me feel just great.

"Ezra was already planning to leave the Amish," I pointed out glumly.

"Do you think the media will care?"

I really didn't.

"Does anyone besides Lapp know?" I asked, hoping it was contained.

"Not that I know of. Not sure even Lapp knows for sure. He's suspicious. He pulled me aside to speak to me about it. Worried for Ezra's soul, of course."

"Naturally. So tell me what you want me to do."

Grady glared at me as if to say, *Now I'm supposed to fix this?* "Well, first of all, I'm gonna have to talk to Ezra. See if he backs up your version of things. Make sure it was *mutual* in absolutely every fucking sense of the word."

I held my tongue and nodded. I would have done the same in his position. A police officer had authority. That could be dicey when it came to matters of consent.

"Assuming that's the case, then I might be able to refrain from telling the chief about this. Poor guy doesn't deserve the ulcer. But you are not to see Ezra again, not till this case is well closed. With any luck, we can keep this thing under wraps, but no more taking the risk. Is that clear?"

I sat back and closed my eyes, feeling sick. "Come on. That's not fair. What if we—"

"You guys lay off until you solve the case, period. Once the dust settles, if he's not involved, we'll help him get out of there if that's what he wants, and then I really don't care what you two do. But I don't want one of my detectives seeing an Amish man while he's still Amish. And definitely not someone linked to an open case. This is nonnegotiable. Unless you want to turn in your badge right now."

I really didn't. I was frustrated as hell though. "What if the case goes cold? What if it's open for years?"

"Sounds like motivation to me," Grady said with a bit of snark.

"Can I at least see him long enough to explain why I can't be with him for a while?"

"Nope. I'll explain it when I talk to him."

I pleaded with Grady silently. He leaned over his desk and frowned at me. "There's one way out of this, Harris. Solve the goddamned case."

"Without talking to any Amish people," I said drolly. "What's next, one arm tied behind my back? Blowing a kazoo?"

A hint of a smile tugged at the corner of his mouth. "You said when I interviewed you that you liked a challenge. Welcome to Lancaster. Now, if you'll excuse me, I have to go see Ezra Beiler." He shook his head in disgust and grabbed his coat.

"Kiss him for me," I said as Grady went out the door.

He huffed a laugh. "Oh my fucking God." He slammed the door only a little on his way out.

He really was the best boss I'd ever had. I hated him.

CHAPTER 14

The Bloody Bower

I couldn't stand thinking about what Grady was saying to Ezra. I went home feeling pretty bad. It felt like someone had stolen my wallet, keyed my brand-new car, and told me I had to get a tetanus shot all in the same day.

Ezra.

I hoped Grady didn't make Ezra feel like he'd done anything wrong. He'd had enough guilt heaped on him in his life. And I hoped Ezra understood this separation was only temporary.

God. He was a grown man. I was being ridiculous.

I took my phone to bed with me, but he didn't text. When I was sure Grady could no longer be there, I sent him one.

> **Sorry. It's just till we solve the case.**

I got back a quick response.

Yeah. Don't like it tho.

I HATE it. Miss you.

He didn't reply.

The next morning, I stopped in Grady's office to fish around for how Ezra had taken it, what Grady had said, what Ezra had said. Grady just grunted at me. "Morning, Harris. Get to work." Then he firmly shut his door in my face.

I figured that meant that, whatever Ezra had told him, it hadn't gotten me fired.

I tried to solve the case.

Two weeks went by. Somehow March had snuck up on me and our snowy winter turned into a soaked early spring. It rained as if the heavens were crying.

I spoke to every one of the "clients" who'd contacted Jessica through that Craigslist ad, or at least all the ones we could trace. About ten of them had actually gotten to meet the girls. The others had apparently not satisfied Jessica's criteria and had been declined. When I spoke to the ones who did meet up with them, their stories of how things went down matched Larry's pretty well. We checked out alibis. We checked backgrounds for any link to Grimlace Lane—and found none. Larry, meanwhile, sat in jail on the drug charge. I wasn't able to dig up anything more substantial to tie him to the murders, and several more interviews with him just ended up pissing off the both of us.

I was frustrated being stuck on the Craigslist angle. I knew our best lead was Katie selling her story about abuse, but I couldn't do much about that due to my ban from seeing any of the Amish. I plagued poor Grady until I think he was about to ban me from talking to him too, maybe making it nice and legal with a restraining order.

"Have you talked to Isaac Yoder again about that whole birthmark comment? Don't you think that's suspicious?"

"I've talked to him. Twice. He can't even stomach the thought that Katie was abused. He didn't know."

"What about her older brothers?"

Grady shook his head. "I gave you the audio interviews. They don't seem guilty to me. If they are, they're lying their pants off."

"It didn't sound like you grilled them that hard, though."

"Harris—"

"What about Amos Miller?"

"It's not him."

"How can you be so sure? It was his barn. He's an older man and he lived close to the Lapps. He had opportunity."

A grand rolling of the eyes.

"What about Aaron Lapp? Katie cleaned house for them for years."

"Miriam Lapp swears she was always with Katie when she was in the house. I got the feeling she didn't particularly trust Katie. So even if Lapp *would* have, which I highly doubt, he never had the opportunity."

I wasn't convinced on that score. Miriam couldn't have been there *all the time every time* for all those years. But I had to admit to myself that my dislike for Lapp could be coloring my suspicions.

"What about a grandfather? Uncle? Older cousin? She has to have dozens of them."

"What if Katie wasn't abused at all? What if she was making up a story to get money?" Grady said. I knew he was goading me though. Mostly.

"I don't believe that. And neither do you."

And so it went.

On Saturday night, when there wasn't one more thing I could think of to do at the station, I went home and went to bed early. I was all caught up on my sleep now that Ezra wasn't around. I hated it.

I lay there staring at the ceiling and gave in to an irresistible urge to call the man. After all, Grady had said I couldn't *see* Ezra. Talking on the phone wasn't seeing him, right? I'd been a good Girl Scout for two weeks. I needed this.

"Hey," I said.

"Hey."

For a moment, we just listened to each other breathe.

"You know I don't want this, right?" I told him morosely.

"All right. You solved the case already?"

"No, babe. But I'm doing everything I can. How are your plans going?"

"Got my social security card in the mail. And I looked at a couple of places I could maybe rent. Places where I can have the mules. Ain't cheap though."

"Yeah? Where are they?"

"One's south of Mount Joy. One's near Stevens."

Stevens was too far away.

"Can't afford it yet." Ezra sounded a bit low.

"If I moved out of this place, I could pay half." My chest hurt just saying that. God knows, I hadn't planned on saying any such thing.

There was a long pause. "Don't think you mean that, Elizabeth."

I sighed. "I dunno. Right now the idea of being able to see you every day is pretty sweet."

Ezra's voice was dry. "What about after two months? Maybe it'll sour by then."

"I like you sweet *and* sour."

"You ain't even seen me sour yet, Detective Harris." I could hear the hint of a smile in Ezra voice. I'd give anything to be able to see that tiny, wry tilt to his lips right now. And then kiss it away. Being with Ezra had revved me all up again, gotten me used to being held, being touched. Now I'd been forced to go cold turkey. It wasn't fair.

"Well, maybe you could text me a few of those addresses you're looking at. And maybe I could just happen to drive by and take a look."

Ezra was quiet again. "All right."

"Good then."

I could feel his confusion and doubt over the phone, wondering if I was stringing him along. Or maybe I was just projecting my own fears about what he was feeling.

"Ezra, I can't see you right now because it would be a mess for the police department if the press found out about us. You see that, right?"

A shaky breath. "I see it."

"It'll pass. I want to be with you."

"Okay."

I waited. "Is that all you've got for me, farm boy?"

"I'm glad you want to be with me," he said solemnly.

I snorted. "Nice. Thanks a lot."

"And I want to be with you more than anythin'."

"Yeah?"

"Yeah. I'm really missin' the smell of you."

There was a teasing heat in his words that sent what was already a perked-up libido, just from the sound of his voice, all the way to eleven.

"Damn," I breathed. "I wish we had Skype."

"Sky?"

"Skype. Have you ever had phone sex?"

"What now?" He sounded very confused.

I smiled. "Not you having sex with a phone. Two people having sex *over* the phone."

"How could we . . . ?"

I explained to him the principle of the thing and got a strangled reply. "I knew there was a reason I shoulda installed a lock on my bedroom door."

I grinned, unreasonably happy to have made him suffer a little. "Well, someday we'll try it. Someday when you're not living with your sister. To be honest, it doesn't quite live up to the real thing though."

"Bet it beats Parcheesi."

I laughed. "What?"

"Been playing way too much of it with Martha in the evenings."

"Yes, I think we can safely say it beats Parcheesi." I sighed, wishing I could reach through the distance between us and touch his hand as it held the phone—anything.

"If that's what you English get up to, I think I understand why cell phones are forbidden 'cept for work."

I laughed.

"Well." His voice was heavy with things he didn't say.

"Good night, Ezra. Send me those addresses."

He hesitated as if there was something he wanted to say, but he didn't. "Good night, Elizabeth."

After we hung up I had the most terrible feeling. What if this case never ended? What if Ezra changed his mind about leaving the Amish? What if we were never together, in the flesh, again?

It was like having the stomach flu. No matter how bad the end might be, or what terrible things you might have to go through to get past it, at this point, I was willing to face it all just to have this done so we could get to the other side and things could be better.

I needed it to be done.

———

It must have been the sound of rain battering my bedroom windows, along with my stress about the case, but I dreamed again of drowning.

I was in the water looking for Katie. I knew she was there, but the water was muddy and I couldn't see her. I searched around for her with my hands, blindly. I kept thinking, *I need to go up for air*, and I kept deciding just one more step, just let me reach this way. And then I realized I'd left it too late, and I was losing consciousness.

I woke up suddenly and sat up in bed. I wanted to go out there *right now*. It was a lingering panic brought on by my dream, that Katie was in the creek, she was drowning. I knew, of course, that Katie was long dead. There was no one I needed to save in Rockvale Creek. But I couldn't sleep anymore either. I looked at the clock—it was half past midnight.

I got dressed, got in my car, and headed toward Grimlace Lane.

I had no plans other than to drive around the area, make sure nothing looked amiss, and to use the quiet time to think about the case. That, and glean what hollow satisfaction I could just from driving by Ezra's house. But as I drove down a country road on my way there, I got behind a slow car. It was a sedan, and in the glow of my headlights I could see a young guy driving. His arm was around a girl who was seated as close to him as possible. They had no interest in going over twenty miles an hour.

After a few frustrating minutes, the car rolled into a pullout with an irritating nonchalance. I passed it.

I pushed the gas pedal, glancing behind me at the car, which seemed content to sit where it was for a while. It reminded me of something—Ezra turning the mule and buggy into a pullout while we were on our way to the farmers' market that day in February. I came to the next intersection and sat there, thinking. In the dark of night, in the heavy rain, I sat at a stop sign in the middle of farm country. If it had been the summer, I'd be serenaded by the sound of crickets and the glow of fireflies. In the

March rain, the staccato beat of raindrops supplied the soundtrack.

Jessica hadn't been killed in the Millers' barn. She'd been killed elsewhere and then, already cold, stiff, and dead, guided through the water of the creek to her final resting place.

She could have been killed anywhere, we'd agreed. She could have been killed in a Klein's Dairy truck—except we'd found no trace of it—or at the park where Larry Wannemaker took his lunch break—though blacklight tests there had found no blood. She could have been killed on any of a million country roads, like the one back there. When we hadn't found footprints in the snow exiting the creek toward the road, we hadn't followed up heavily on that theory.

I turned my car and headed for Ronks Road.

I started at Route 30. From there I followed Ronks south, toward the area of Grimlace Lane. I remembered from the map—it was a few miles before Ronks curved and parallelled Rockvale Creek for a time. I passed a pullout too close to 30 and kept going. Then I saw one on the right side of the road. I had a sense the creek was over there. I lowered my car window, but the rain made it impossible to hear the sound of moving water. I was pretty sure I was still downstream of the Millers' farm. I pulled into the dirt area. In my headlights I noted muddy wheel tracks and hoofprints from earlier in the day. This pullout was used by buggies.

I parked and got out, grabbed a flashlight from my glove compartment, and flipped up the hood on my windbreaker. The pullout was roughly curved and framed by trees. There was enough gravel to keep the dirt from completely turning to mud, but the footing was slick and wet. The rough shapes of larger rocks shone in the flashlight's beam. I walked to the woods, the trees foreboding in the dark and the rain. I pressed on, and a few minutes later I was on the bank of Rockvale Creek. Or, to be honest, the bank was submerged, flooded from the recent rain, and I was as close as I could get to it without wading.

I shone the light upstream. I could make out nothing but trees, but I knew the farms on Grimlace Lane lay in that direction.

Jessica was hit in the back of the head while turned away, then finished off with suffocation. She'd lain somewhere, in the snow, for ten to twelve hours before she was moved via the creek.

Why had she lain outside? Why not in a car trunk?

I had a deep, intense burning in my gut. I wanted to search this area. I wanted a forensics team here, now.

I looked at my watch. It was a little after one in the morning. If I called a forensics team out in the middle of the night, in the rain, and it turned out to be a false lead, I'd never hear the end of it. Grady would say it could wait till morning. After all, we were well past those critical first few days. But the rain . . . The heavy rain was going to wash away any evidence that might be left, if it hadn't already.

I drove to the Lancaster Police Station. Some facilities stayed open twenty-four hours including, thankfully, the Equipment Rec office. The female officer who worked the night shift got what I asked for and signed me out with no words wasted. At least, until she looked at her log.

"Huh. Third time on this metal detector, Detective Harris," she said with a quirked brow. "This a kink of yours?"

"You know what they say: Third time's the charm."

"Well if you find RoboCop with that thing, bring him back here. He's hot."

I smiled. "The original or the remake?"

She snorted like I was out of my mind. "You kiddin'? Peter Weller all the way."

I gave her a high five and lugged my stuff out the door.

———

By the time I got back to the pullout it was almost two-thirty. I started getting tired on the way back, and I contemplated the wisdom of what I was doing—as opposed to, say, going back home to bed and returning in the morning. But I wanted to at least do a quick pass with the luminol to see if I could find any traces of blood. If I did, that would be a good reason to pull the forensics team out bright and early. So I parked my car at the pullout, took my flashlight and the newly mixed spray bottle of luminol powder and H_2O_2 liquid, and got to work.

Once I was there, with the potential for discovery on every patch of ground, my energy and excitement returned. The rain had eased off to a sprinkle, which made the work slightly more rational. It was quite dark out, so if there was anything to react to, the luminol would glow blue. I sprayed it at various places around the pullout. I got reactions immediately and I was excited until I remembered that luminol detects iron and also reacts to fecal matter. There was plenty of horse manure in the pullout, both old and new. They showed up as round blue blobs. But near the edge of the clearing I found a patch that was sprayed out in a pool—it was a shape I recognized from plenty of crime scenes. I'd bet anything it was blood, blood that had soaked into the dirt and gravel of the pullout and was probably nothing more than a darkish stain during the day.

I followed the blobs that trailed from that patch into the trees.

I searched for an hour, tantalized to keep going by bread crumbs of blue glow on leaves and on the ground in the woods, getting closer and closer to the creek bank. And then I found it. There was a pile of brush with bits of blue glow on it. When I moved some of the brush aside, I found the bower. I could almost picture Jessica lying here—a large patch of deep blue marked where her head had been. Here, the killer hid her after she was dead, roughly covered by brush and blanketed by snow. She'd lain here in the cold for hours until he came back and dragged her into the creek. But I was sure this area had been searched the day we'd found the body and no footprints found. The snow would have hidden his tracks from earlier in the day, when he'd killed Jessica, but not from that night, when he'd moved her. Which means he had to have walked back through the creek to pick up the body. *Smart.* But where had he come from?

I took photos with my phone, even though they really didn't turn out. I felt a burning sense of satisfaction. Luminol is like

God's eye, revealing the invisible blotches of sin. I had a fleeting sense of being an avenger.

Then I went and got the metal detector.

I was still obsessed with the idea of the phone. I searched in a wide swath around the area but found nothing. Of course, this was where *Jessica* had been killed, not Katie. And Katie was the one who'd had the phone. But I couldn't get the damn thing out of my mind. At last I stood at the edge of the creek and looked north.

It was time to stop, I knew that. But I was wide-awake now, adrenaline in my blood and the scent of victory in my nose. *I'll just go upstream far enough to see how far this is from the Millers' farm.*

That's what I told myself. I went back to the car and put on the chest-high waders I'd checked out at the station. I stuck the spray bottle of luminol down inside my waistband. Carrying the metal detector across my shoulders, I waded into the creek.

Rockvale Creek was running very high—and it was cold. I walked for a good ways. I had to stay thigh deep, because the sides of the bank that were newly flooded were riddled with branches and bushes and debris. The rush of the current around me was like an embrace that wanted to pull me down. Adrenaline or not, exhaustion was threatening to put an end to my midnight adventures. Then I hit the first chicken-wire barrier.

I saw it, stretching from the sides of the creek bank, mere seconds before I ran into it. I stopped. I had to be on the property line of a farm with livestock, though whether or not it was one of the farms on Grimlace Lane remained to be seen.

The water was so high the chicken-wire fencing disappeared in the middle of the creek, its top underwater. It was like an invitation. *There's no barrier here, keep going.* I waded to the middle and pushed the fencing down farther with my hand and allowed the water to push me over it, the rubber of the waders catching only a little on the wire. I kept going.

After the third chicken-wire fence I crossed I started to recognize the area. I waded out and climbed up the creek bank. In front of me was a pasture, the grass low but already greening up in the March rain. Beyond that was Aaron Lapp's big red barn and new, ranch-style farmhouse. The night was silent except for the sound of the running creek and the increased beat of the rain, coming down hard now.

I'd used the metal detector at the Millers' and at Ezra's place, but not here. I swung it off my shoulders and gave silent thanks when I turned it on and it was still working. I started to search.

I found nothing along the creek bank, so I followed the animal trail across the pasture toward the barn, swinging the metal detector along the way. I'd been banned from Grimlace Lane, so I wouldn't be able to come back and search in the day. But now? No one was here to see me. I was interacting with no one.

I reached the barn having found nothing but three large nails and an old metal buckle. I turned the metal detector off and stood there.

The Lapp house was silent and dark. The barn loomed like a living presence. Aaron Lapp would be incensed to find me here. Which was why I'd likely never have this opportunity again.

I thought of the laws governing police searches of outbuildings. It was iffy territory. But the Lapp barn was at least a hundred feet from the house and not marked in any way, either by fencing or signage, as private. In the normal course of my job, I would not hesitate to check it out if I had good reason to do so. Even so, I knew Grady wouldn't like it.

But I thought of Jessica, her body left unclaimed in that barn, and of Katie, who was lost in the river. And I thought, more self-ishly, of Ezra. *This needs to end.* I went inside.

The Lapps had four horses in one large free stall at the end of the barn, and two cows in a stall on the other side of the aisle. They were rough shapes in the dark, unalarmed by my presence. There was a light switch just inside the door. *Dare I risk it?* The part of the barn I was in faced away from the house. Still, I decided to stick with the flashlight.

The aisle was apparently used for feeding, with long food troughs on either side that opened onto the stalls and large plastic bins of grain. I ran my flashlight over everything and ran the metal detector briefly around the food bins—nothing.

The aisle opened onto a larger room with a cement floor, steel plates lay over what appeared to be channels for manure, and several rusty chutes disappeared into the upper story. I figured the metal detector was going to be useless in a place like this, but I did run it in the shadows along the wall, under a wooden cabinet that sat up off the floor, around a large bin of firewood. The readout spiked. I ran it around the wood bin again—the metal detector was reacting to the back of it.

It was probably a large metal hinge or even nails. I told my-self that, but my stomach twisted with anxiety. I put the metal detector down and shone the flashlight inside the bin. It was a large container, around five feet long and four feet high. It was made of rough boards, well aged, and filled with chopped wood and twigs sized to burn in a wood stove. The back of the bin was taller than the front and some of it showed over the logs. It looked normal—unusually clean even. I debated turning on the light so I could get a better look. Then I remembered the spray bottle of luminol I'd tucked into the waders. I pulled it out and sprayed the top of the woodpile and the back of the bin and turned off the flashlight.

The back of the bin had an apple-sized smear of blue glow—blood.

A body would fit in that bin. In fact it would be a good place to hide it until it could be disposed of. Was that blood Katie's? Jessica, I was fairly certain, had been killed at that pullout, hidden in the woods there until the killer could return and drag her body downstream to the Millers' barn. But Katie? Had Katie been killed here?

I propped my flashlight up on a nearby ledge so it shone over the wood bin, and I started removing logs.

CHAPTER 15

Drowning

I found the phone with the hot pink cover in the woodpile, where it had slipped down through the top layer of logs some time ago, probably the previous October. I stood there holding the phone in my hand. I hit the power button, but of course the battery was long dead. I knew as soon as I picked it up that I shouldn't have touched it. I had to put it back, call Grady, and get the forensics team in here. I could stand watch outside, make sure no one got a chance to move it before—

The light in the barn went on.

I turned. Aaron Lapp stood in the doorway blinking at me. He looked like he'd hastily dressed in his black pants, suspenders, and a worn blue shirt. His hair was wild around his head from having been asleep. His eyes narrowed in anger as he registered who I was and what I was doing—standing in his barn and going through his woodpile.

"Get. Off. My. Property," he said, through gritted teeth.

I felt a hot wave of fear. I had no backup. No one knew I was here, on private property in the most secret part of night. I hadn't worn my gun, had no reason to think I'd need it. And I was pretty sure I was looking at the man who had killed Katie Yoder and Jessica Travis. How much further would he go to hide his crimes? And then I realized—I was a police officer, an ex-member of the NYPD, and I had years of self-defense training on Aaron Lapp. I was not a girl he could bash on the back of the head. I wasn't going to be afraid of him.

In fact, I was pissed.

Instead of dropping the phone back where I'd found it, I held it up. "Did you know this was here? I'm betting you didn't, or you would have gotten rid of it. You know what's on it though, don't you?"

He looked at the phone with a frown. "You . . . That does not belong to me. I don't know what you're talking about."

"It's Katie Yoder's phone. The batteries are dead, or we could take a little look at what's on here together. But you know, don't you? That's why you killed her. Last fall, she took a video of the two of you messing around and she was going to sell it to the papers."

Aaron wiped his face and left his hand clasped over his mouth as if to hold in words or the contents of his stomach. I could see panic and calculation in his eyes as his gaze moved from my face to the phone in my hand and back again.

"You didn't mean to kill Katie, did you?" I said, unable to re-sist pushing him. "Did you catch her making the video? You hit her on the back of the head in a rage and then you had to finish it, didn't you? You hid her body in the woodpile until you could get rid of it, and the phone fell out. Bad luck. Where did she tape the two of you?" I looked around. "Not here, surely. It's a bit too open. You'd take her someplace more private."

Aaron still said nothing, but I saw his eyes move to a door at the back of the room.

"Back there?" I asked. The phone still in my hand, I went to the door and pushed it open. Behind it was a little workshop, maybe eight feet by ten, with no windows and a concrete floor. An array of tools was organized neatly on a pegboard, and a worktable and chair was against the wall. It smelled of oil, Pennsylvania dirt, and age. It smelled just like my grandfather's workshop, the scent stirring memories long forgotten. I walked in and looked around, found a light switch and pulled it, lighting a dim yellow overhead bulb. It flashed with the generator, casting flickering shadows.

Aaron stood in the doorway. "You have no right to be here," he said, but his voice had lost all of its hubris. It was almost a whisper. He looked afraid for the first time since I'd met him.

I knew I was grandstanding. I knew I should just leave and call Grady. I shouldn't question Lapp, not without the Miranda and witnesses and a lot of other hoops having been jumped through. But I just wanted him to admit it, goddamn it. I wanted him to admit that he'd sexually abused Katie Yoder, probably from the time she was eleven years old. After all his judging of Ezra—*of me*—I wanted him to goddamn well acknowledge that he himself was a pedophile. I wanted to at least see it on his face.

"I bet she put it here," I said, noticing a rough wooden shelf opposite the worktable. I went over and put the phone on the middle shelf, on its side, facing out. "She came in before you, didn't she? She set up the phone and she called you in here."

Aaron's knees started to go out. His face was utterly white like he might faint. He leaned heavily on the door frame, then staggered over to the worktable and fell into the chair. "God help me," he muttered.

"Did you see the phone while you were touching her? Did you get suspicious when she tried to get you to talk about it? Or maybe afterward she gloated about it, showed you the evidence?"

I took the phone and put it in my pocket for safekeeping. I walked to the doorway and stood there looking at him. Aaron's utter despondency was starting to sink in through my anger. He was slumped in the chair like a rag doll, his face drained of color, his eyes shut, his breathing labored. Maybe that was all the acknowledgment I was going to get. Maybe it was enough. I studied him. It made me sick to think about what he'd done to Katie in this room.

"It's not what you think." He opened his eyes to look at me. "She was . . . so beautiful. So young. And she liked it. Liked the attention, wanted to be held and petted. I always . . . she enjoyed it too. She was greedy for it. When she got older, she wanted me to leave my wife—demanded it! I would never, never do that. So Katie, she put an end to it. I repented of this sin years ago already." His eyes were distant. "It was a pair of earrings, that first time. Some cheap, gaudy things some Englishwoman had given her in town, like you hand a biscuit to a dog. Katie had them on, cleaning up, here in the barn. When I saw them I was angry but I felt this . . . lust. The world out there. It just won't leave us alone."

I closed my eyes. I tried to filter through what he was saying.

Aaron had taken her young, far too young. But later on it must have been mutual enough, in Katie's mind, that she had expectations. She'd wanted Aaron to leave his wife, given him an ultimatum? Cut off their affair? Maybe when Katie was out meeting up with men from Craigslist, she'd already been over Aaron Lapp. If so, she must have come back one last time, one last time to get her twenty-five-thousand-dollar video, and maybe her revenge too. And that had been a fatal mistake.

"I don't think the law is going to care that you repented of it, Lapp. It was pedophilia while it was going on, and then, in October, it was murder."

"No." There were tears in Aaron's eyes. "We . . . She did come to me. Last year. Tempted me to do it again. And I gave in, God help me. But I never . . . I didn't—"

His words cut off abruptly. I saw his eyes widen in shock, looking at something behind me. But I saw it a moment too late. There was no time to turn or even raise my arm. There was no time for anything before something smashed, with force, into the back of my head.

The pain was the worst thing I'd ever felt—like burning fire wrapping around my skull and shooting down my neck. It was vicious and deep, a dangerous blow, maybe fatal. I knew this on some level, knew I needed help, medical help, but mostly there was just the pain. It was so bad it stole my breath and every scrap of energy. My stomach rebelled in a wave of nausea and my vision went as soft as black cotton.

I was on the concrete floor. There was another whiff of that smell, the smell of my grandfather's workshop, and I wondered if that would be the last thing I would ever smell. Then I knew nothing more.

"She told me she was leavin'. She told me that day," Miriam Lapp was saying matter-of-factly.

I sat on the chair in her kitchen writing it down, writing and writing. The page in my notebook was white as snow and it was getting longer and longer. It was surely getting in the way on the kitchen floor.

"She told me to say good-bye to her family," Miriam said as she flipped bloody pancakes in a heavy iron skillet on her stove. They looked . . . bony. Like pieces of a skull. I didn't want to look at them.

"And then what happened?" I asked, wanting to make sure I wrote it all down. I had to get everything just right. I could hear an argument in the next room and I wished they'd shut up so I could concentrate.

The notebook page was dragging behind me. I worried that it would get wet in the snow and that all my hard work, everything I'd written down, would be ruined and become unreadable. If that happened, I'd never be able to solve the case. It would never end and Ezra would walk away from me. He'd tell me it was over if I couldn't give him what he wanted.

"Stop," I tried to say. "Let me pick up the paper. Just stop for one second."

She was taking off my clothes. It was cold, so cold, and my head hurt so bad I wanted to die. My chattering teeth woke me up and my body convulsed with shivers.

"Don't," I muttered, looking up at her hard face. *Take me to a hospital. I'm sick, so sick. Just let me sleep, please.*

Someone rolled me onto my side in bed. Why was the bed so cold? It was wet too, slick and clammy. Disgusting. I wanted to protect my face from the cold, but my arms were stuck behind me. And then I rolled off the side of the bed into water, deep water. And I was drowning.

Black water. Freezing cold. My feet struck the bottom—toes scraping against stone. I was moving fast in the current. My knee struck a rock, and there was pain, but the pain was distant, like it was happening to someone else.

That scared me. The cold water stung my head where I felt a dull, frighteningly deep, and brutal ache. I had a bad head wound. If I was no longer fully feeling pain in my lower body, that was not good. *Head trauma.* My body was shutting down. But in a moment, I stopped worrying about my head wound because the only thing that mattered, the only thing in the whole world, was my need for—

Air. Air, air, air, air—

My feet found the bottom again and pushed up of their own accord, from some deep survival instinct. My head broke the surface of the water.

I gasped, choking, my lungs surging with blessed oxygen. I tried to bring up my hands to stabilize myself in the water so I could keep my head up, but they didn't move. For a moment,

I feared they were paralyzed and then I felt the rope. *Tied. My hands are tied behind me.* My head was dragged under again by the rush of water. And my body slammed into something that yielded slightly and scraped my skin.

Chicken-wire fencing. It was submerged because of the flooding. Air was once again the only thing I cared about. Maybe I could use the fencing. I had no clothes to catch on it—my body was nude. But I used my feet to get purchase in the little sections of wire and pushed myself up. My head broke the surface again.

I gasped, drinking in air. My mind and body filled with one clear imperative: I didn't want to die. There'd been days when, weighted down by grief and discouragement, I would have accepted death without a struggle. But not now. I wanted desperately to live. I didn't realize how much I'd healed from Terry's death until that instant, when suddenly there was so much to live for. Death would be a cruel and unwelcome thief.

I tugged at my bonds. I was weak, incredibly weak, and growing weaker in the freezing water. I couldn't undo the ropes around my wrists or even hang on to the chicken wire with my feet. The current pushed me relentlessly and the wire bent under my body. The barbs on top scraped deep into the skin of my stomach as the water dragged me over the top.

No.

I fought for some purchase on the fencing, but it was gone, well gone. Then it was just me under the water again, my searching legs finding no bottom, my damaged head leading the way under the current's surge with no ability to stop or even bring up my arms to protect it. I'd hit another rock. Even the thought of anything touching my head filled me with panic. I was going to drown.

The sides of the creek. The creek isn't that wide.

The thought gave me hope. With the last burst of energy I had, I fought the current and tried to swim to my left, twisting my body and kicking with my legs, all the while trying to keep my head up. It was hard. I was moving forward more than I was moving left. But I fought on, kicking my legs, ignoring the numbness and broken feel to my knee. I went under. My lungs burned, needing air, but I resisted the urge to try to fight my way to the surface and kept pushing left. If I stopped now, any progress I'd made toward the bank would be lost in an instant.

And then I felt the touch of pebbles under my toes. One more hard push and my feet found the bottom. I again resisted the terrible need to push up and find air, refusing to let my feet leave the earth, sure I'd never find it again if I did. I dug in my frozen toes and forced my legs to walk. A moment later my head broke the surface, my feet still on the rocky creek bed.

It was a victory as sweet as any I'd ever had, that moment of feeling that I'd accomplished something, that I'd fought for, and won, both ground and air. I was saved.

And then the current pulled my feet off the slippery stones, and my head under the water.

I fought again for the shore, but my body was so weak, it barely obeyed my commands. Who would believe a mere creek could rush so fast? Be so dangerous?

It isn't. The creek isn't that wide. You can make it the shore. Just do it. Do it!

I thought of Ezra working on his rockers, steady and strong, the way he looked driving his buggy, petting Horse. I remembered the sight of him naked in my bed, his long blond hair like silk on the pillow. I saw the line of his jaw; the tiny, ironic lift at the corner of his mouth; his kind, sweet eyes.

I drifted, losing thought, losing myself. I might never have returned except that my shoulder slammed, hard, into something. The pain brought me back to my senses. It was a fallen tree, partially submerged. And my head had popped out of the water. I gasped in lungfuls of air and when I exhaled I was screaming.

"Ezra! Ezra!" I didn't sound like myself. It was desperate, hoarse screaming. "Ezra!"

It was raining, raining hard, the drops striking my face. The current began to push me along the log, determined to send me on my way, maybe to the Susquehanna where I would finally wash up, like Katie had, on Robert Island. I had no way to cling to the log. My legs ran under it into clear water and could not rise high enough to catch hold. My hands were bound. I pushed my shoulders into the bark as hard as I could, trying to stay put.

"Ezra!" I screamed.

I stopped moving, a small branch bracing me and bending under the strain. Where was I? I remembered crossing one fence; had I crossed others? Was I still near the Lapps' farm? Ezra's? Or was I far downstream by now? I searched the creek banks but it was dark and there was something wrong with my eyes. Everything was blurry and doubled.

Concussion. Dear God, I'm badly hurt.

The twig bent further. I slipped another inch down the log.

A kind of resignation stole over me. I was going to die after all. There was nothing I could do about it. I wished I'd been able to tell someone about the Lapps. I wished I'd been able to get justice for Jessica and Katie. And I wished, more than anything, that I didn't have to leave *him*.

Something lighter came into my view of the bank, something large and moving. It took me a long moment for the shape to coalesce enough to recognize what it was.

It was a horse. No, it was Horse. He was watching me.

"Ezra," I said. "Ezra."

I must have scared Horse, and I couldn't blame him. He turned and stormed away.

But that meant I had to be on Ezra's land, didn't it? If I could just make it to the bank, maybe work my way along the fallen tree . . . The branch that had snagged me bent further, threatening to give way, and my body was moved another inch toward the middle of the creek.

No, not this close. Please. Give me strength.

The branch gave way.

———————

"I called an ambulance. They're comin'. Hang on, Elizabeth. *Gott im himmel*, please."

The voice was anguished—and familiar. My eyelids seemed to weigh a hundred pounds each, but I forced them open a crack. Ezra's face loomed over me. It was fuzzy but it was undeniably his face.

"Hey," I said. My voice croaked like a dying bullfrog.

"Oh, thank the Lord!" Ezra's hand wiped at his mouth, his eyes. He was shaking so hard I could see it, even though I couldn't see much.

"Don't," I said. *Don't cry. It's fine.*

"Oh, Elizabeth. Your head . . . I thought. Who hurt you like this?"

I wished he didn't sound so upset. I was happy, so happy. I wasn't dead, and Ezra had found me. There was even a heavy coat laid over my body. I wasn't warm, but I was out of the water, I was on solid ground. I wasn't fighting for air. Didn't he know how amazing that was? That everything in the entire world had to be all right now? But then I remembered I had something I needed to tell him, something important.

"Miriam Lapp. Tell Grady."

"Oh Lord. Oh no." He sounded disbelieving, horrified.

"The phone," I said, despite my chattering teeth. "In the woodbin. Grandfather's smell. Solved the snow. I mean, the case. I solved the case, Ezra. Where are my notes?"

"It's okay," he said, rubbing my arms and legs under the coat, trying to warm me up. They were starting to prickle and hurt where the numbness was wearing off. "Rest now. The ambulance comes soon."

"But I solved it. I solved the case."

"I knew you would. I had faith."

His face swam a little more into focus and I could see the emotion in his eyes, still damp with fear, but full of so many other things as well—relief and love. So much love.

"I have faith in you," I said. And yeah, I had a concussion and I'd just nearly died, but I meant it. I meant every word.

In the end, what else was there to have faith in? Not in the fairness of life, or in a perfect world, or the goodness of man. What else, but the ones we love?

CHAPTER 16

Snake in the Grass

I was in the hospital for two days. They stabilized my knee, salved and bandaged my rubbed-raw wrists and various cuts and bruises, and stitched my head back together and watched for it to explode. It didn't.

The doctors told me the creek had saved my life. The cold water lowered my blood pressure, stopped the bleeding, and kept my brain from swelling inside my cranium like a soufflé. Ironic, that the thing that almost killed me had ended up saving my life. Or maybe that's just the way it works.

Ezra came both days to see me. He had an English driver drop him off at the hospital in the middle of downtown Lancaster and wait in the cafeteria while we visited for a few hours. He was a little shy about holding my hand at first, but I clung to him even when people entered the room, not letting him retreat. I think he was surprised when the nurses didn't pay any attention to us. God love those Lancaster General nurses. Ezra was still dressed

Amish, and they knew I was a cop, so they had every reason to be confused. But in fact, they seemed particularly smiley about the two of us. It was nice. I was done hiding.

Ezra told me about the small farm he'd gone to see the week before. He showed me pictures on his cell phone.

"Only a fifteen minute drive to Lancaster. In a car, that is," he said, not meeting my eyes.

"I need thirty days to get out of my lease," I replied.

He smiled and nodded once. I smiled back. Screw it. If Grady and the police department didn't like me living with Ezra, they could find another detective.

I thought it would be all right though. Because when Grady came to see me, he yelled at me for about five minutes for going into the Lapps' barn on my own, and then told me they'd never have solved the murders without me. He and the chief were grateful. "Grateful" is a word I very much like to hear from my bosses. As long as there isn't a "but" attached. Grady also said he was glad I'd survived my stupidity because he "needed me."

"Hell yeah. You really, really do," I said.

He rolled his eyes. "Don't let it go to your head, Harris. But—"

"But?"

"But yes, I do. You're a hell of a detective."

That was the kind of "but" I liked to hear.

———

The case caused the kind of hue and cry Grady had feared. Jim Johnson broke the story about Katie's abuse and murder in the *National Tattler* and it spread fast. It even made the national news, on some talking-heads show where they brought in experts to talk about sexual abuse of young girls in religious communities. They had to put an armed cop on my door to stop the reporters. Ezra Beiler's name was never mentioned. Everyone in Lancaster County was in shocked disbelief over the arrests. Fortunately, the police department had every leg to stand on. They'd found Katie's phone and traces of blood in the Lapps' kitchen and barn. More important, Miriam and Aaron Lapp had surrendered themselves willingly.

The day Miriam Lapp made a full statement was my first day back at work. She'd asked for me to be there, and I'd insisted on it, even though Grady wanted me to take more time off. I wanted to hear what she had to say. I deserved to hear it.

And Katie and Jessica deserved for it to be heard.

"It was last October. Katie come to clean house. I sent Sarah, Job, and Rebecca out to the barn to get the corn and eggs ready for market. Told 'em not to come in till it was done. I wanted to talk to Katie alone."

Miriam Lapp spoke slowly and calmly. Only her stiff back, the pallor of her face, and hands twisting a handkerchief in her lap betrayed any emotion. She looked straight ahead at nothing as she spoke. She'd been in jail for a few days, but she'd requested, and been allowed, her own clothes for what she'd called her "public confession." With her white bonnet and black dress, and with the Amish elders in the room, it reminded me of a scene from some medieval trial.

We were in the largest conference room the police station

had. Miriam had said she'd tell everything, but she wanted the church elders present, and Aaron—in handcuffs and with a warden at his side—and Katie's parents and Jessica's mother too—and me. She wanted to confess and she only wanted to do it once, she'd told Grady. One of our techs was filming it with a small camera on a tripod and there was a stenographer there too, and two armed men outside at the door. Grady was taking no chances.

"Always knew what was goin' on between her and Aaron. She didn't hide it. She goaded me with it. Smiling at him when he came in and givin' me these knowing looks. She was only a girl when it started. It was a terrible thorn in my side for years. Aaron, he wouldn't let me fire her. Said people would talk. Said Katie might tell stories. But he didn't give it up. Whenever I saw Katie head out to the barn, I knew. . . ." She twisted her handkerchief tighter and took a deep breath. Aaron stared at the floor, his face drawn and troubled.

"I bore it. I didn't chide my husband. I knew I was never . . . never pretty. And after Rebecca was born, the doctor said I'd not have another. I was hurt for a good while. Inside. Couldn't . . . I figured that ruined me for Aaron.

"Then God heard my prayers. Katie stopped going out to the barn. 'Twas two years before, 'bout. Aaron . . . he come back to me after a time. Thank the Lord. I thanked God with all my heart." She squeezed her eyes shut tight.

"Then, that last October, Katie come to work one day and I knew. She had this look in her eyes and color on her lips. She went out to the barn and stayed out there a good, long while. When she come back in she was pleased as anythin'. Humming as she worked, and she give me these looks. . . ."

"I knew it was startin' up again. I couldn't bear it. And I . . . I knew Katie'd been wantin' to leave, see. So next time she come over, I made sure the children was out of the house. Aaron was gone visitin'. I offered Katie money if she would just go. Go to the city. Leave us alone. I offered three hundred dollars, my pin money I saved up for Sarah's weddin'."

Katie's mother, Hannah, and her father, Isaac, sat listening with closed eyes. I had the feeling they were praying. The pain on their faces was not obvious, but that just made it worse.

"You know what she done? Katie? She laughed at me. Said she had a lot more money than that, twenty-five thousand dollars that she was gonna get from the papers when she told her story. Said she had video of her and Aaron, that she'd gotten him to confess everything. She was gonna . . . she was gonna . . ." Miriam's small blue eyes grew red with tears. She wiped at them with her handkerchief and pushed on. "Don't see? She meant to bring Aaron down, ruin him, ruin me, ruin our children's lives, and Hannah's too. She was gonna shame the whole community."

She took a moment to get herself back under control. Everyone stayed silent and grim, waiting for the rest of it. This confession felt as much our punishment as hers.

"We was in the kitchen. I was at the stove brownin' some onions, and Katie, she sat at the table shellin' beans when she told me 'bout the video. I wasn't angry. I didn't think 'bout it. I just knew I had to stop her. Knew it was up to me." Miriam's eyes had gone a bit glassy, as if reliving the scene, and her voice grew more impassioned. I knew what was coming, but there was no way to be prepared.

"I took the skillet off. Scraped the onions onto a plate, like any other time. Then I hit her on the head with it. So hard. It was like . . . like it wasn't even my arm. Like I was the hand of God."

Hannah Yoder made a small sound and Isaac Yoder squeezed her arm tight.

"And then . . . there she was on the floor. . . ." Miriam continued, her voice faint. "So much blood. I made sure she was dead. Like this." She covered up her nose and mouth with her hand and held them there. I'd seen a lot of things as a cop, but seeing Miriam Lapp make that gesture was one of the most horrible things I'd ever seen.

"Couldn't move her far in daylight. So I sent the children to the neighbor's for some flour and I drug Katie out to the barn and put her in the wood bin. Covered her up. That night, when everyone was sleepin', I drug her to the creek and God took her away. It seemed like . . . like that flood was there to help me. Like this was all part of God's plan, to stop Katie and not allow this shame to be brought on all of us. You see?"

Miriam finally looked up. She looked at Hannah, as if pleading for understanding. But Hannah stared steadily at the floor.

"What about Jessica?" Grady asked. He was seated on a chair in front of Miriam.

Miriam touched her throat. "Can I have some water?"

Grady nodded, and Hernandez got up and left the room. He returned a moment later with a plastic cup full of water. Miriam drank it all almost daintily, then gave Hernandez the cup. He sat down again.

"The day it happened with Jessica," Miriam continued, once again in an eerily calm voice. "I went to the market. I come out to the buggy with my shoppin' and there stood this blonde girl, an

English. I'd seen her once before, in that same market with Katie, and Katie must have told this girl who I was. Because she come up to me that day in January and said she was scared Aaron had done somethin' to Katie. She knew all about it, even 'bout the video. She thought it was Aaron what killed Katie. 'Maybe it was an accident,' she said to me. 'Maybe he didn't mean it.'"

Aaron was staring at Miriam, grim and shaking his head like he couldn't believe what he was hearing. Miriam went on. "Don't know what she wanted me to do 'bout it. Don't know if she was lookin' to find Katie, or maybe turn me against my husband or what."

"I told her to get in the buggy so's we could talk. No one saw us. I started drivin' home, but I didn't know what to do. I couldn't bring her to the house, couldn't let her talk to Aaron or the police. So I prayed. I prayed so hard for wisdom the whole time I was drivin'.

"That's when it come to me. I said I had to check one of the horses that it was walkin' funny, and I pulled over. She got out and was standin' there looking at the road when I come up behind her with a rock. I done her just the same as I done Katie. I didn't want to, but . . . I had to do it."

Her voice was getting wet-sounding. She paused for a moment, blowing her nose and swallowing.

"You struck Jessica in the head with a rock? What happened then?" Grady prompted once she seemed under control.

"I hid her there by the creek till I could figure out what to do."

"Why didn't you leave her there? Why did you put her in the Millers' barn?" Grady asked in a neutral voice.

"Maybe I should have left her. But I meant to do just what I done with Katie. Send her down the creek. That night I put on some of Grandad's old clothes and boots what was in the attic, in case someone saw me. I walked down the creek to get her. Had to go under the fences. But once I got to Jessica and got her in the water, I realized she weren't gonna go far. The creek was too low. Guess I wasn't thinkin' clearheaded. Then I was stuck. I was afraid she'd be found too close to our place.

"I prayed again and it come to me, standing right there in the creek with Jessica's body, to put her at the Millers'. I knew no one would suspect Amos Miller or his. And he didn't have a dog or nothin'. I thought . . . if she was put in the barn like that, make it look like it had been . . . been about sex, the police would think the English had done it. It seemed like the sort of ugly trick they would do. It made no sense for an Amish to do somethin' like that."

She was right. That was just what we'd thought. If Katie's body hadn't been found, if my gut hadn't made me keep pushing . . .

"You carried Jessica's body across that field? Both of you soaking wet?" I asked, before I could remind myself that this was Grady's show.

Grady shot me a look but he didn't interfere. Miriam glanced at me, then away, probably not liking the reminder of her crimes in the big bandage around my head.

"Ja. It was very hard. I prayed for strength every step, and I thought of my children, of what would happen to them if that video of their father were seen, if . . . ." She swallowed hard. "If their mother was caught. *God* gave me the strength to do it."

I wanted to laugh at that—or vomit.

"You do realize that another man was about to be wrongly convicted of this crime?" Grady asked bluntly.

Miriam frowned, twisting that handkerchief in her lap. I wanted to believe she was insane, but maybe the truth was worse, that she wasn't crazy, just someone with religious delusions who'd made some really horrendous decisions.

"Ja. I knew. When it was over, I put it in God's hands, if I was caught out or not. If someone else had gone to jail, well . . . I'm sure God wouldn't've let anyone suffer who was a true innocent. Katie and . . . and that Jessica too. They were harlots, whores. And Detective Harris is . . . a worldly woman. You see, God wouldn't have let me hurt anyone but the wicked."

Okay, I was wrong. She was totally insane.

"Tell us what happened that night with Detective Harris," Grady prompted.

Miriam took a deep breath. "I also do confess that I struck Detective Harris over the head with a skillet and intended to do her the same way. Only Aaron wouldn't let me finish her by takin' her breath. It was my idea to put her in the creek, let God decide her fate. I pushed Aaron till he agreed. It weren't his fault. I told him we had to, for the sake of the children. And Detective Harris looked nearly dead anyhow."

I looked at Aaron. Even if he hadn't known about the murders, even if he hadn't been the one to strike me on the head, he could have stopped his wife from dumping my naked body in freezing water. But he hadn't. Maybe he'd bought into her let-God-decide-her-fate bullshit. Maybe he'd hoped it would all go away, that his position in the community could be salvaged. He put his hand over his eyes and slumped forward. I felt sorry for him. But I didn't forgive him.

Miriam finally raised her eyes to look around the room pleadingly. "I'm a sinner. And I do confess it. I asked God to forgive me. And I ask my family, and my good neighbors, and for the church to forgive me. What I done was wrong, terrible wrong. But I did it for you, to save the scandal. And Katie, you know what she was. You know I was driven to it."

Hannah finally looked at Miriam, her face set hard. She stood up slowly and, without a word, turned her back. Isaac, looking more sad than angry, did the same. Aaron just stared at the floor, face unreadable.

The Amish bishop, with his long white beard and black hat, stood slowly and when he spoke it was with a terrible gravity. "Miriam Lapp. The law will sentence and judge you in this life, and God in the next. As for the church, you have violated our most sacred beliefs with destruction, deceit, and murder. It was not for you to punish Katie Yoder, or the young girl who came to you for help. As for Detective Harris—" He looked me in the eye. I saw genuine regret and sorrow on his face. "Please accept our sincere apologies for what was done to you, including the day we asked you to be removed from the investigation. We should not have interfered, and the harm that came to you in our community causes us great sorrow."

He waited, as if really asking me for forgiveness. I found that I held no grudge against the Amish in my heart. I gave the bishop a brief nod. He bowed his head at me.

"Thank you. As for you, Miriam," the bishop continued, "I

forgive you, but I cannot accept your confession at face value. You say you repent, but true repentance can only come out of true understanding of what you did wrong and the harm it did yourself and others. And I don't think God has touched your heart yet so. We will pray for you."

With that, the bishop nodded to his men and the Amish filed silently out of the room, not looking at Aaron or Miriam. Miriam seemed surprised at not having been accepted back into the fold, at being left alone. I couldn't help feeling gratified about that.

A warden went to Miriam, helped her to her feet with a strong hand, and put cuffs on her. As she was being led from the room, Aaron looked up at her.

"Miriam, forgive me," he said. "My sin with Katie put you in a terrible place, confused and befuddled your mind. This is my fault."

"I forgave you long ago," Miriam said, in a simple voice, as though surprised. It was the last thing she said before the warden led her out the door.

On October 10, LeeAnn Travis held a memorial for Katie and Jessica. It was at a pavilion at Paradise Community Park, and Hannah Yoder, along with a host of other Amish women, provided food. It turned out to be a beautiful fall day, and the park was full of Amish who had come to show their solidarity. Dotted among the black dresses and black-and-white bonnets were teenagers from Jessica's high school and a few of us from the police force too. The local press turned out, and even one of the major networks, but they respectfully kept their distance.

The bishop of Katie's church gave a brief prayer. He talked about how Katie and Jessica had become friends despite being from different worlds, about how Jessica had never given up on finding Katie, and how her determination to find her friend had eventually led Jessica to her own death. It was moving to hear him acknowledge that—that Jessica and Katie's friendship had been sincere and deep. Like Ezra, Katie had been a square peg unable to fit into the prescribed round holes of the Amish life, and in Jessica she'd found someone who accepted her as she was, someone who understood, someone with whom to dream of escape.

I'd thought a lot about the girls in the seven months since it had all gone down. I'd thought about what Katie had planned to do, selling a video of her and Aaron Lapp. It had been a nasty act. But when I considered her minimum-wage jobs, how she'd cleaned houses from the age of eleven, worked at the farmers' market, and then sold her body for seventy-five dollars to strangers in an effort to save up that pouch full of money, I couldn't judge her. She was fighting her way to a new life in the only way she knew how. And maybe she felt, too, that Aaron deserved exposure, deserved to have his abuse of her seen by the world. I couldn't blame her for that either.

Aaron's abuse was exposed in the end—documented at his sentencing hearing and reported in all the major papers. He admitted to all of it, and Miriam too. They never stood trial because they did not contest their crimes. Aaron was sentenced to ten years for child abuse and conspiracy to murder. Miriam got twenty. But the video Katie had made never went public. The phone belonged to LeeAnn Travis, and it was up to her whether or not to release the footage to the public. She decided not to, despite being offered an obscene amount of money for it. The Amish community, and especially Hannah and Isaac, had been good to LeeAnn. They'd gone to her home to apologize right after Miriam Lapp's confession, and they'd befriended her since. LeeAnn didn't hold a grunge, and neither did the public. In fact, tourist season was bigger than ever in Lancaster County that summer, with all the curiosity-seekers coming for a closer look at where it had happened. Grimlace Lane had been getting a lot of traffic. Fortunately, Ezra didn't live there anymore.

Hannah Yoder came up to us after the prayer. Her eyes were red but she looked at me kindly. To my surprise, she put her hands on my upper arms and briefly pressed her cheek to mine before pulling away. "Elizabeth, I haven't had a chance to thank you before now. We're so grateful to you for bringing home our Katie and . . ." She paused, her face pained as if the words hurt. ". . . and for helpin' me understand her . . . why she was the way she was. Thank you."

I didn't know what to say, and I didn't trust my voice anyway. I managed a simple reply. "You're welcome, Hannah. If there's ever anything I can do for you or your family, please call me."

She nodded with a sad smile and even gave a nod to Ezra too before walking away. "You okay?" I asked him as we stood at the edge of the crowd.

"Yup. I'm good." He wasn't though. I could see the strain in his shoulders. We knew it would be hard to come to this, but he'd wanted to do it anyway. As we expected, the Amish all ignored Ezra, though of course they recognized him, despite his jeans and blue blazer. Their loss. Ezra was the best, most appealing human being on the entire freaking planet. Of course, I could be biased. I suppose it wasn't as bad as it might have been. Though they ignored Ezra, no one gave us dirty looks.

Ezra went to talk to Mike Grady and his wife, Sharon, while I said my good-byes. LeeAnn Travis gave me a long hug and I got one from Katie's little sister Sadie. Katie's parents, Hannah and Isaac, were polite, and Isaac shook my hand. But there was an undeniable reserve in them that set them apart. That was fine. Ezra and I didn't belong in their world, and we were just fine in our own.

———————

Ezra was quiet that evening. He did his chores out in the barn with our six-month-old golden retriever named Rabbit while I cooked a quick stir-fry. The police department had given those involved with the Grimlace Lane case the afternoon off to go to the memorial, and it was a treat to be home early on a Friday night. The farm we rented was small, just twelve acres, but it had a barn that opened onto a ten-acre fenced pasture and a place for Ezra's kitchen garden. Martha had decided to return to their parents' home and remain Amish. Neither of us was really surprised. She didn't have the burning need Ezra had to break free, and the pull of family and the familiar was just too strong.

Ezra wore different clothes these days, but there was still a grounded simplicity about him, like the wildflowers and weeds that crowd around the white pasture fence. It was a simplicity that spoke of the past and of home to me, like the smell of my grandfather's shed. Pennsylvania was home to me. Ezra was home.

I thought Ezra's solemn mood that evening was due to the Amish gathering at the memorial and the way he'd been shut out of it, the way his own family hadn't acknowledged him. Sometimes I wondered if he ever regretted his choices. But then we had a dinner full of heated looks and low words. He made love to me that night with fire and passion and a heart full of love, and it seemed to me that he didn't regret a thing.

We had a good life together, a wonderful life. As far as I was concerned, I wasn't going to take a single minute of it for granted.

Ezra fell asleep and so did Rabbit, hogging the foot of the bed. But I was too wound up from the memorial. I put a coat on over my pajamas and went to sit on the back porch. Horse came to the fence and looked at me and then, seeing I was just fine and, furthermore, was not Ezra, went on his way to roam in the dark with the dozen other mules Ezra was raising.

The copper beech tree in the pasture shook its limbs, its dying leaves *shrrr*ing in a light breeze. The clouds parted and the moon broke out, creating light and shadows. An image of Terry came to me from out of the blue. It felt as if he stood there under the copper beech tree, watching me. For the first time, the thought of Terry did not fill me with rage or fear or guilt. In my mind, Terry was smiling.

I smiled back. *I still miss you*, I thought, *but I'm happy*.

Maybe there is no such thing as a perfect place in life, or a perfect person. But we are granted perfect moments, I think.

I went back inside to join Ezra and savor this one.

Keep reading for a special preview of
Jane Jensen's next Elizabeth Harris novel . . .

IN THE LAND OF MILK AND HONEY

Coming soon from Berkley Prime Crime!

PROLOGUE

Lancaster County, Pennsylvania, March 2015

"Mama! Mama!"

The strained cry pulled Leah from a fevered dream in which she'd been sewing and sewing. The stitches fell apart, disintegrating as she frantically worked. It was something important and she had to finish it . . . a bridal dress.

No. A shroud.

"Mama!"

Leah sat up in bed. Beside her, Samuel was asleep. She touched his forehead. It was still hot and dry with fever. But it wasn't Samuel who had called for her. It had been a child's voice. She left her husband to his fitful rest and went out into the hall in her white cotton nightgown and bare feet.

Coming! she thought. She left the reassurance unspoken

because it was the middle of the night, and she didn't want to wake the rest of her children.

A shining band of lantern light peeked out from under the door of the upstairs bathroom the children all shared.

She knocked lightly. "*Hast du mich gerufen?*" she asked, low. *Did you call me?*

"Mama!" Breathless and weak, the cry came from behind the door. Leah opened it.

On the floor by the toilet lay Mary. She was pale as snow. Her thirteen-year-old body had recently begun to develop a woman's shape, but she looked years younger now. Her long dark hair, loosened for bed, was sheeted around her, damp and oily at her brow. Her eyes were closed. One of her hands twitched weakly, as if it wanted to reach for her mother. The smell of vomit and bile hit Leah in the face, sharp as the January wind on the open fields. The lid of the toilet was open, small amounts of bile the only evidence of Mary's heaving. Her stomach was empty, poor thing. But the back of her nightdress was stained brown.

"Oh, Mary!" Leah fought her own nausea, exacerbated by the smell, and bent to help her daughter. She managed to get Mary sitting up and stripped off her soiled nightgown and undergarments. She cleaned Mary with a wet rag and bundled all the stained cloth up together. Leah enumerated the tasks in her head. She had to take the bundle down to the laundry room, open up the little window in the bathroom to air it out, then see to it that Mary was put into a clean nightgown and settled back into bed, and, oh yes, given a glass of water to drink while Leah watched. The doctor said water was important, especially with all the vomiting and diarrhea, but it was hard to get the children to drink it. When they did, it often came right back up.

Mary was trembling like a leaf in the breeze, her eyes bleary. But at least she was able to sit up by herself. Leah draped her in a few towels to keep her warm and went to fetch a clean nightgown.

As she passed the boys' room she heard the muffled sound of crying—miserable, lonely gasps. She hesitated, wondering if she should first get Leah's nightgown, but the sound was too worrying. She pushed open the door to the boys' room.

"Aaron!" She hurried to the child's side. Six-year-old Aaron, who looked so much like his papa, especially with their identical sandy-colored Amish haircuts, was sitting up on the lower bunk. He was crying, quietly but full-out, his mouth gaping wide.

She pulled him into a hug and checked his forehead. His fever seemed to have broken for the moment. His skin was clammy and covered with sweat.

"*Was is das?*" she tsked quietly. Across the room in the other set of bunk beds, Mark, her twelve-year-old, had his back turned, asleep on the upper bunk. The bottom bunk the boys used for playing—at least until little Henry outgrew his crib.

"*Ich hatte einen Albtraum,*" Aaron sobbed. A nightmare.

Leah felt a touch of relief. At least Aaron was not as sick as Mary, or as he himself had been earlier that evening. Maybe he was on the mend. Maybe they all would be soon, and her own nightmare would end. "*Es war nur ein Traum. Schlafen tu.*" *It was only a dream. Go back to sleep.*

She tucked Aaron in, his eyes already drooping, and straightened up from the lower bunk. Her back ached, deep and low, and she put a hand to it, rubbing. Chills ran through her, shaking her so hard the wooden boards beneath her feet creaked. Dear God, let this terrible flu pass soon. She should fetch her shawl. But first—Mary's nightgown.

She turned to go, but decided to check on Will first. He was in the bunk above Aaron's. Her fourteen-year-old had been very ill all day, refusing food and going to bed at six o'clock after dragging himself through the daily chores. The cows had to be milked, no matter that the entire family was sick as dogs.

She stepped closer to the top bunk and went up on her tiptoes, reaching a hand out to touch William's forehead. He was a barely distinguishable shape in the dark. Her fingers touched wetness, partially dried and sticky. It was around his mouth, which was slack, open, and felt oddly firm. The smell of something foul came from where her fingers had been. Alarmed, she drew back her hand and paused for only a moment before reaching for the Coleman lamp on the bedside table. She turned it on. Keeping the other boys asleep was no longer the foremost concern on her mind.

"Will?" She blinked as her eyes adjusted to the light. She stepped on the lower bunk and pulled herself up to look at her son.

A moment later her scream echoed through the silent house like a gunshot.

CHAPTER 1

I pulled into the driveway at the Yoders' farm and turned off my car. I forced myself to sit still for a moment instead of hopping out immediately. I needed to get my head out of my current caseload and go-go mindset before I could appreciate Amish hospitality.

It was late March. The weather had warmed early this year, and the signs of spring were everywhere. The dark brown wooden fence along the Yoders' pasture contrasted with the brilliant green of new grass and the white and purple of early blooming crocus. The late-afternoon light was just turning golden and soft. Several fawn-colored Jersey cows were eagerly tugging up mouthfuls of the new growth, completely engrossed. And the little decorative windmill in the center of the kitchen garden on the other side of the gravel drive spun in a light breeze. The garden was still in its winter hibernation, dormant but cleared. I imagined it held its breath in expectation.

This was why I'd moved back to Lancaster County. Every once in a while I had to remind myself of that before I got bogged down with head-in-the-sand-itis. Feeling better, I grabbed Sadie's present and headed for the house.

Sadie Yoder had turned seven a week ago. This was the first chance I'd had to come by, sneaking out early from an afternoon of tedious paperwork. I'd debated what to get her. Ezra said dolls were acceptable for the Amish, as long as they were modestly attired. No Glam-Rock Barbie for Sadie then. But I didn't want to reinforce the "grow up and have lots of babies" message, for no reason other than my core streak of feminism and innate rebellion. So I settled on a game of Chutes and Ladders.

I'd struck up a tentative friendship with the Yoders, specifically Hannah and two of her daughters, Sadie and Ruth. We were odd bedfellows—a female police detective and Amish womenfolk. But we'd shared a tragedy. Or, rather, the Yoders tragically lost their daughter Katie, and I'd found her killer. I'd nearly died in the process.

There was guilt and gratitude on their side, and I couldn't even begin to untangle the mare's nest of motivations on mine. I felt protective of Katie's younger sisters, bonded to the family through the sympathy and pain of Katie's murder case—and I was curious. I wanted to learn about Hannah's way of life. Of course, I lived with Ezra, who was ex-Amish. But he couldn't tell me what it was like to be an Amish wife and mother, and he didn't like to talk about his life before anyway.

Also, if I were perfectly honest, I simply liked coming here. It made me happy. I went up the porch stairs and knocked on the door.

"Hallo, Elizabeth!" Hannah opened the door and welcomed me inside with a smile. She always looked so young for a mother of eleven, slightly built, her dark hair pulled back tight under a white cap and her face without a trace of makeup. Her plain, royal blue dress was covered with a large black apron that had traces of flour on it.

"Hi, Hannah." I smiled. I wanted to give Hannah a quick hug, but refrained. Instead, I held up the gift. "I brought Sadie a birthday present."

"Ocht! You spoil her!" Despite her words, Hannah seemed pleased. "We're making strudel. Would you like to cook with?"

"Sure." Being in the Yoders' kitchen was soothing. And it would be fun to surprise Ezra by learning how to make something from his childhood.

The kitchen was crowded with girls and young women. The pine center table had been cleared and covered with wax paper, rolling pins, and large bowls of dough and chopped apples. Sadie's face lit up when she saw me. She ran over to give me a hug around the hips. The others all said hello. Sadie's older sisters, Ruth and Waneta, who still lived at home, were there, as well as Miriam, who was grown now and had children of her own. There were two young women I didn't know. Before I could introduce myself, my dark pantsuit was covered by an apron and I was clutching a rolling pin. *En garde.* I bit my lip and refrained from saying it. They wouldn't find it funny.

The sheer volume of strudel they were preparing came as no surprise by now. I'd seen Hannah cook before. Not only did the Yoders have a large family, but they always made extra, either to freeze or to share with the community at some get-together or another. And the two young women I hadn't met before had probably come over to make batches for their own households. Cooking in a group made things a lot more fun.

We rolled out the dough, cut it into large square sheets, sprinkled on a sugar-cinnamon mixture, added raisins and nuts to some and not to others, and layered on small slices of apple before rolling them up and brushing the tops with melted butter and powdered sugar. The bushels of last fall's apples were from cold storage, according to Hannah. Those that hadn't been eaten over the winter had to be used up before they went bad. They were a tough-skinned green variety, and they were pared and chopped in an endless assembly line. And while trays of rolled strudels sat and rose in the warm kitchen, more and more and more were made.

It was a repetitive task that soothed me after a long week of work. This past week I'd investigated a man who'd killed his wife accidently during a heated argument, a Jane Doe found near the highway, and a baby whom I suspected had been abused rather than suffering crib death. It all melted away under the steady motions and the pleasant singing in complicated-sounding German words.

I couldn't contribute much to the singing or the conversation. With the older Amish, most of my life was topic non grata. I was living in sin with Ezra Beiler who was, in any case, an Amish man who'd taken the church vows and then left the Amish, and was therefore shunned. And my work as a homicide detective wasn't something Hannah cared to have her girls learn much about, even if she did respect it. But Sadie, as usual, had a million nonsensical questions for me like *Do you like grass?* and *Do you have red birds at your house?*

The last strudels were rolled. A few of the dough logs were stuffed into the warm oven, but most were wrapped in cling film for later baking. Hannah's guests left with cheerful good-byes and boxes bursting with strudel. Sadie opened her birthday present, thanked me for the "most wonderfullest gift" and ran off with Ruth and Waneta to play the game before supper.

I washed the dough off my hands at the sink. The window above the basin overlooked the fields outside. The sun was sinking and I saw Hannah's husband, Isaac, and two of her boys heading home on a plow pulled by two horses. It was getting late—time to let Hannah get to their evening meal. Besides, the sight made me long sharply for Ezra, who would be ending his own day about now.

"Thank you for allowing me to stay," I told Hannah. "This was just what I needed to relax."

Hannah was placing two wrapped, unbaked strudels into a bag for me to take home. She paused, an odd look on her face, like she wanted to say something but wasn't sure if she should.

"What is it?" I asked.

Hannah looked troubled. "I meant to speak to you. . . . It is about a bad business."

"Of course." I stepped closer to Hannah and leaned against a counter, making it clear I was happy to listen.

Hannah sighed. "There ist some trouble lately, among the people in our church. Now a boy has died."

"Trouble? What kind of trouble?"

"My friend Leah Hershberger, her whole family is sick. They called in a doctor, and he said it was the flu. But . . . there has never been such a flu. So sick they were, and her son William, only fourteen and strong before now—he died from it."

"I'm sorry, Hannah." It was disturbing. There'd been word in the news that the flu season was particularly virulent this year. Everyone at the station had been given a flu shot last November. But this was the first I'd heard about a local child's death. Of course, if he'd died from a virus it wouldn't have come to the homicide team.

"Another family, the Knepps, got ill such like too. I hoped maybe, you could look into this?" Hannah asked, her face uncertain.

I didn't understand. "How do you think I could help? It sounds like a case for a doctor, not the police."

Hannah tugged at her cap self-consciously, her eyes downcast. "Some believe it is not a normal sickness but *hexerei*, a curse."

I blinked rapidly as my mind tried to catch up. A *curse?*

Hannah looked up, her face hopeful. "There is a man, a *brauche* man. He holds a grudge against our church. Maybe if you could just look things over, say what you think. I don't know what to believe myself, but if it is a curse . . . I don't ask for myself, Elizabeth, but for Leah and her children, and for my own children too."

I felt out of my depths, like the floor had gone wonky beneath my feet. A *curse?* What could I say?

"I . . . would be happy to take a look into the boy's death."

Hannah's face lit up with a grateful smile. "I knew you were a *gut* friend to us. Thank you."

Lancaster General Hospital was a big and open space, surprisingly modern and new. I was used to the old hospitals in Manhattan, with their cramped corridors and smell of centuries past. Like all things in Pennsylvania, this hospital's corridors were extra wide and its ceilings extra high, as if its citizens could be counted on to be oversized, families overblown, as if posterity could only get bigger. There was something endearingly optimistic about that.

The optimism was nowhere evident in the patient room I entered.

Samuel Hershberger and his young son Aaron shared a large room, each in his own bed. Both were sleeping.

Samuel looked to be in his early forties. His long bangs of brown hair and unkempt beard clearly identified him as Amish, even though he wore nothing but a hospital gown under the blankets. He must have lost a lot of weight, because the skin on his face appeared to be laid over the skull—drawn, loose, and colorless. An IV drip fed steadily into his veins. He appeared to be resting peacefully. I knew what it would take to get an Amish farmer like Samuel Hershberger into the hospital—near death. The loss of their son William must have been a wake-up call.

Aaron was quite young, maybe five or six. He was turned on his side and, although clearly ill, had healthier skin tone than his father. He would probably make it, I thought. I certainly hoped so.

I decided not to wake them. There wasn't much Aaron could tell me, and Samuel looked too sick to disturb. Instead, I went off in search of their doctor. This wasn't how I'd planned to spend my Saturday off, but a promise was a promise.

———————

"I can't say for certain what it is," Dr. Kirsch said, being perfectly blunt about his ignorance.

Thanks to my badge, I'd gotten the doctor to speak to me about the Hershbergers. I left out the fact that my investigation was in no way official.

"My best guess is it's a particularly virulent viral infection. But these things often remain undiagnosed. Both Hershbergers' blood work show severe hyperchloremic acidosis, which can result from prolonged diarrhea and vomiting. We're giving them IV fluids. It's the best we can do for now. They should pull through fine."

"Do you know why the fourteen-year-old son, William, died?"

"Dehydration, possibly kidney or liver failure. I doubt there'll be an autopsy. There usually aren't with the Amish unless it can't be avoided. His mother said the whole family had been sick for three days, and William wasn't keeping liquids down. He worked on the farm that day too. His body just gave out."

Kirsch was an older man, early fifties, stocky, with a superior air. He clearly was a busy man and not overly curious about the medical mystery of the Hershbergers.

"If it's a viral infection you don't recognize, wouldn't it be the procedure to call in the CDC?" I asked.

Dr. Kirsch looked incredulous. "Well . . . no. Not without a lot more evidence that it's something unusual. It's flu season. There are dozens of common viruses going around. If we called the CDC every time we had a patient with flu symptoms, we'd need a CDC the size of the U.S. military."

"But a boy died."

Kirsch squinted impatiently. "There have been over forty deaths from flu so far this season alone in the U.S. It's tragic, but it happens. Dehydration can be very dangerous."

I pulled out my notepad—not because I really needed it, but to reinforce the message that I wasn't some dim relative he could bully. "Mrs. Hershberger says the entire family came down ill at the same time, overnight. There were also severe chills and tremors. Isn't that unusual for the flu? People in a family would normally get sick in waves, not all at once."

"It depends on when and how they were exposed to the virus." Kirsch leaned forward, elbows on his desk. He seemed to be taking me a bit more seriously, but I sensed defensiveness in his tone. "If they were all exposed to someone who had the virus, say, at the same church meeting, it's conceivable they would fall ill at the same time. And chills and shivering are to be expected with severe flu."

"What exactly did their blood work show?"

Dr. Kirsch opened the file on his desk. "About what you'd expect. Electrolyte abnormalities, hemoglobin and red blood cell counts are elevated, and the acidosis . . . that's all typical for severe dehydration."

"Does it actually show the virus?"

"Viruses are detected via a swab culture, not blood work."

"And was a swab culture done?"

He gave a subtle huff. "No. Confirming the influenza virus via a swab test wouldn't change the treatment."

"I understand. Still. I's dotted and t's crossed—you understand. Is it possible for you to administer a swab test now and confirm that it's influenza? Just for our records?"

Kirsch frowned. "You understand that we're conservative on our use of tests since these patients are not insured. It's not in their best interest to rack up avoidable expenses."

I gave Dr. Kirsch a brittle smile. "Run the test on Samuel Hershberger, please, doctor. Text me with the results today."

Ezra was working in the garden when I got home from the hospital. As I parked the car my text alert went off.

> Rapid flu test negative in both Hershbergers. No
> Influenza A or B virus present.

I read the message twice.

I typed in Meaning it's not the flu?

The reply took seconds. Inconclusive. Likely the virus has left the system and now it's complications. Treatment same.

Well. That wasn't very helpful. I'd been hoping for something concrete to report to Hannah. I sighed and got out of the car, stretching my back. I took the opportunity to check out my partner like a shameless hussy.

Since leaving the Amish a little over a year ago, Ezra had

changed in many ways. He never had taken to T-shirts, but he loved jeans. In the warm April afternoon, he wore a denim button-down work shirt with the sleeves rolled up and a pair of jeans that clung to his narrow hips and long legs. I preferred his blond hair long, and he indulged me by keeping it shoulder-length. He had it tucked behind one ear, revealing his handsome face as he hoed between the rows.

The first time I'd seen Ezra, he'd been standing in his barn, his back to me, lost in a private moment of sorrow. Now, as then, he could make me forget to breathe. I gave in to the urge to go over and give him a hug.

"I'm covered in dirt," he warned, though his arms were welcoming.

"Uh-huh. You're so sexy when you're working in the garden."

Ezra's lips quirked. "'Tis so? Guess that explains why the Amish have so many children."

I laughed, feeling my mood lift like someone had pumped helium into it. "I suppose that could be a factor, though the lack of birth control might have something to do with it." I breathed him in for a moment and stole a kiss. Our golden retriever, Rabbit, panted happily and wove around our legs.

"Any news?" he asked.

"The doctor says Samuel and Aaron Hershberger will recover, so that's good. Unfortunately, the diagnosis is vague. Can I help you out here?"

"No. I was about to stop for the day. Need to do some chores in the barn already."

"Shall I make stir-fry?" On weeknights, Ezra usually cooked

for both of us since I worked late, so on the weekends I liked to take care of him. I went to pull away, but Ezra tightened his arms in one last squeeze.

"Sounds good," he murmured into my ear. The nuzzle of his lips on my cheek held a lovely promise for later. I smiled.

———

"What's a *brauche* man?" I asked Ezra as we relaxed on the couch after dinner.

"Where'd ya hear that word?" Ezra sounded amused.

"Hannah Yoder. She said people thought the Hershbergers had been cursed by a hex-something. And she mentioned a *brauche* man."

Ezra settled down deeper into the couch and pulled me closer. "Ah. Well, a *brauche* man does a kind of magic. Sometimes it's called powwow."

"Magic?"

"They use prayers and plants and whatnot, but some say it's magic all the same. You go to them when you're sick or there's a problem with an animal, or bad weather. They say special prayers and give you medicine that you take or . . . like bundles or tokens that you put under your bed or in the horse's stall. Things like that."

"Sounds like voodoo, or maybe a witch doctor. I didn't know the Amish had a folk magic like that."

"Oh, ja. Have you not seen our hex signs? These are old beliefs, coming from Germany. But not many think anything of it anymore. My grandmother used to go to an old powwow woman."

"Yeah? Your grandma did?" I sat up so I could see Ezra's face.

"Yes." His face was serious, but his eyes twinkled.

"Okay. What did this powwow woman do for your grand-mother?"

"Treated aches and pains. Though maybe there were other things she used powwow for too. My father didn't approve. He'd grumble about 'the work of Satan' and 'being in league with the devil.' Some don't like powwow, even when it's a *gut* church member that does it. But my grandmother just complained louder about her pain and didn't stop goin'."

"She sounds like a character."

"She was a woman who knew how to get her way. You didn't cross her. Reminds me of someone else I know." Ezra was smiling as he told this story, but suddenly his smile faltered and pain darkened his eyes.

I'm sorry. I'm sorry you lost all of your family in one blow.

I didn't say it out loud, but I lay against his chest and squeezed him tight. Just when I thought the anguish of being shunned had passed, it could crop up again. It probably always would. I still missed my own parents at times, and they were dead. They didn't live fifteen miles away and refuse to acknowledge I'd ever been born.

"So . . . a powwow man could hypothetically curse someone and make their crops fail or make them sick?"

Ezra shrugged. "Hex signs are to protect from curses. So yes, I guess the Amish believe in such things. Do you?" He sounded genuinely interested in what an English person—that is, some-one who wasn't Amish—might make of it.

"Hmmm." I thought about it. "I think there are people who *believe* they can lay curses, and send a lot of bad intent your way.

But I don't think it could actually hurt you unless you knew about the curse and believed in it too. Then you might have a psychosomatic response."

"What does that mean?"

"If you expect to become sick, really, truly believe it, it can make you sick."

Ezra's body, so lanky and relaxed beneath mine a moment ago, grew tense. His hand had been stroking my arm. It stopped.

"Did I say something wrong?"

Ezra bit his lip, then shook his head. "Sometimes I wonder at how easy it is for you to dismiss anything outside of us humans, anything outside the mind. Not sure if I should admire you for it or just feel brokenhearted."

Leave it to Ezra not to pull punches. He didn't say things he didn't mean, and rarely held back on the stuff that was hard to hear. Religion, faith in God . . . it was something Ezra struggled with. He couldn't be Amish any longer, but he wasn't an atheist at heart either. In his upbringing there was no such thing as a middle ground. Unfortunately, I had no faith of my own to give him as an alternative. I'd seen too much out there as a cop, experienced too much of my own heartbreak when my husband had been brutally murdered, to believe in an omnipotent being who directed man's fate and cared.

I cupped Ezra's face. "I don't dismiss everything outside of us. God . . . I don't know. But faith and love . . . absolutely. *Curses* though?" I put a funny twist on the final words, hoping to get him to smile.

It worked. He huffed. "Ja, okay. Maybe curses don't work. Or I'd have killed off a few of my mules a hundred times over."

"Not to mention our furnace."

Ezra nodded solemnly. "It's a right bugger."

"And the shower."

"The hot water runs the other way when I get in there. Don't do a lick of good to yell at it." He was all laconic irony now.

I bit back a smile, playing the game. "And I've heard you say some not very nice things to our stove once or twice."

"The flame on that right front burner has it out for me."

I relaxed back into him with a laugh. I breathed in the warm scent of his shirt, felt the hard muscles shift under the cotton, and felt heat stir inside me. "I missed you today." I raised my head to kiss his neck.

"Yeah?" His hand stroked my arm once more, but this time there was an electric intensity to it. He pressed up into me ever so slightly, causing my body to immediately heat, preparing for him.

Someday, our mutual attraction, the love we had for each other, and, yes, the quite lovely sex, might not be enough. It might not be a glue strong enough to hold us together. We came from such different worlds. I feared that day. But for now, I'd take all of Ezra I could get.

2-16